WITHD
No longer the property of the
Boston Public Library.
Sale of this material benefits the Library.

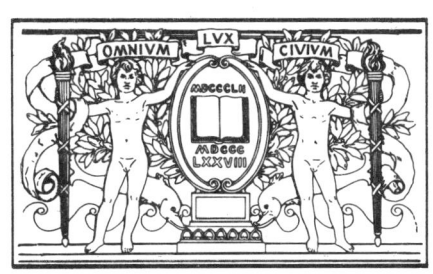

BOSTON
PUBLIC
LIBRARY

WINTER'S CRIMES 17

WINTER'S CRIMES 17

edited by
George Hardinge

St. Martin's Press
New York

All rights reserved. Printed in the United Kingdom. No part of this book may be used or reproduced in any manner whatsoever without written permission except in the case of brief quotations embodied in critical articles or reviews. For information, address St. Martin's Press, 175 Fifth Avenue, New York, N.Y. 10010.

Library of Congress Catalog Card Number: 72-623690

ISBN 0-312-88244-0

First published in Great Britain by Macmillan London Limited

First U.S. Edition

10 9 8 7 6 5 4 3 2 1

CONTENTS

Editor's Note	7
A Thumb on the Scales by Jon Breen	11
Kindness by Celia Dale	27
The Perfect Alibi by Paula Gosling	35
The Secret Lover by Peter Lovesey	49
The Last Place on Earth by James McClure	63
Chicken Feed by Jennie Melville	83
A Light on the Road to Woodstock by Ellis Peters	99
The Birthmark by Julian Symons	125
The Casebook Casanova by Miles Tripp	143
The Man Who Nursed Grievances by Michael Underwood	159
A Wise Child by John Wainwright	175
The Gallows by Ted Willis	189
Every Tale Condemns Me by Sara Woods	205

WINTER'S CRIMES 17.
Collection copyright © 1985 by
Macmillan London Limited

The stories are copyright respectively:
Copyright © Jon L Breen 1985
Copyright © Celia Dale 1985
Copyright © Paula Gosling 1985
Copyright © Peter Lovesey Limited 1985
Copyright © Sabensa Gakulu Limited 1985
Copyright © Jennie Melville 1985
Copyright © Ellis Peters 1985
Copyright © Julian Symons 1985
Copyright © Miles Tripp 1985
Copyright © Michael Underwood 1985
Copyright © John and Avis Wainwright 1985
Copyright © Ted Willis Limited 1985
Copyright © Probandi Books Limited 1985

Editor's Note

For the last collection of the *Winter's Crimes* anthology that I expect to edit personally a few more words of introduction are needed than were called for in the earlier ones.

This time I decided – perhaps something of a sentimental gesture – to invite only friends who have regularly been published by Macmillan to contribute. So this volume is in the nature of an 'imprint muster' and the imposing high standard achieved here is one more witness to the imagination and craftsmanship of gifted friends.

The story by Jon Breen does not come in this category, since he and I have never met, though I have published with enthusiasm and admiration his first three crime novels. He offered it to me and I accepted it.

Once again the stories have all been written especially for this volume and will not have appeared anywhere in the English language in 'Commonwealth' territory countries before our publication date. One possible exception is *A Light on the Road to Woodstock* by Ellis Peters – but then anyone of discrimination will be more than content to read for a second time this enthralling introduction to Brother Cadfael. And Peter Lovesey's *The Secret Lover* will have appeared in September 1985 in a Macmillan collection.

It has been my custom in these Editor's Notes to express a profound gratitude to the writers who have done the creative work that resulted in a book being published. That gratitude is more deeply felt than ever when such a gathering of friends contribute. And in my opinion this 'imprint muster' need yield nothing to its predecessors, it is a spirited, powerful and varied collection.

George Hardinge

Jon Breen

A THUMB ON THE SCALES

Capital punishment? No, you can't draw me into that argument. There's a lot to be said on both sides, and I've argued them both in my time on editorial pages and in bar-rooms like this one, but you guys are getting too wrought up. Calm down. We can't solve it here, right? Have another drink, and let me tell you a story that has something to do with capital punishment, though I'm not sure whose side it supports.

I covered a good many murder trials in my newspaper days, but the most interesting may have been Clayton Foxworth's for the murder of his wife, not so much for the trial itself as . . . Well, let me start at the beginning.

It was in the early Seventies, right after the Supreme Court had effectively ended capital punishment in the United States, at least for a while. Andy Cutshaw, the clerk of Judge Francis Middleton's court, was a drinking buddy of mine and one of my most reliable Informed Sources. The night before the Foxworth trial was to begin, we were sharing a drink in a little tavern near the courthouse.

'It was a lousy time to strike down the death penalty,' Andy muttered. 'If anybody ever deserved to die for his crime, it's Clayton Foxworth. I mean, if he's guilty, of course.'

'You think he'll get a fair trial in this town?' I asked. 'Or, maybe more to the point, will the State get a fair trial in this town?'

'Of course it'll be a fair trial!' Andy said, fiercely protective like he's a mama lion and the American justice system is his cub. 'What else would he get in Judge Middleton's court? The judge is the fairest man I've ever known.'

'No doubt. But you know how much weight Foxworth carries in our fair city, Andy.' The defendant's mattress factory was a major employer in the small Mid-Western city. Foxworth was also a leading figure socially, supporting most of the city's cultural and charitable activities. Less visibly, he was said to be a political power.

'Justice will be done,' Andy said, lugubriously staring into his beer. As always, he seemed to have a cloud over his head, a permanent melancholia, as though some personal tragedy had affected his whole life. His entire existence was tied up in Judge Middleton's court.

I went on, 'They say the DA only brought the prosecution because the case was too strong to ignore, and he may not be too anxious to pursue it as hard as he might. The guy that's doing the prosecuting, Willard Craven, is no dynamo, and Foxworth is spending a lot of money on that hotshot out-of-town lawyer, George Ealing, compared to whom F. Lee Bailey is shy and self-effacing. And the media, my paper excepted of course, have not treated the case even-handedly. They've mostly given Foxworth a white hat and his wife a black garter belt.'

Andy gave me a murderous look. 'Watch how you talk about her.'

I was taken by surprise. 'Did you know Mrs Foxworth, Andy?'

He sighed. 'Years ago, I used to go to the café where Stella was a waitress. Just to see her. That was long before she married Foxworth. We got to know each other pretty well. I almost asked her to marry me – closest I ever came to taking that step. I think she would have done it, too. But I guess I loved a bachelor's routine existence more than I loved her. Crazy, huh? I wish I had asked her. She'd still be alive. I'd have quit smoking a lot sooner than I did, because Stella would have made me, and I wouldn't be dying right now . . .'

I just gaped at him. 'Dying? Andy, I didn't . . .'

'Nobody knows. Not even the judge. It's inoperable cancer.' He looked at me abruptly. 'I don't have to tell you this is all completely off the record, do I? About me knowing Stella and this other thing, too. I want to keep working as long as I can, and the judge would . . . You won't tell him, will you?'

'No, Andy, I won't tell anybody.'

'I'm not looking forward to hearing *both* sides in this trial make out Stella as some kind of promiscuous tramp, but I think that's what'll happen. She wasn't like that at all.' He downed his beer.

'But justice will be done in this case. You can bet on that.'

The next few days would tell. The Foxworths had had a marriage that was stormy and controversial from the first. As a former waitress, she was hardly in his social stratum, and there were rumours throughout their marriage that he was cruel to her or she was cheating on him, depending on which set of gossips you chose to listen to. At the trial, there was sure to be ample testimony on both sides.

On the evening of the murder, Foxworth had come home from one of his numerous charitable committee meetings to find his wife on the floor of their living room shot to death. He immediately called the police. To them, he theorised that she had been visited by a lover or surprised a burglar. That nothing was missing kind of let out the second theory.

Two hours before Foxworth arrived home, neighbours had heard a loud explosion, which later was pretty well accepted to be the shot. Naturally they all thought, or wanted to think, it was something other than what it was. A car backfiring maybe. So no one reported it.

Foxworth appeared to have an airtight alibi for the time of the killing. He actually *had* been to that committee meeting at a downtown hotel. On closer examination, though, the police discovered he had been away from other members of his committee for a period of about fifteen minutes, long enough for him to drive back to his house, kill his wife, and return to rejoin the committee at the hotel. There were even a couple of members of the committee who thought he seemed out of breath and nervous on his return. The others disputed that, however.

There was no real evidence he'd actually made that trip back to his house with one exception: the testimony of an eyewitness, a neighbour who said she had seen Foxworth leaving by the back door of the house shortly after the shot.

There was even a fairly solid motive: a piece of land Foxworth needed to expand his factory was in his wife's name, and she was refusing to co-operate with him on it. It was rumoured that Foxworth wanted a divorce to marry somebody else and Stella had offered him the land or the divorce, but not both. The identity of the other woman, if any, was never brought out, but the prosecution could use Foxworth's humiliation about his wife's rumoured infidelity to strengthen the possible motive.

The first day's testimony was mostly the technical stuff, not too interesting unless you were really wrapped up in courtroom give-and-take for its own sake. I usually am, but this time I kept turning my eyes and thoughts to Andy Cutshaw at the court clerk's table, down below the judge's bench. Did he look sick? I didn't think so, no more than usual. He was a skinny little guy anyway, and he always looked miserable.

He did look, though, as if the proceedings were difficult for him, as though his personal sense of involvement was hard to keep under control. If you weren't looking for the signs, though, I don't think you'd have known.

The second day of the trial was one of the big ones. The neighbour, Mrs Harmatz, gave her testimony.

Willard Craven, the assistant DA, a bulky guy in his thirties with the tired, slow-talking courtroom manner of an octogenarian, was asking his questions. Normally, one of his questions would have been enough to put half the court to sleep, but today everybody was alert. The witness was a dignified lady in her seventies, not much like the village busybody the defence would probably try to paint her.

'Mrs Harmatz, do you recall where you were on the evening of the seventeenth of March last?' Craven asked.

'Yes. I was at home, watching television.'

'Tell the court and the jury what occurred on that evening.'

'Well, at about nine thirty, I heard a very loud bang. I remember it made me jump.'

'Could you tell where the noise had come from?'

'It sounded as if it had come from the Foxworth house next door, but I couldn't be sure.'

'Did you go to investigate?'

'Yes, I went to my back door, opened it, and looked across at the back door of Mr and Mrs Foxworth's house.'

'You could see their back door from your own?'

'About the top half of it. There is a fence between our properties, but it is only about five and a half feet high, and my back porch is somewhat elevated from the ground. So I can see about the top half of their back porch.'

'Was their porch light turned on?'

'Yes, it was.'

'What did you see then, Mrs Harmatz?'

'The door swung open, and Mr Foxworth appeared in the doorway. I saw his face for a moment after he opened the door. Then he switched the light off and disappeared from sight.'

'Disappeared where?'

'I believe he remained outside. But in the darkness it was hard to be sure.'

'What did you do then?'

'I returned to my living room and started watching television again.'

'Did Mr Foxworth speak to you?'

'No.'

'Did you speak to him?'

'No.'

'Is there any doubt in your mind that it was Mr Foxworth you saw?'

'I'm certain that's who it was.'

'And you said this was at nine thirty?'

'Almost exactly.'

'How can you be so sure of the time?'

'I had just finished watching Julia Child on the educational TV station. They always bring her programme from nine to nine thirty. When I returned to the house, the next programme was just beginning. I heard the shot . . .'

George Ealing, Foxworth's attorney, was on his feet. 'Objection, Your Honour. It is the witness's conclusion, not supported by evidence, that she heard a shot.'

'Sustained,' said Judge Middleton. He told the witness, quite kindly and patiently, that she must testify only to what she knew of her own knowledge.

'I'm sorry, Your Honour. I heard the loud noise just as Julia Child was finishing her dish for the night, and when I looked out the back door, it was almost precisely nine thirty.'

'I have no more questions,' said the prosecutor. He lumbered to his table and sat down, as if wearied beyond his years.

The out-of-town hotshot leaped to his feet, as though he couldn't wait to get at Mrs Harmatz.

'What was Julia Child cooking that night?'

'I don't remember,' she said simply.

'You remember the other events of the evening quite vividly but not what Julia Child was cooking?'

'The other events of the evening were far more memorable.'

'I see.' Ealing spoke in rapid, clipped tones, making no effort to establish a friendly rapport with the witness. He differed in this from most other trial men I've seen in action, but it was his style and it seemed to work effectively for him. So did the use of seemingly random questions, unannounced changes of subject, and the variations in delivery of a baseball pitcher.

'Do you wear glasses?'

'Yes, for reading.'

'Were you wearing them that night?'

'I wasn't reading.'

'Were the Foxworths good neighbours?'

'I suppose so. I didn't see them much.'

'You didn't see them much?' Ealing echoed with elaborate surprise.

'No, but frequently enough to know them when I saw them.'

'Do you usually try out Julia Child's recipes?'

That one seemed out of left field to me, and I thought Craven could have objected, but he stayed in his chair.

'Sometimes I do.'

'Did you try out the one she did that night?'

'No.'

'How do you know you didn't if you don't remember what it was?'

Before Mrs Harmatz could answer, Craven belatedly lumbered to his feet to object to the irrelevancy of this line of questioning. The judge sustained him, and the defence attorney leered at the jury as if he and they were aware he'd made some telling point here. Whatever he and they knew, it surely escaped me.

Returning to the attack, Ealing said, 'Don't most persons over seventy wear their glasses all the time?'

Craven objected that the witness had no way of knowing the state of the vision of most people over seventy, and again he was sustained.

'Have you ever been told to wear your glasses all the time?'

'No.'

'Does it worry you that your glasses make you look old?'

'I *am* old.' This got a laugh from the spectators.

'Did you ever have a dispute with the defendant?'

'What do you mean a dispute?'

'An argument, a quarrel, a disagreement.'
'Not that I recall.'
'Did you ever call the police on the Foxworths?'
She thought for a moment. 'Once he had a dog that barked too loud, late at night. I believe I did once call the police about that, after discussing it personally with Mr Foxworth and seeing no improvement.'
'You don't call that a dispute?'
'It was a minor matter. You can call it a dispute if you want to.'
'What about the leaves from his tree falling on your lawn, Mrs Harmatz?'
'I never called the police about that.'
'But you were angry about it?'
'No, not angry.'
'Upset about it, then?'
'Upset is too strong a word.'
'But you did object.'
'I mentioned to Mr Foxworth that I wished he would do something about his leaves, yes.'
'And did he?'
'I believe he did. It was years ago. He cut the tree down.'
'Isn't it true that your neighbours have been a constant source of irritation to you, Mrs Harmatz?'
'Certainly not. You've mentioned two incidents in twenty years.'
'How long have you had vision problems, Mrs Harmatz?'
'I don't have vision problems.'
'But you wear glasses.'
'For reading. And many people wear glasses. That doesn't mean they have vision problems.'
'If they didn't have vision problems, why would they have to wear glasses?'
Craven objected to defence counsel's argumentative question, and again the out-of-town lawyer leered at the jury as if he'd made a telling point.
'Is it true, Mrs Harmatz, that while your neighbours capitulated and got rid of their dog and cut down their trees, they never removed their ivy plant?'
'I don't know anything about their ivy plant.'
'Isn't it a fact that you objected to their ivy plant on the

grounds that it was giving you roof rats?'

She hesitated. 'Yes, that's true. I had forgotten.'

'Forgotten? The ivy plant is still there, isn't it?'

'But the roof rats are gone,' she replied, over-sweetly. 'I must have been mistaken about their ivy plant. It was less of a problem than I thought.'

'Is it not a fair statement, Mrs Harmatz, that it is the imagined problems created by your neighbours that have led you to make this false accusation against Mr Foxworth?'

'Objection, Your Honour,' said Craven, with less heat than I thought was warranted. 'That is a beating-your-wife type of question. It cannot be answered.'

Ealing continued in the same vein for a while longer, alternately impugning Mrs Harmatz's motives and casting doubt on her ability to see what she said she had. On redirect, Craven asked one question.

'Mrs Harmatz, would a barking dog, a few leaves, and a roof rat or two be sufficient provocation for you to bear false witness against a neighbour?'

'Nothing would be sufficient to do that, Mr Craven, neighbour or not,' she replied.

The consensus of the press was that Mrs Harmatz had been a very damaging witness. A few thought, however, that George Ealing had created enough of an illusion of doubt to influence some of the more gullible members of the jury. The defender's flashy style, like something out of a TV lawyer show, presented a distinct contrast to the soporific performance of Prosecutor Craven. But would a jury of intelligent people acquit a man of murder because of his lawyer's superior skills as an entertainer.

The trial bore on. The weapon used in the crime was identified as Foxworth's own, normally kept in a desk drawer in their house. The fact he'd had an opportunity to leave the committee meeting long enough to commit the crime was established pretty solidly and with much care to detail. But the only solid evidence was the eyewitness testimony of Mrs Harmatz. Would the jury believe her?

After three days of presenting its case, the prosecution rested and the defence took over. Ealing's strategy seemed to be to capitalise on the blackened reputation of the victim, indicating that she regularly entertained lovers in the house in her husband's absence; this brought more observant neighbours into play but no flesh-and-blood lover. The prosecution had needed her infidelity to bolster the motive, but the defence seemed to need it even more to suggest an alternate killer. The evidence seemed inconclusive to most of us, obviously trumped up to some. During this phase of the trial, Andy Cutshaw the court clerk grew more and more morose. I thought he was actually starting to look as sick as he claimed to be. His face looked grey.

Andy and I continued to meet for an occasional drink as the trial went on. One of those evenings, he reached down to look for something in the briefcase he always carried into court with him. It fell open and I noticed that the court clerk was carrying a handgun among his papers. It seemed totally out of character to me.

'How long have you been packing a rod, Andy?' I asked as lightly as I could manage.

He gave me a thin grimace. 'Self-protection,' he said with heavy irony, as if he and I both knew he had little reason to want to prolong his life.

During a trial, Andy was scrupulous about what he could discuss and what he couldn't. Though he was privy to a lot of confidential information, he didn't consider it ethical to pass it along to me. About courthouse gossip and out-of-court activities he had no such compunction. Our discussions of the Foxworth trial had to be superficial, but I could read between the lines well enough to know that he considered Foxworth guilty as hell and, whether he admitted it or not, he shared the feeling of some of us that the rich man was about to get away with murder, the beneficiary of Ealing's dramatic manner and tricky cross-examination as well as his own status in the town. Because of his past association with the victim, I thought Andy felt a personal enmity towards Foxworth.

It was that night, after I'd left Andy and gone back to my apartment, that it first occurred to me that the court clerk might intend to take the law into his own hands. I'll admit a reporter needs a vivid imagination, and mine started heating up with a vengeance, much as I tried to dismiss the possibility from my mind.

The next day, George Ealing called Clayton Foxworth to testify in his own defence. The defendant was a big, impressive-looking man who maintained the air of a pillar of the community even when on trial for murder.

'Mr Foxworth, do you recall what you did on the evening of your wife's death?'

'Yes, very well. I attended a meeting of the city symphony funding committee at the Warnecke Hotel.'

'What time did you arrive at the hotel for that meeting?'

'Shortly before eight o'clock.'

'And what time did you leave the meeting?'

'Eleven thirty.'

'Arriving home when?'

'About eleven thirty-seven.'

'It was about a seven-minute drive?'

'That's right.'

'Would that be your normal driving time from the Warnecke Hotel to your house?'

'For me it would. I'm a rather slow driver.'

'Did you leave the Warnecke and return home at any time during the evening?'

'I did not.'

'Did you leave the meeting of the committee at any time during the evening?'

'Yes, at about twenty past nine, I believe.'

'What did you do?'

'I went to the men's room down the hall from the conference room.'

'How long were you in the men's room?'

'About ten to fifteen minutes, I think. I wasn't feeling well. I had a bad stomach. I'd seen my doctor about it just a couple of days before.'

'Did you have any other reason for being in there that long?'

'I had one of the committee reports to read, and I wanted to read it in peace.' That got a titter from the crowd. 'The bathroom is one of my favourite places to read.' This got, you should pardon the expression, a belly laugh.

With one of his usual dramatic changes of pace, the defence attorney asked simply, 'Mr Foxworth, did you kill your wife?'

'No, I did not.'

'Were you aware of your wife's dalliances with other men?'

'Yes, but . . . I forgave them. All of them. I loved her.' His voice broke over that a little bit. Faked or not, it was effective theatre. 'She was somewhat younger than I was, and I knew that . . . Well, I turned a blind eye to them. I just hoped she would be discreet about them.'

I could sense Andy's anger as he listened to this. To someone who didn't know him, he wouldn't look any different sitting there among his exhibits. But I could tell he was keeping a tight rein. Andy was convinced Foxworth was guilty. And he could bring a gun into court with him. He wouldn't be searched entering the courtroom, and he always had his briefcase . . .

Ealing asked Foxworth about the alleged land problems, and he admitted he and his wife had disagreed over the use of the land. But he ridiculed the idea that this was enough to provoke him to kill her. He denied he had wanted to divorce his wife.

The cross-examination of Foxworth by Willard Craven wasn't much. Not what it should have been, I thought. Yes, there was a door to a fire escape near the men's room where Foxworth had gone, but no, he hadn't used it to go downstairs to his car. Yes, he'd parked his car on a side street where he might have driven it off without being seen, but no, he hadn't. Yes, he could have driven home in four or five minutes, but he never drove that fast. Yes, he could have parked his car in the back alley, entered his yard through the back gate (unseen, he hoped, by his neighbours), killed his wife, and left the same way. But he hadn't. No, no one had seen him in the men's room, but it wasn't a full-scale men's room, just a small one for the convenience of people using the meeting rooms, for use by one at a time. No, he didn't recall telling anyone that his wife's intransigence over the parcel of land would ultimately have ruined his business, and the suggestion was absurd.

When the cross-examination ended, there was about forty-five minutes to go until the afternoon recess. In that time, the defence wrapped it up, calling Foxworth's doctor to testify to his stomach trouble, something that indeed could have kept him in the bathroom for an unusually long period of time. Ealing even had a witness from the symphony committee to swear that Foxworth had returned from the men's room with more apparent knowledge of that one particular report than he'd had when he started out.

With that, the defence rested. Craven had no rebuttal

witnesses to call, and Judge Middleton set the following day for closing arguments.

Andy didn't turn up at the tavern that night, but I drank my share anyway.

The next morning, as I sat listening to the summations, my suspicions started niggling at me again. I felt as sure as Andy did that a not-guilty verdict would be the wrong one, but shooting Foxworth would be murder . . .

The closing arguments were about what the rest of the trial had led us to expect. Assistant DA Craven summed up the evidence in a clear, well-organised manner, but he was about as boring as a participant in a murder trial could possibly be. Everything was there – motive, means, opportunity – but he didn't really bring his case to life.

The defence summing up was where the fireworks were. Ealing ran down Mrs Harmatz's testimony, characterising her as a half-blind, disgruntled crank nursing imaginary grievances against Foxworth. It didn't work for me, but who knew what the jurors might swallow? He had great sarcastic fun with the idea that Foxworth would put together such an elaborate but chancy alibi. All he had to do was to be seen or have his car be seen by someone along the way and the whole thing would have been blown to smithereens. The police theory was likened to something out of the *Columbo* TV show, just then gaining popularity. The killer, Ealing suggested, could have been a regular visitor of Mrs Foxworth who knew where to find the gun.

Of course, the prosecutor got the last word, but even then Craven didn't seem to make that much of an impression. Viewed dispassionately, the case against Foxworth looked good, but would the jurors look at it that way or would they be dazzled by the defence attorney's pyrotechnics? Ealing was a courtroom magician who could make a handful of air look like multi-coloured scarves.

Again, I was starting to think about Andy's gun. Maybe he did just carry it for protection and had no idea of using it. But as Judge Middleton charged the jury, I felt I could almost read Andy Cutshaw's mind. I remembered his repeated insistence, almost like a litany, that justice would be done and the secretive look that accompanied the statement. He felt as I did that it would be a miscarriage of justice if Foxworth got off. If there was a verdict of not guilty, I was convinced Andy was ready to put a thumb on the scales of justice and pull the trigger of that gun, killing Foxworth. Andy's own life, almost gone anyway, meant nothing to him, but he was determined to avenge Stella, that pretty waitress he'd once known.

During the time the jury was out, I'd have liked a chance to talk to Andy, but he disappeared with his briefcase back into the area of the judge's chambers. I can see you asking why I didn't blow the whistle on him, tell the security guard to search his briefcase and see if he really had the gun. I think the answer is that a part of me agreed with what he wanted to do. I wouldn't admit it to myself, of course, but every time I got close to saying something I told myself it was ridiculous and would just cause embarrassment for both of us. It was only when court was in session, and I really could do nothing, that the feeling came over me the most strongly.

The jury had only been out a couple of hours when we all returned to the courtroom to hear the verdict. I tried to catch Andy's eye at the clerk table, but he wouldn't look my way. He seemed to have his hand on something under the table, something no one was in any position to see. I was almost starting to feel like a potential accessory to murder, and I didn't like the feeling. I decided that if the verdict was not guilty, I had to leap across the room at the clerk table fast enough to keep Andy from shooting Foxworth. Sure, I knew I might get shot myself, but that was what I got for not doing something sooner. I tensed myself to spring.

'Ladies and gentlemen of the jury, have you reached a verdict?' Judge Middleton asked.

'Yes, Your Honour,' said the foreman.

'And what is your verdict?'

Foxworth and his lawyer were on their feet. It crossed my mind what a big target the defendant made.

'We find the defendant guilty as charged.'

I felt myself relax. That settled that. Justice was done. No need ever to know if Andy really intended . . .

And at that moment, Andy Cutshaw stood up, aimed his pistol carefully, and shot Foxworth in the heart. The bailiff and two cops wrestled him to the floor, but it was too late. Foxworth was dead.

Looking back, I realise I had Andy figured all wrong. He insisted on his firm belief in our justice system, and he really did believe except for one little flaw: that Supreme Court decision that wiped out capital punishment. If the jury had said Foxworth was innocent, he'd have gone along with no question, however he might have felt privately. But if they found him guilty, Andy Cutshaw was going to be his executioner, make sure he got the punishment the Supreme Court said he couldn't have. That's what Andy said in a widely quoted confession.

What does that say about capital punishment? Now, fellows, I told you I wasn't going to take sides on that issue. Let's have another drink.

Celia Dale

KINDNESS

That's right, dear, come and sit down for a bit, take the weight off your feet. You're on your feet a lot, aren't you, I've seen you about, 'specially lately. I often sit here when the weather's nice. It's nice in the sun and I can watch the world go by. I see a lot of what goes on, I can tell you – although, of course, no one takes no notice of an elderly lady like me.

That's what we call it now, isn't it. We don't say 'old' any more, it doesn't sound nice somehow. 'Elderly's' more dignified somehow, although I daresay it means just the same to you young people. 'Old folks' now – that's a term I can't abide. As if elderly people were just bags of rubbish, old clothes, jumble. That's why 'elderly' sounds nicer, leaves us our self-respect.

Oh yes, I know what you're thinking, dear. You're thinking you're in for a long moan about how everything's changed for the worse, how much better it was in my young days, how young people nowadays have it all their own way. Well, I'll tell you something – I'm sorry for you young people, I really am. Yes, I am, I'm sorry. You just don't know what life's all about, with your discos and glue sniffing and Social Security. You don't never face up to what real life's all about, like what it was when I was a girl. We learned what's what better than you lot nowadays, we was really up against it when I was growing up.

My Dad was away in the war – the Great War, that is – and when he come back there was the Depression. There was five of us at home. My Mum used to go out cleaning, and my word, what she couldn't make out of a scrag of mutton and some carrots and turnips and that you wouldn't believe. Talk about making money stretch – and nourishing with it. We was all of us healthy, 'cept Annie, she was the youngest, she suffered from her legs and her chest, bronchial she was and her legs never was really strong.

She passed away just before the war – the last war, that is – and I must say I was glad in a way. She was spared all the Blitz and that.

Mind you, we had our good times in the war. We lived near the docks and of course they caught it from old Adolf right from the start. But we used to go down the Underground every night, had our own pitch, blankets, pillows, snacks and that, and there was ever such a nice crowd down there. We used to have sing-songs and buskers and games of housey-housey. Oh, we had some good times down there, I can tell you.

Of course, we never knew what we'd find when we come up again in the morning. Whole streets'd be down and you never smelled anything like the smell of wet soot and brick and gas mains and burning. But we was all together, one big family somehow, right from Their Majesties down. There was none of this nastiness we get nowadays, all this mugging and demos and violence. We had respect, and hopes for better times.

It's the kiddies I feel sorry for now. I mean, take what's been happening round here just lately. Three of them gone, and the police chasing round like their tails was on fire, getting nowhere. You never had this sort of thing when I was a kiddie. We used to go out and play in the street till all hours and not a bit of harm came to us. But nowadays you can't let a kiddie so much as run down to the sweet shop without wondering whether you'll ever see her again. Shocking.

I love kiddies, dear. I've had two of my own and I've got three grandchildren – yes, two boys and a girl, that's nice, isn't it. But I don't see them because my daughter and her hubby, they went to Canada, oh back in the nineteen sixties it was. Well, there wasn't much prospects for them here, never mind all that talk about Swinging Britain and that, so they emigrated, a place near Vancouver, and the kiddies was born there. So I've never seen them, though I've got photos, of course.

Well, I couldn't hardly find the fare, could I, dear, just on my pension and the Supplementary. I get my heating and some of my rent, and there's Senior Citizens' clubs where you get a nice dinner three times a week. I'm still pretty active although my legs give me a bit of trouble – well, they would at my age, wouldn't they. But my arms is still strong, I do all my own housework and laundry and cooking. I've just the one room, dear, with a kitchenette. It's on the ground floor and near the shops, so I manage to get out most days and look after myself. I've got one of them trolley things on wheels to help with the shopping. And when it's fine I like to sit out on this seat here near the school and watch the world go by. I often have a nice chat with someone passing by, like you and I are. And I like to see the kiddies.

My other one? Well, Kevin was in an accident on his motorbike out in Margate one Bank Holiday. He was mad about his motorbike, used to go out with his friends all done up in black leather and that, he looked lovely. He was in that place where Mr Tebbitt was, Stoke something, but they couldn't save him. Twenty-two he was and ever so good-looking.

Yes, it was sad. My hubby'd gone off by then, you see, so I was just on my own. That's why I said just now you young people don't know what real life's all about, you're not trained to stand up to things like we was.

Like I said, it's the kiddies I'm sorry for. They're just not being prepared for the kind of things that can happen to them. Illness and wars and that, let alone getting old and being left on your own. I blame the parents.

You're not married, dear, are you – you're not wearing a ring, although that don't signify nowadays. When I was a girl we took pride in our rings, showing we was married. It gave us respect. That's what's missing these days – respect. I daresay you think I'm just a silly old woman going on about how things have changed for the worse, that I'm losing my marbles just moaning on. But let me tell you, we older people aren't stupid, you know. We've seen it all and we can see where it's going and some of us are a great deal cleverer than you'll ever be. No offence meant, dear, but it makes me mad to be pushed on one side like I was daft. Just because I'm elderly don't mean I'm stupid. In fact, you'd be surprised at just how sharp I am, although I says it.

And I really mean it – I'm really sorry for the kiddies growing up in the kind of world we've got nowadays, and their parents don't do nothing about it. What's a kiddie growing up nowadays got to look forward to, I ask you – kidnappings and murders and riots and all this nuclear threat. All these transplants and test-tube babies. Single-parent families. We used to call them unmarried mothers and that was something to be ashamed of, and the man took his share if you could catch him. Nowadays they don't even *want* to get married, not even if there's a kiddie.

So no wonder I get upset, sitting here on this seat in the lane by the school and watching all those lovely little kiddies coming by on their way home. They're only little, it's the Infants' gate that lets out just up the corner there, no more than five or six most of them, all colours too nowadays. And d'you know, half of them have to go home on their own! I tell you no lie, half of them don't have no one to meet them, they just come out of the gate and toddle off on their own. Their silly cows of mothers can't even be bothered to turn up at the gate to collect them, and those that do just hang about chatting and giggling, all done up in dirty old jeans and jumpers the dustman would sniff at, not a scrap of make-up, hair all anyhow, no pride in themselves – it makes you wonder just how those kiddies ever got born, it really does. Their kiddies just mill about, never a kiss or a hug like mine used to get, while their mums just stand there nattering to their friends till at last they go off with their fag-ends and their bottoms and the poor little kiddies trailing along behind.

But a lot of them don't even have that. I've watched all through the summer, I can tell you, whenever the weather's been nice. I've sat on this seat in the quiet, there's not much passing to and fro in this lane here, it's a kind of cul-de-sac they call it, and I've seen which little ones go by on their own, up to the path at the end there and into the housing estate, and it's made my heart bleed to think what kind of a world they'll grow up into and what kind of a life they'll have. I tell you, it won't be worth living.

Yes, dear, it makes my heart bleed to think of all the neglect and pain and sorrow in store for those little kiddies – lovely kiddies, their hair all shining and their cheeks all rosy, so small and trusting, like flowers really, lovely innocent flowers . . .

They most of them like sweets. The first one, the little girl, she came and sat down beside me when I called her and I gave her a fruit gum. She wasn't a bit shy, rather cheeky really, like some of them are. I remember she asked was I a granny and I said I was and she said her granny worked in a supermarket every day and sold people money – wasn't that killing, I had to laugh! I suppose she meant the check-out, they call it.

Next time I gave her one of my tablets for sleeping. They look like sweets really unless you know, and then I asked her would she like to help pull my trolley back to my home like it was a dolls' pram, and of course she would. By the time we got there she was quite drowsy, so I laid her down and put a plastic bag over her little head. And afterwards I packed her up in the trolley and when it was dark I took it out to the Common and put her away nicely right in some bushes.

The next one was just the same – I expect they none of them had the kind of grannies like I am, elderly and comfy-looking and kind, so they was really glad to come with me. And of course all kiddies like sweets.

And they'd never been warned! Just think of that, those silly young cows of their mothers had never said to them Don't ever take sweets from strangers or go home with a stranger! Just think what might have happened to them if it hadn't been me but some terrible sex maniac – they'd have been interfered with, beaten up, terrified, it won't bear thinking of! They was happy as lambs with me, and spared all the nastiness to come.

So you do see, don't you, dear, that it's because I love kiddies that I can't let them grow up in the kind of world we're making for ourselves. I'm doing them a kindness. It's a pity I haven't saved more, but there's plenty of time, if I'm spared.

Come to the station? What station's that, dear? Well, fancy that, I'd never have thought it, not with your jeans and your T-shirt and that! And if you don't mind my saying so, dear, the police is a funny job for a nice girl like you to be in . . .

Paula Gosling

THE PERFECT ALIBI

'Two beers, Charley.'

It was a corner bar not too many steps from the Precinct Station, and the Sergeant and the Rookie, coming off an arduous tour, were in need of a little restorative refreshment. They carried their glasses to a booth and settled in with a sigh each, one tenor and brief, the other long, low and grateful.

'Gets worse every day,' said the Sergeant.

'You said that yesterday, Sarge.'

'Yeah, and I'll probably say it tomorrow, smart-ass. So? I got my rituals, you got yours.' The Sergeant's voice was filled with the gravelly sediment of many years' service, and the Rookie grinned.

There had been a rush of business just before they'd come off duty, to say nothing of a fist-fight breaking out between a man and wife, and a visit from Granny, who had been reporting the same B & E for fifteen years – lost, one diamond tiara (she was the *real* Princess Anastasia). The Sergeant had a special report sheet he pulled out for her, like clockwork, and wrote everything down with a leadless pencil, going over the old words so many times that they were wearing thin in places. It was, he said, her only entertainment – and it allowed them to keep an eye on her, for she was frail and lived alone.

There were a lot of people in this slum precinct that the Sergeant kept an eye on. Currently, one of them was the Rookie, who showed promise, but was inclined to be swept away by the excitement of it all. As far as he was concerned the Sergeant was the fount of all wisdom, and he was always ready to listen to another story. The Sergeant was flattered by this, naturally, being a childless widower and lonely, but he saw it as his duty to select incidents that would instruct rather than amuse. One day this freckle-faced bundle of energy would be in charge of a case, and he didn't want to see it go down the toilet just because the kid forgot the basics. In some ways, the young man's good looks would be useful – nothing disarms a female suspect quite as much as a handsome arresting officer. The Sergeant didn't have that advantage, being thick in the middle and thin on top. However, the evening stretched ahead and, for some reason, the boy was in the mood for more learning.

Many steps, the Sergeant always told him, many careful steps make a case.

He was telling it to him again today.

'Take, for instance, the line-up,' he said. The Rookie frowned with frustration. They'd had a line-up that morning, in an attempt to identify a mugger, and, as happened so often, the witness hadn't been certain enough to make an identification.

'Waste of everybody's time,' the Rookie complained.

The Sergeant shrugged. 'People don't like to make mistakes, don't like to take responsibility. They see all them scowling faces, they get confused. But sometimes that works for us, too.'

'I don't see how,' the Rookie said. 'A lawyer can really milk a failure to ID.'

'Sure. But I'm not talking about failure, here, I'm talking about a wrong ID altogether, see? Take, for instance, the Excelsior diamond robbery in 'fifty-six,' the Sergeant continued. The Rookie, smiling, leaned back to listen. This was History. He hadn't even been *born* in '56, for crying out loud.

'Torn down now, the old Excelsior Building. Was over on Third and Oakland, I think. Or was it Third and Elm?' the Sergeant mused. 'Anyway, it had a lot of ... Fourth and Oakland, that was it. Fourth and Oakland.'

'Where the McDonald's is,' the Rookie said, encouragingly. He knew the location, he was on the ball.

'Yeah, yeah, where the McDonald's is,' the Sergeant agreed. The Rookie nodded.

'The Excelsior Building,' he repeated, as if taking notes.

The Sergeant looked gratified. 'Yeah. Right. Well, it had a lot of jewellery wholesalers and diamond merchants in it, the Excelsior, and one morning we get a call that one of the biggest, called the Excelsior Diamond Exchange, had been ripped off. So, over we goes, and the place is like an anthill, people running

The Perfect Alibi

around and yelling, everybody scared to death and like that. See, the minute they come in and hear the Excelsior has been ripped off, they figure *they* been ripped off, too, so we got to go from office to office, the whole damned building this is, looking, checking, and like that, okay?'

'Yeah, I got the picture.' The Rookie could see it, he really could, a wave of blue surging through the corridors, and the plain-clothes dicks in those hats with the big brims they wore in the Fifties, taking notes, talking out of the side of their mouths, the whole bit. Two years in the Academy and two years on the beat had not dimmed the Rookie's childhood images. Now was now, now was a bitch, but then, *Then*, cops were cops. The Sergeant was rolling on.

'So we do our thing, and we get to this little guy named Samuels, *his* name I remember to the day I die, and he says to us he was working late planning to cut a big diamond – did you know they take weeks to figure out how to do it? – and he maybe sees the thief. Gives us a description. Right away we're lucky, because this description, it had to be Buddy Canoli. He had him cold, down to a scar on the back of his left hand, which he saw as Canoli was on his way up the stairs.'

'If this guy was in his office, how could he see somebody going up the stairs?' the Rookie interrupted.

'He left the door open to get a breeze, it was hot, okay?'

'Okay.'

'It was August.'

'*Okay!* Summer, diamonds, Buddy Canoli. I got it.'

'Right. So we pull in Canoli. He's got spit for an alibi, so we put him in a line-up with some guys we pull in from the street plus a few cops for flavour, and what do you think?'

'Samuels identifies a cop?'

'No. *No.*' The Sergeant looked disappointed in his protégé. 'He identifies one of the guys we pull in from the street, name of Whitney. Don't forget *that* name, either. Walter Whitney. Anyways, this guy is *like* Buddy Canoli, I give you that, tall and thin and a lot of dark curly hair, plus on the back of his left hand, he has a birthmark. Not a scar, but close enough, maybe, for a nitwit like Samuels, who swears this is the guy he sees going up the stairs the night before.'

'Swell,' sympathised the Rookie.

'Yeah, right. Well, there we were, we had Canoli cold, we *knew* he did it, and he knew we knew, and he walks out laughing. I was burned. To add to which, you know the regulations, I got to check this poor guy Whitney's alibi out, right?'

'What regulations?' the Rookie asked, nervously. Another one he must have missed.

'The one which states if a person is identified on a line-up, we got to check them out, is which one,' the Sergeant told him, impatiently.

'Oh, yeah, that one,' the Rookie said, vaguely, trying to pin it down in his mind.

'Right. Well, obviously, this Whitney is pretty boiled about the thing himself, respectable guy and all that. It makes him nervous, it would make anybody nervous, but I get him calmed down. You know, have a coffee, stuff like that.'

'Yeah, sure,' the Rookie agreed. Stuff like that he could do standing on his head.

'So, Whitney tells me he was home alone like ten million other people. He's separated from his wife, who's gone back to her mother in Chicago, he leads a quiet life, all that. Fine, I don't argue, I got no reason to doubt him, do I? He goes on his way, I pick up a phone, call the caretaker of his particular apartment building which I happen to know personally, ask is this Whitney on the up and up, very casual, and the caretaker – what do you think he says?'

'Whitney is a nutny?' the Rookie suggested.

'Nah. But Whitney is not being a truthful person. Like he says, he lives alone, all that. Only Whitney *wasn't* home that night because the caretaker has to go up there about the air-conditioning which Whitney told him was broken, and when he goes up he gets no reply. Goes up twice, too.'

'Maybe Whitney was asleep.'

'Caretaker has a pass key. Went in, fixed the air-conditioner, no Whitney.' The Sergeant looked triumphant.

'Jeez. So why was he lying?'

'Exactly what I want to know.'

'Yeah, right!'

'So, I go down to where this Whitney has an office, he's some kind of accountant, and I say, look, friend, you weren't home on the night in question, anything to say about that, and he gets very

The Perfect Alibi

nervous again and he closes the door and asks me to sit down. Turns out he's shagging his secretary on the night in question, but he doesn't want to put it on the record because his wife is on the look-out for anything she can get on him for a divorce, which would ruin him financially. He points to a picture of the wife on his desk, and she is one mean-looking old broad, that's for sure. One of those thin hard mouths, you know, the kind that bites and hangs on for keeps?'

The Rookie nodded. They'd picked up a hooker the other day who'd had a mouth like that and had done exactly what the Sergeant said. The marks were still on his arm. He looked at the Sergeant warily, to see if he was kidding him about that, but the old man's eyes were misty with remembering, so he let it go.

The Sergeant was continuing. 'Well, Mr Whitney, I says to him, we can be discreet. If you'd said that to me right away and explained, I could have saved some shoe leather. He apologises, asks me if I want to speak to his secretary and confirm it, and I say, well, okay, if you insist, and so he calls in this little red-head from the outer office and says tell this man about last night.'

The Sergeant smiled. 'She was a cute little thing, name of Marylou Mason, and she blushes, which tells me nearly all I want to know right there, but she speaks her piece all right, and says, yes, they were together all night, so I say thank you, Miss Marylou Mason, and I come away and write up my report.'

'Is that it?' asked the Rookie, finally, when the Sergeant took time out to drink some beer.

'No,' the Sergeant said. 'We keep on at the thing, but we can't get a hold on Buddy Canoli on account of no solid forensic evidence and no ID from friend Samuels the near-sighted diamond king, and so the case stays open. We're stuck, we have to move on to other things, and gradually the subject fades away, so to speak.'

'Gee,' said the Rookie. 'That was interesting.' His voice was bleak with disappointment.

'I ain't finished yet,' the Sergeant growled.

'Sorry.' The Rookie brightened again.

'Right. So a few months later, we got to do another line-up, and we pull in some guys from the street as usual. This was, I think, maybe November, now. And guess who is third from the right?'

'Whitney?'

'No, *Samuels*, dumbo. But seeing him reminds me of the case, so to speak. Nobody IDs *him* for robbery, though. Damned shame, would have served him right. Point is, because the whole thing comes back to me, my mind is aware, you know? And the next thing is, I spot Whitney in a restaurant a few days later. Only he's thinner, so I don't recognise him at first. Especially wearing a five hundred dollar suit, when before it was thirty-seven buck numbers off the rack. Well, he spots me and suddenly lunch is over. I say hello, Mr Whitney, to him, as he goes by, being a friendly type. He gives me the fish-eye and goes out of the place like his ass was on fire.'

'Aha!' the Rookie pounced on this as evidence of something sinister. He was nearly chewing hunks out of the beerglass, trying to second-guess the story. The Sergeant sighed. Where do they get all this energy? he wondered, and pressed on.

'Well, he goes off so fast, he forgets his coat, see? I notice the waiter pick it up and take it to the manager, so, being a swell guy, as you know, I decide to take it around to Whitney's office for him, as it's only around the corner. But it's not his office any more, I discover. He's moved uptown, they tell me. So, uptown I go, 'cause I'm now stuck with this damned coat, and sure enough, there he is. Set up in some fancy office with a new secretary and all very nifty. He makes like he didn't see me in the restaurant, acts all surprised, very nervous, too, wants me to get out of sight. I don't like to be put out of sight, you know? I got my pride.'

'You bet.'

'So I look around, I get like, expansive, you know, just to needle the stuck-up bastard. I say, business must be good, this is nice. He says yes. You must have some pretty fancy clients, now, I say, not like the old days. Yes, he says, and no, he says. He obviously wants me gone, so I figure what the hell. I say here's your coat and he says thank you, and that's it and goodbye.'

The Rookie's eyes showed disappointment again. 'Is this going to be another one of your stories about how no matter how hard you work on something it never comes right?' he asked, suspiciously. 'Are you just building me up for the big let-down?'

'Would I do that?' the Sergeant asked, his eyes twinkling.

'You did last week, said it was a salutary lesson,' the Rookie grumbled. 'You got it in for me, I sometimes think. I'm not as dumb as I look.' He caught the Sergeant's eye, and grinned. 'I know, I know – I couldn't be. Okay, go on.'

'Right.' The Sergeant leaned back. 'I thought to myself about this new office business, and the new suit, and the new secretary, even classier than the one before, and how it all must have cost him an arm and a leg, so I ask around, and what do you think? Seems that Whitney suddenly has a lot of money to spend a few months back. And this new money of his makes an appearance right after the Excelsior robbery. Hey! I begin to think, maybe – just maybe – that little weasel Samuels made the right identification after all! Maybe it wasn't Canoli who ripped off the Excelsior, but *Whitney*, instead.'

'Son of a bitch,' the Rookie breathed.

'I tell all this to the Captain and he says follow it up, things being what they were and him not liking a big case dangling unfinished like it was. So I go around to Whitney's bank and say what about all this money in August? And they say what about it? And I say was it cash. And they say, no, it comes by cheque from some insurance outfit in Chicago, which stops me, cold. What can I say? Oh, I say. They tell me he's got three accounts now, one personal with his wife, one for the business, and one for what's left of this big lump of money, which ain't much, but they don't let me look at no details because I ain't got no court order, only nosiness and my badge.'

'Bastards,' the Rookie growled.

'You got to go by the rules,' the Sergeant said, pointedly, then relented. 'But that doesn't mean you have to go by the main road, either.' The Rookie lit up. He knew the Sergeant wasn't going to give up *now*.

The Sergeant let his halo glitter for a moment, then went on. 'I went around to Whitney's apartment, which was as new and fancy as his office. I ask to speak to his wife. The guy on the Security desk, who happens to be an old cop I know, tells me Whitney's wife has left him, and I say, again? And he says as far as he knows this is the first time, and now Whitney, the bastard, leads the life of Riley with a new girl every week. He doesn't seem to think too much of Walter Whitney, and I decide maybe I should push this button a little. Well, I say, I don't blame Whitney for kicking up his heels after having a wife that looks like a bad-tempered ant-eater, and this is the right tack because my old friend gets real mad, all of a sudden, and I wonder what's going on here? Mrs Whitney is a lovely girl, he tells me in a loud voice, and who should he proceed to describe to me but Marylou Mason, Whitney's old secretary.'

'No!' said the Rookie, with highly satisfactory surprise.

'Yeah. My old friend gets pretty excited about it – I guess sitting at a Security desk in the lobby of some fancy building all day is kind of boring, at that – and bangs his fist even. He didn't deserve her, he says. Turns out she was nice to my old buddy, and looked a little like his grand-daughter, you know? This kind of thing is a big help when you're pushing a witness, believe me. Anyway, he gives me her new address, which is a little dump on Nineteenth. I think maybe I'm lucky at last, and I go over there. Sure enough, it's little Marylou, and boy, is she sour on Whitney. I ask her about the alibi she gave Whitney for the night of the Excelsior job and eventually she breaks down and says it was all a lie.'

'Got him cold!' said the Rookie, banging his own fist down on the table top and nearly knocking over his empty beerglass.

'Jesus,' said the Sergeant. 'Don't *do* that, you'll give me a heart attack one of these days.'

'Sorry,' said the Rookie, looking around to see if anyone had noticed. One had – the new girl from Records who was sitting in the corner with some other clerks. She was laughing at him. He turned his attention back to the Sergeant and tried to look as if they were on to something big. 'Go on.'

The Sergeant, who had seen the girl in the mirror at the back, and knew how the Rookie felt about her, went on. ' "So tell me the truth," I says to Marylou, all braced to hear about the robbery. "He wasn't with me," she says, "he went to St Louis to meet someone he told me would mean big money. I got the feeling it was some kind of fast deal with this 'insurance business' he was getting into." '

' "What kind of business is that?" ' I asked her.

' "I don't know, but there were some very funny people involved. He wouldn't let me stay in the office when he talked to them. I think they must have been criminals or something. He thought I was stupid, but I'm not. He was always talking big, like he was so tough and knew what was what. He said when he got back we could get married, and we would be on easy street. He

The Perfect Alibi

always bragged about the important people he knew, but *I* never met any." You could see he'd cut her up pretty bad, emotionally, you know? Poor kid. I hate guys like that.'

'Me, too,' said the Rookie.

'But I had to go on. Was it like he promised, I asked her, and she says yes and no. The money showed up, all right, and he married her quick enough, and put her into that fancy apartment, but that was it. Like he had her where he wanted her and so he wasn't interested any more. He never talked to her, never took her anywhere, or introduced her to anyone, expected her to stay home alone all day. She'd only lied for him because she thought he loved her, but now it seemed to her like the lie had been all he'd really wanted her for. Seemed to me, too. After a while, she says, there started to be other women and she couldn't stand that, so she ups and leaves. Didn't take anything with her either, but what she stood up in. Marylou was a real nice girl. She's a grandmother, now, would you believe? I put her on to another retired cop I know ran a security firm and she married his son. Anyway, I ask her will she tell the truth about Whitney in court, and she says, sure, as far as she's concerned he's a rat and we can have him.'

'But a wife can't testify against her husband,' interrupted the Rookie.

'Sure she can, if she wants to,' the Sergeant said. 'The law says that a wife can't be *forced* to testify against her husband. That's a big difference.'

'And had Whitney gone to St Louis that night?' the Rookie asked, feeling this foray into jurisprudence wasn't getting them anywhere.

'Yeah, just like she said. She'd booked the ticket herself, using the name Mason, and drove him to the airport.'

The Rookie's eyes lit up. 'Ah,' he said, with great emphasis. 'But did she actually *see him get on to the plane?*'

The Sergeant's expression was a patient one. 'Yeah,' he said. 'She did.'

'Oh,' said the Rookie. 'Damn. But why didn't Whitney just *say* he'd gone to St Louis the night of the robbery?'

'I'm coming to that, dammit. She waved him bye-bye at around six that night, and as far as she was concerned, that was where he had been, St Louis. That was what she had been lying for him about – going to St Louis. If she couldn't maintain the first lie for him, that they'd spent the night together, say because she was worried about her reputation or something, she could *still* give him an alibi because she'd seen him leave town, right? He had *two* alibis, one behind the other. He figured that was perfect.'

'Right,' said the Rookie, but he sounded dubious, which pleased the Sergeant.

'Yeah, right. How did he know he was going to *need* two alibis?'

'I was just going to say that.'

'I thought you were.' The Sergeant smiled kindly. 'Because you know and I know that planes not only fly *into* St Louis – they also fly *out* of St Louis. He had plenty of time to turn around and come back – the Excelsior job wasn't pulled until around midnight.'

'And did he take another plane out?'

'As a matter of fact, he did. After I left Marylou, I called St Louis and confirmed that "Mr Mason" took a flight out almost immediately after he got in. Bingo. A few days later, we arrest Whitney. I get a commendation, and that's how the line-up can sometimes work for you, although not always the way you expect it will.'

'So you broke the Excelsior case all on your own?' the Rookie said, much impressed. 'That's real good.'

The Sergeant shook his head. 'Hell, no. Deakins and Brady broke the Excelsior case, got Canoli cold through a fence that traded the information in exchange for a light sentence.'

'But you said . . .'

The Sergeant leaned forward and tapped the table. 'The trouble with you is, you don't listen. Many careful steps make a case. I had to check Whitney out because of a false identification. He lied, so I had to go on checking. He told me he lied because he didn't want to drag the girl into divorce proceedings. That was another lie. Marylou said he married her as soon as he got back from his trip to St Louis. A trip *in* that was just a blind to cover another little trip *out*. He came into a lot of money very soon after this second little trip, which happened to take place the night of the Excelsior job, which is how he happened to come to my attention in the first place by getting identified in the line-up the next day.' He was beginning to wheeze, slightly. 'I wouldn't have had to check him out, otherwise, would I?' The Sergeant leaned back, waved to the bar-tender for another two beers, then watched the Rookie expectantly.

The Rookie was confused. 'But you said he didn't *do* the Excelsior job.'

The Sergeant sighed. 'He didn't. Walter Whitney had a third and even more perfect alibi for the night of the Excelsior robbery. He was in Chicago. Murdering his wife.'

Peter Lovesey

THE SECRET LOVER

'Pam.'
  'Yes?'
  'Will you see him this weekend?'
  Pam Meredith drew a long breath and stifled the impulse to scream. She knew exactly what was coming. 'See who?'
  'Your secret lover.'
  She summoned a coy smile, said, 'Give over!' and everyone giggled.
  For some reason, that last session of the working week regularly turned three efficient medical receptionists into overgrown schoolgirls. They were all over thirty, too. As soon as they arrived at the health centre on Saturday morning, they were into their routine. After flexing their imaginations with stories of what the doctors had been getting up to with the patients, they started on each other. Then it was never long before Pam's secret lover came up.
  He was an inoffensive, harassed-looking man in his late thirties who had happened to walk into the centre one afternoon to ask for help. A piece of grit had lodged under his left eyelid. Not one of the doctors or the district nurse had been in the building at the time, so Pam had dealt with it herself. From her own experiences with contact lenses, she had a fair idea how to persuade the eye to eject a foreign body, and she had succeeded very quickly, without causing the patient any serious discomfort. He had thanked her and left in a rush, as if the episode had embarrassed him. Pam had thought no more about him until a fortnight later, when she came on duty and was told that a man had been asking for her personally and would be calling back at lunchtime. This, understandably, created some lively interest in Reception, particularly when he arrived at five minutes to one carrying a

bunch of daffodils.

At thirty-three, Pam was the second youngest of the medical receptionists. She exercised, dieted and tinted her hair blonde and she was popular with many of the men who came in to collect their prescriptions, but she was not used to floral tributes. In her white overall she thought of herself as clinical and efficient. She had a pale, oval face with brown eyes and a small, neat mouth that she had been told projected refinement rather than sensuality. Lately, she had noticed some incipient wrinkles on her neck and taken to wearing polo-necked sweaters.

Under the amused and frankly envious observation of her colleagues, Pam had blushingly accepted the flowers, trying to explain that such a tribute was not necessary, charming as it was. However, when the giver followed it up by asking her to allow him to buy her a drink at the Green Dragon, she had found him difficult to refuse. She had stuttered something about being on duty after lunch, so he had suggested tomato juice or bitter lemon, and one of the other girls had given her an unseen nudge and planted her handbag in her hand.

That was the start of the long-running joke about Pam's secret lover.

Really the joke was on the others. They hadn't guessed it in their wildest fantasies, but things had developed to the extent that Pam now slept with him regularly.

Do not assume too much about the relationship. In the common understanding of the word, he was not her lover. Sleeping together and making love are not of necessity the same thing. The possibility was not excluded, yet it was not taken as the automatic consequence of sharing a bed, and that accorded well with Pam's innate refinement.

So it wasn't entirely as the girls in the health centre might have imagined it. Pam had learned over that first tomato juice in the Green Dragon that Cliff had a job in the cider industry which entailed calling on various producers in the West Midlands and South-West, and visiting Hereford for an overnight stay once a fortnight. He liked travelling, yet he admitted that the nights away from home had been instrumental in the failure of his marriage. He had not been unfaithful, but, as he altruistically put it, anyone who read the accounts of rapes and muggings in the papers couldn't really blame a wife who sought companionship elsewhere when her husband spent every other week away on business.

Responding to his candour, Pam had found herself admitting that she, too, was divorced. The nights, she agreed, were the worst. Even in the old cathedral city of Hereford, which had no reputation for violence, she avoided going out alone after dark and she often lay awake listening acutely in case someone was tampering with the locks downstairs.

That first lunchtime drink had led to another when Cliff was next in the city. The fortnight after, Pam had invited him to the house for a 'spot of supper', explaining that it was no trouble, because you could do much more interesting things cooking for two than alone. Cliff had heaped praise on her chicken *cordon bleu*, and after that the evening meal had become a fortnightly fixture. On the first occasion, he had quite properly returned to his hotel at the end of the evening, but the following time he had introduced Pam to the old-fashioned game of cribbage, and they had both got so engrossed that neither of them had noticed the time until it was well after midnight. By then, Pam felt so relaxed and safe with Cliff that it had seemed the most natural thing in the world to make up the spare bed for him and invite him to stay the night. There had been no suggestion on either side of a more intimate arrangement. That was what she liked about Cliff. He wasn't one of those predatory males. He was enough of a gentleman to suppress his natural physical instincts. And one night six weeks after in a thunderstorm, when she had tapped on his bedroom door and said she was feeling frightened, he had offered in the same gentlemanly spirit to come to her room until the storm abated. As it happened, Pam still slept in the king-size double bed she had got used to when she was married, so there was room for Cliff without any embarrassment about inadvertent touching. They had fallen asleep listening for the thunder. By then it was the season of summer storms so, next time he had come to the house, they had each agreed it was a sensible precaution to sleep together even when the sky was clear. You could never be certain when a storm might blow up during the night. And when the first chill nights of autumn arrived, neither of them liked the prospect of sleeping apart between cool sheets. Besides, as Cliff considerately mentioned, using one bed was less expensive on the laundry.

Speaking of laundry, Pam took to washing out his shirts, underclothes and pyjamas. She had bought him a special pair of bottle-green French pyjamas without buttons and with an elasticated waistband. They were waiting on his pillow, washed and ironed, each time he came. He was very appreciative. He never failed to arrive without a bottle of cider that they drank with the meal. Once or twice he mentioned that he would have taken her out to a restaurant if her cooking had not been so excellent that it would have shown up the cook. He particularly relished the cooked breakfast on a large oval plate that she supplied before he went on his way in the morning.

So Pam staunchly tolerated the teasing in the health centre, encouraged by the certainty that it was all fantasy on their part; she had been careful never to let them know that she had invited Cliff home. She was in a better frame of mind as she walked home that lunchtime. It was always a relief to get through Saturday morning.

As she turned the corner of her street, she saw a small car, a red Mini, outside her house, with someone sitting inside it. She wasn't expecting a visitor. She strolled towards her gate, noticing that it was a woman who made no move to get out, and whom she didn't recognise, so she passed the car and let herself indoors.

There was a letter on the floor, a greetings card by the look of it. She had quite forgotten that her birthday was on Sunday. Living alone, with no family to speak of, she tended to ignore such occasions. However, someone had evidently decided that this one should not go by unremarked. She didn't recognise the handwriting, and the postmark was too faint to read. She opened it and smiled. A print of a single daffodil, and inside, under the printed birthday greeting, the handwritten letter C.

The reason why she hadn't recognised Cliff's writing was that this was the first time she had seen it. He wasn't one for sending letters. And the postmark wouldn't have given Pam a clue, even if she had deciphered it, because she didn't know where he lived. He was vague or dismissive when it came to personal information, so she hadn't pressed him. He was entitled to his privacy. She couldn't help wondering sometimes, and her best guess was that since the failure of his marriage he had tended to neglect himself and his home and devoted himself to his job. He lived for the travelling, and, Pam was encouraged to believe, his fortnightly visit to Hereford.

Presently the doorbell chimed. Pam opened the door to the woman she had seen in the car, dark-haired, about her own age or a little older, good-looking, with one of those long, elegant faces with high cheekbones that you see in foreign films. She was wearing a dark blue suit and white blouse buttoned to the neck as if she were attending an interview for a job. Mainly, Pam was made aware of the woman's grey-green eyes that scrutinised her with an interest unusual in people who called casually at the door.

'Hello,' said Pam.

'Mrs Pamela Meredith?'

'Yes.'

The look became even more intense. 'We haven't met. You may not even know that I exist. I'm Tracey Gibbons.' She paused for a reaction.

Pam smiled faintly. 'You're right. I haven't heard your name before.'

Tracey Gibbons sighed and shook her head. 'I'm not surprised. I don't know what you're going to think of me, coming to your home like this, but it's reached the point when something has to be done. It's about your husband.'

Pam frowned. 'My husband?' She hadn't heard from David in six years.

'May I come in?'

'I suppose you'd better.'

As she showed the woman into her front room, Pam couldn't help wondering if this was a confidence trick. The woman's eyes blatantly surveyed the room, the furniture, the ornaments, everything.

Pam said sharply, 'I think you'd better come to the point, Miss Gibbons.'

'Mrs, actually. Not that it matters. I'm waiting for my divorce to come through.' Suddenly the woman sounded nervous and defensive. 'I'm not promiscuous. I want you to understand that, Mrs Meredith, whatever you may think of me. And I'm not deceitful, either, or I wouldn't be here. I want to get things straight between us. I've driven over from Worcester this morning to talk to you.'

Pam was beginning to fathom what this was about. Mrs

Gibbons was having an affair with David, and for some obscure reason she felt obliged to confess it to his ex-wife. Clearly the poor woman was in a state of nerves, so it was kindest to let her say her piece before gently showing her the door.

'You probably wonder how I got your address,' Mrs Gibbons went on. 'He doesn't know I'm here, I promise you. It's only over the last few weeks that I began to suspect he had a wife. Certain things you notice, like his freshly ironed shirts. He left his suitcase open the last time he came, and I happened to see the birthday card he addressed to you. That's how I got your address.'

Pam's skin prickled. 'Which card?'

'The daffodil. I looked inside, I'm ashamed to admit. I had to know.'

Pam closed her eyes. The woman wasn't talking about David at all. It was Cliff, *her* Cliff. Her head was spinning. She thought she was going to faint. She said, 'I think I need some brandy.'

Mrs Gibbons nodded. 'I'll join you, if I may.'

When she handed over the glass, Pam said in a subdued voice, 'You *are* talking about a man named Cliff?'

'Of course.'

'He is not my husband.'

'What?' Mrs Gibbons stared at her in disbelief.

'He visits me sometimes.'

'And you wash his shirts?'

'Usually.'

'The bastard!' said Mrs Gibbons, her eyes brimming. 'The rotten, two-timing bastard! I knew there was someone else, but I thought it was his wife he was so secretive about. I persuaded myself he was unhappily married and I came here to plead with you to let him go. I could kill him!'

'How do you think I feel?' Pam blurted out. 'I didn't know there was anyone else in his life.'

'Does he keep a toothbrush and razor in your bathroom?'

'A face-flannel as well.'

'And I suppose you bought him some expensive aftershave?'

Pam confirmed it bitterly. In her outraged state, she needed to talk, and sharing the trouble seemed likely to dull the pain. She related how she and Cliff had met and how she had invited him home.

'And one thing led to another?' speculated Mrs Gibbons.

'When I think of what I was induced to do in the belief that I was the love of his life . . .' She finished her brandy in a gulp.

Pam nodded. 'It was expensive, too.'

'Expensive?'

'Preparing three-course dinners and large cooked breakfasts.'

'I wasn't talking about cooking,' said Mrs Gibbons, giving Pam a penetrating look.

'Ah,' said Pam, with a slow dip of the head, in an attempt to convey that she understood exactly what Mrs Gibbons *was* talking about.

'Things I didn't get up to in ten years of marriage to a very athletic man,' Mrs Gibbons further confided, looking modestly away. 'But you know all about it. Casanova was a boy scout compared to Cliff. God, I feel so humiliated.'

'Would you like a spot more brandy, Mrs Gibbons?'

'Why don't you call me Tracey?' suggested Mrs Gibbons, holding out her glass. 'We're just his playthings, you and I. How many others are there, do you suppose?'

'Who knows?' said Pam, seizing on the appalling possibility and speaking her thoughts aloud. 'There are plenty of divorced women like you and me, living in relative comfort in what was once the marital home, pathetically grateful for any attention that comes our way. Let's face it: we're secondhand goods.'

After a sobering interval, Tracey Gibbons pushed her empty glass towards the brandy bottle again, and asked, 'What are we going to do about him?'

'Kick him out with his toothbrush and face-flannel, I suppose,' Pam answered inadequately.

'So that he finds other deluded women to prey on?' said Tracey. 'That's not the treatment for the kind of animal we're dealing with. Personally, I feel so angry and abused that I could kill him if I knew how to get away with it. Wouldn't you?'

Pam stared at her. 'Are you serious?'

'Totally. He's ruined my hopes and every atom of self-respect I had left. What was I to him? His bit in Worcester, his Monday night amusement.'

'And I was Tuesday night in Hereford,' Pam added bleakly, suddenly given a cruel and vivid understanding of the way she had been used. Sex was Monday, supper Tuesday. In her own way, she felt as violated as Tracey. An arrangement that had seemed to be considerate and beautiful was revealed as cynically expedient. The reason why he had never touched her was that he was always sated after his night of unbridled passion in Worcester. 'Tracey, if you know of a way to kill him,' she stated with the calm that comes when a crucial decision is made, 'I know how to get away with it.'

Tracey's eyes opened very wide.

Pam made black coffee and sandwiches and explained her plan. To describe it as a plan is perhaps misleading, because it had only leapt to mind as they were talking. She wasn't given to thinking much about murder. Yet as she spoke, she sensed excitedly that it could work. It was simple, tidy and within her capability.

The two women talked until late in the afternoon. For the plan to work, they had to devise a way of killing without mess. The body should not be marked by violence. They solemnly debated various methods of despatching a man. Whether the intention was serious or not, Pam found that just talking about it was a balm for the pain that Cliff had inflicted on her. She and Tracey sensibly agreed to take no action until they had each had time to adjust to the shock, but they were adamant that they would meet again.

On the following Monday evening, Pam received a phone call from Tracey. 'Have you thought any more about what we were discussing?'

'On and off, yes,' Pam answered guardedly.

'Well, I've been doing some research,' Tracey told her with the excitement obvious in her voice. 'I'd better not be too specific over the phone, but I know where to get some stuff that will do the job. Do you understand me?'

'I think so.'

'It's simple, quick and very effective, and the best thing about it is that I can get it at work.'

Pam recalled that Tracey had said she worked for a firm that manufactured agricultural fertilisers. She supposed she was talking about some chemical substance.

Poison.

'The thing is,' Tracey was saying, 'if I get some, are you willing to do your part? You said it would be no problem.'

'That's true, but –'

'By the weekend? He's due to visit me on Monday.'

The reminder of Cliff's Monday assignations in Worcester was like a stab of pain to Pam. 'By the weekend,' she confirmed emphatically. 'Come over about the same time on Saturday. I'll do my part, I promise you, Tracey.'

The part Pam had to play in the killing of Cliff was to obtain a blank death certificate from one of the doctors at the centre. She had often noticed how careless Dr Holt-Wagstaff was with his paperwork. He was the oldest of the five practitioners and his desk was always in disorder. She waited for her opportunity for most of the week. On Friday morning she had to go into his surgery to ask him to clarify his handwriting on a prescription form. The death certificate pad was there on the desk. At twelve fifteen, when he went out on his rounds, and Pam was on duty with one other girl, she slipped back into the surgery. No one saw her.

Saturday was a testing morning for Pam. The time dragged and the teasing about her secret lover was difficult to take without snapping back at the others. She kept wondering whether Dr Holt-Wagstaff had noticed anything. She need not have worried. He left at noon, wishing everyone a pleasant weekend. At twelve thirty, the girls locked up and left.

When Pam got home, Tracey was waiting on her doorstep. 'I came by train,' she explained. 'Didn't want to leave my car outside again. It's surprising how much people notice.'

'Sensible,' said Pam, with approval, as she opened the door. 'Now I want to hear about the stuff you've got. Is it really going to work?'

Tracey put her hand on Pam's arm. 'Darling, it's foolproof. Do you want to see it?' She opened her handbag and took out a small brown glass bottle. 'Pure nicotine. We use it at work.'

Pam held the bottle in her palm. 'Nicotine? Is it a poison?'

'Deadly.'

'There isn't much here.'

'The fatal dose is measured in milligrams, Pam. A few drops will do the trick.'

'How can we get him to take it?'

'I've thought of that.' Tracey smiled. 'You're going to like this. In a glass of his own buckshee cider. Nicotine goes yellow on exposure to light and air, and there's a bitter taste which the sweet cider will mask.'

'How does it work?'

'It acts as a massive stimulant. The vital organs simply can't withstand it. He'll die of cardiac arrest in a very short time. Did you get the death certificate?'

Pam placed the poison bottle on the kitchen table and opened one of her cookbooks. The certificate was inside.

'You're careful, too,' Tracey said with a conspiratorial smile. She delved into her handbag again. 'I brought a prescription from my doctor to copy the signature, as you suggested. What else do we have to fill in here? *Name of Deceased*. What shall we call him?'

'Anything but Cliff,' said Pam. 'How about Clive? Clive Jones.'

'All right. Clive Jones it is. *Date of death*. I'd better fill that in after the event. What shall we put as the cause of death? Cardiac failure?'

'No, that's likely to be a sudden death,' said Pam, thinking of post-mortems. 'Broncho-pneumonia is better.'

'Suits me,' said Tracey, writing it down. 'After he's dead, I take this to the Registry of Births, Marriages and Deaths in Worcester, and tell them that Clive Jones was my brother, is that right?'

'Yes, it's very straightforward. They'll want his date of birth and one or two other details that you can invent. Then they issue you with another certificate that you show to the undertaker. He takes over after that.'

'I ask for a cremation, of course. Will it cost much?'

'Don't worry,' said Pam. 'He can afford it.'

'Too true!' said Tracey. 'His wallet is always stuffed with notes.'

'He never has to spend much,' Pam pointed out. 'The way he runs his life, he gets everything he wants for nothing.'

'The bastard,' said Tracey with a shudder.

'You really mean to do it, don't you?'

Tracey stood up and looked steadily at Pam with her grey-green eyes. 'On Monday evening when he comes to me. I'll phone you when it's done.'

Pam linked her arm in Tracey's. 'The first thing I'm going to do is burn those pyjamas.'

Tracey remarked, 'He never wore pyjamas with me.'

'Really?' Pam hesitated, her curiosity aroused. 'What exactly did he do with you? Are you able to talk about it?'

'I don't believe I could,' answered Tracey with eyes lowered.

'If I poured you a brandy? We *are* in this together now.'

'All right,' said Tracey with a sigh.

Sunday seemed like the longest day of Pam's life, but she finally got through it. On Monday she didn't go in to work. That evening, she waited nervously by the phone from six thirty onwards.

The call came at a few minutes after seven. Pam snatched up the phone.

'Hello, darling.' *The voice was Cliff's.*

'Cliff?'

'Yes. Not like me to call you on a Monday, is it? The fact is, I happen to be in Worcester on my travels, and it occurred to me that I could get over to you in Hereford in half an hour if you're free this evening.'

'Has something happened?' asked Pam.

'No, my darling. Just a change of plans. I won't expect much of a meal.'

'That's good, because I haven't got one for you,' Pam candidly told him.

There was a moment's hesitation before he said, 'Are you all right, dear? You don't sound quite yourself.'

'Don't I?' said Pam flatly. 'Well, I've had a bit of a shock. My sister died here on Saturday. It wasn't entirely unexpected. Broncho-pneumonia. I've had to do everything myself. She's being cremated on Wednesday.'

'Your sister? Pam, darling, I'm terribly sorry. I didn't even know you had a sister.'

'Her name was Olive. Olive Jones,' said Pam, and she couldn't help smiling at her own resourcefulness. After she had poisoned Tracey with a drop of nicotine in her brandy, all it had wanted on the death certificate was a touch of the pen. 'We weren't close. I'm not too distressed. Yes, why don't you come over?'

'You're sure you want me?'

'Oh, I want you,' answered Pam. 'Yes, I definitely want you.'

When she had put down the phone, she didn't go to the fridge to see what food she had in there. She went upstairs to the bedroom and changed into a black lace négligé.

James McClure

THE LAST PLACE ON EARTH

The building breathed you in. You were wheeled down a ramp by the ambulance men, passing rockeries and lily ponds, and then across a patio of crazy-paving the colour of cornflakes. You peered over your toes, which gave twin peaks to the grey blanket covering you, and saw the huge glass doors marked clearly *IN*. The other set of doors did not have *OUT* on them.

You approached the *IN* doors. They remained closed. Then, with a loud and sudden sound, like a swimmer's gasp for air, they opened inwards, leaving you no time to think before the sky overhead vanished. You saw a pine ceiling, had a glimpse of a tropical fish tank, and the doors wheezed slowly shut again, clenching their jaws.

The visitor arrived at the wrong moment. His aunt had just had a suppository inserted. So he went through to the lounge of the hospice and sat down in front of the television set. The early evening news was on.

'Forty-three people are believed to have died today,' said the newscaster, as a film clip began, 'when a gas leak caused an explosion in this block of flats in South London.'

The dying, seated on either side of the visitor, shook their heads and tut-tutted and one said, 'Now, isn't that terrible? What is the world coming to?'

They had forgotten.

But one old man sat with his back to the television set, and toyed with his lighter, cigarette packet and a thick glass ashtray, while his urine dripped steadily down a tube into the clear plastic bag at his side. This old man looked angry and more interesting than the others.

So the visitor rose, wandered into the adjoining chapel, where magazines and paperbacks were kept beside the hymnals, and chose himself something that would serve as an excuse for changing seats. It was a May 1976 copy of *Country Life*.

'Evening,' said the visitor, as he sat down opposite the old man's wheelchair. 'You don't mind?'

The old man seemed to ignore him.

The visitor dipped the magazine each time he turned a page, sneaking quick glances across the low coffee table. He noted a middling mottled brow, dense brown hair protruding from each ear like mattress stuffing, full lips that were pale and striated, with gleams of scarlet in the cracks. He studied the weathered hands and their chipped fingernails, the ragged scar across the back of the right wrist such as barbed wire might make. He wondered where, in that heavy-limbed body, a dread thing was growing.

If one wanted to picture cancer cells, his aunt's doctor had said, then simply imagine a handful of thistle seeds tossed into a bed of poppies, and these thistles thrusting upwards, flourishing.

'What I mind,' said the old man, 'was not stopping.'

The visitor glanced up. 'Not stopping?' he said. 'Smoking, you mean?'

'Not stopping at home, more like!'

'You don't like it here?'

'Bah!'

'Oh, I don't know. When you compare it with –'

'I should've stopped outside and taken one more look.'

The visitor put down the magazine and leaned forward. 'I'm sorry,' he said, 'not quite with you.'

'The universe,' snapped the old man, pointing to the top of the coffee table. 'Right? And here, what they calls the solar system. Big ashtray's the sun, ciggie packet is this bleedin' planet, and that's me, a cheeky little blighter of a lighter, comin' in between! That's how we were, three score and more, with me shadow on the ground to prove it.'

The visitor nodded.

'Got bugger-all shadow now,' said the old man.

There was a soft bubbling from the tank of tropical fish over on the left. The visitor glanced that way, and then round the room. It was large and warm and very unhospitalish. The walls and ceiling were lined with pine in the Swedish manner, and the furnishings suggested the lounge of a comfortable if modest hotel. In one corner, there was a small alcove where hot and cold drinks were always available; in another, was the television set with its huge screen, and, to the right of it, hung a neat rack holding brochures that gave some idea of local scenic attractions, concerts, plays and exhibitions. Some stuffed toys, made under the guidance of the hospice's occupational therapist, lolled glassy-eyed on a wide shelf, sharing it with two boxes of Monopoly. Crocheted cushions abounded, so did big-leaved pot plants. The lighting was low, shadowless, and its sources invisible.

'Comfy enough,' said the old man, shrugging as he gave his own glance around. 'But still a bit of a disappointment – y'know, when it comes home to yer, this is the last place on earth.'

Then a grey-haired woman, wearing a chequered smock over drab street clothes, came up to the visitor and said, 'So sorry you wait, but your aunt she is ready for you now.'

The visitor's aunt waved a greeting at his reflection in the window as he entered the room behind her back. She had to lie on her right side most of the time, what with the oozing on her left.

'My sweet,' she said. 'Goodness, are those for me?'

He held out the bouquet in its flower-shop wrapping and wondered why her eyes darted aside before taking a second look.

'Oh, *carnations*,' she said. 'How lovely! So very, very red . . .'

'They come with Chloe's love, too, Aunt Judith.'

'See you give her mine, Richard, and tell her how pleased I am with them. Be a dear, won't you, and see if you can find that volunteer lady to have them popped in a vase right away.'

'The foreign one in the smock?'

His aunt nodded. 'Not *so* foreign,' she chided, knowing her nephew's prejudices of old. 'Mrs Daventry has been in England since only a few years after the war. Hasn't she the most marvellous, deep brown eyes?'

'She looks – ' he began, then stopped himself.

You lay there and wanted to cry out, but the crab had you by the throat.

A new terror seemed impossible, after all you had gone through since the initial, mumbled diagnosis. That moment when a very young doctor, her lower lip trembling prettily, had pushed an X-ray plate into your hands and asked you, as a man of science, to take a look at it. One glance had been enough, and ahead of time your voice had failed. Not even a croak.

Yet there was indeed this new terror, far more terrible than any before, and what was worse, you didn't know the reason for it.

Or even what you had seen to make you so fearful.

'This is my nephew, Richard,' said the visitor's aunt, when Sister Braithwaite came in, as quietly as a nun. 'He brought me the carnations.'

'Gorgeous,' said Sister Braithwaite, sniffing them.

The visitor had to suppress a laugh. There was only one smell in that room, nothing else could compete with it, and nobody could possibly mistake it for the scent of carnations.

'And how is Mr Joliffe today?' said his aunt. 'I do miss our little chats together.'

Sister Braithwaite looked her very straight in the eye.

'Oh, dear, has he?' said his aunt. 'Then is there someone new in his room?'

'Yes, a professor.'

'Oh, really? Not from Oxford, by any chance? My late husband –'

'Leicester University, I believe,' said Sister Braithwaite, retreating to the doorway. 'Well, it's almost time for the drugs round.'

The visitor took this as his cue to look at his wristwatch. 'Half-seven already! Chloe will – '

'Off you go, my sweet,' said his aunt. 'We've had a lovely natter, but I must confess I'm feeling a little tired now.' And she looked at him most accusingly.

'Mrs Daventry has told the voluntary help organiser that she wants to resign,' Staff Nurse Pam Clement remarked to Sister Braithwaite in the day wing, to which they had retreated for a quick cigarette apiece. 'I overheard her ringing her at home only about five minutes ago.'

'That's a bit out of the blue!' said Sister Braithwaite, undoing her silver belt buckle. 'Seemed as happy as a lark at tea time – and of all the volunteers, she's the only one I'd really miss around here.'

Staff Nurse Clement nodded. 'Not a trace of bloody do-gooder in her.'

'Empathy. I know sweet FA about Mrs Daventry, but one thing sticks out a mile: that woman's seen a *lot* of suffering in her time.'

'Making it stranger she should want to chuck it all of a sudden.'

'But don't we all? I'm forever writing out my resignation!'

The two women laughed, and shared the match flame.

'I'll try and have a word with her,' Sister Braithwaite said. 'Perhaps she could do with the support of our stress group. I don't see why it should be restricted to trained staff.'

'God,' sighed Staff Nurse Clement, running a hand over her freckled face. 'I can guess what the talk's going to be about at the next one.'

'Paraplegic, carcinoma larynx, spinal secondaries, no next of kin, eyes that bore holes in you, terrified out of his wits . . . ?'

'Uhuh, Prof Thingy.'

'But it shouldn't be for long. Have you seen the whopping morphine dosage he's on?'

You swallowed your morphine and dreamed great swirling, chaotic dreams with moments of shrill clarity.

Faces.

Thousands of faces, each with an open mouth.

If there were screams, you did not hear them.

One face keeps returning, spinning by, smiling.

Then a huge empty beach and a great stillness, except down at the sea's edge, where a crab has its claws deep in the neck of a thrashing eagle.

That one face.

You awake, and it's looking at you.

But not quite.

The next night, the visitor called at eight to see his aunt again, but first detoured into the lounge. 'And how did today go?' he asked the old man in the wheelchair.

'Boring,' said the old man. 'No flowers?'

'Chocolates. "Boring" in what way?'

'Dead boring,' said the old man, and cackled at the visitor's expression. 'You remind us,' he added, 'of that smarmy doctor what comes round, sort of rubbing his hands like he was soapin' 'em, and says to me, "Well, William, and how are we today?" So I says, "I'm dyin' to get out of here, doc!" You should've seen the face on *him* by the time I was finished.'

The visitor laughed. 'You're a character,' he said.

'No, I'm not, I'm a dying man, son. And different to you, I know what I'm going to die of, no scope for the old imagination.'

'And that's what bores you?'

'Aye, a bit.' The old man nodded at the group around the television set. 'With most of them, it's quite a relief, really, this knowin'. Frightens yer, gets yer dander up, can ruin yer religion if you're that way inclined, but it's still a weight off yer mind – y'know, being certain it won't be no car crash, all trapped screamin' in the wreckage, or Flight Bing-bong to sunny Spain goin' smack into a mountain. Personally, I'd high hopes of another kind.'

The visitor noticed a flare of yesterday's anger return, twisting the striated lips slightly. 'And what were these hopes?' he asked.

'Same as yours, son! Goin' hammer and tongs till the old ticker can't take any more, but the lass with her legs around yer keeps cheerin' you on!'

Beginning to colour, the visitor gave a crooked smile. 'For a moment there, I thought you could read minds,' he said.

'Not just the chocolates.'

'Sorry . . . ?'

'You've also,' said the old man, with a gleam in his rheumy eye, 'brung along a bit o' paper for the old lady to sign . . .'

The visitor stared at him, turned about and walked away, his cheeks burning.

'I spoke to Mrs Daventry this morning,' said the voluntary help organiser, telephoning from home, 'and I think she must just have become over-tired the other day. She tells me she's carrying on as a volunteer as per usual.'

'Are you sure that's all it was?' asked Sister Braithwaite, watching Mrs Daventry pass her desk in the corridor.

'I can't imagine any other reason, Sister.'

'Fine. And by the way, one of your volunteer drivers left a day patient stranded here this afternoon.'

'*Not* that wretched vicar's wife again! Was the patient Mr Gibb?'

You knew what the new terror was. For weeks, you had been preparing to die a particular natural death, and as *unnatural* as that had seemed, it was at least something a man could adjust to. Nobody had a right to so many years, only to live out his allotted span, and this was what, with the help of the hospice, you had expected to do. Yet now you knew you couldn't count on even that any longer.

Your dreams told you so.

'Professor,' a nurse was saying, leaning over so you could look up at her. 'See? I've brought your morphine.'

You shut your mouth tightly.

'You're being very silly, you know! We have got to control the pain. You don't want more pain, do you?'

You nodded.

'You *don't* want your morphine?'

You nodded again.

The ward sister came and gave you your morphine, not by mouth but with an injection. She threw the syringe away. The pain subsided and the dreams began. There was no way of stopping them.

'What has the house to do with my being in here?' demanded Aunt Judith.

The visitor hastily changed the subject: 'Oh, by the way, how is your new neighbour getting on?'

'The professor?' she said, brightening.

'That's right. Has he been across to see you, like Mr Joliffe?'

'Heavens, no. Quite immobile, Madge tells me, and unable to speak as part of his condition. What's fascinating is, he's apparently spent his life in medical research trying to find a cure for you-know-what.'

The visitor felt strongly that his aunt should face up to the word. 'You mean cancer?'

She helped herself to another chocolate.

'Yes, ironic,' said the visitor. 'Must make things a lot worse, too, if you're a medic and know all the options, symptoms, et cetera, what can be done for you and what can't. I know I'd be happier being left in the dark.'

'I won't be left in the dark,' said his aunt, with a sudden show of feeling. 'I was very cross last night when that little nurse tried to put the lights off before I–'

'Hello, my duck!' said a broad, homely woman, wheeling in the drinks trolley. 'Cocoa, two sugars, in a beaker? Or is it your night for a drop of something a bit stronger?' And she winked like a barmaid.

'Madge, you really are naughty!' said Aunt Judith, delighted. 'Whatever will my nephew think I get up to in here?'

Something wasn't right. Sister Braithwaite had experienced this sense of unease once before as a young VSO nurse in a mission hospital in Africa, and the next morning a one-eyed orderly and two orphans were reported missing – he'd stolen the babes to sell for witchdoctor's medicine, the black auxiliaries had said.

'A penny for them, Sue,' whispered Staff Nurse Clement, pausing at the desk in the corridor.

'Sorry?' said Sister Braithwaite, brusquely.

'Be like that . . .' said Staff Nurse Clement with a shrug, walking off.

Annoyed with herself for her rudeness and for giving way to a ridiculous mood she couldn't define, Sister Braithwaite rose and moved with a brisk step, hoping to make amends by seeing to one of the external tumours herself. Pam Clement had admitted in the stress group to finding them particularly distressing.

An unexpected smell coming from the staff changing room made her pause and look in. Staff Nurse Wong was dabbing at a mark on her overcoat with cotton wool soaked in a dry-cleaning fluid.

'Ah, so that's it!' said Sister Braithwaite.

'Sister? My bike chain came off and I ended up with grease everywhere. I noticed this bottle of – '

'Have you managed to fix the bike? If not, ring Security and Max – '

'It's fine now, thank you, Sister.'

Sister Braithwaite remained in the doorway, wishing she could avoid the stereotype but seeing Theresa Wong as inscrutable. That lovely, heart-shaped face, with its neat-as-a-button nose and cherry-pink mouth, never gave one any idea of what was going on in her head. And she politely declined every invitation to join the stress group.

'I noticed when I came on tonight,' said Sister Braithwaite, 'that your Cardexes on the professor were – well, a bit skimpy. Those notes are there to help us pick up the threads, Staff.'

'So sorry, Sister.'

'Why were they like that? Do you have difficulty with that patient?'

'He's –!'

'Yes? Go on, dear . . .'

'He is unusual, Sister,' said Staff Nurse Wong, very evenly and inscrutably.

Again, Sister Braithwaite was aware of her sense of unease.

You dreamed of wards and of operating theatres, of great pain and suffering.

You felt nothing.

The crab, in a head-dress of eagle feathers, sat on its rock.

The visitor made for the exit, thinking how like a spaceship the inside of the hospice could appear at times. It had the same sort of passages in the ward area, the hum of hidden machinery, a small kitchen like a galley, tiny storerooms with everything from bed sheets to ginger ale, neatly stowed, and outside its windows, all eternity.

He glanced into a room and saw the old man there, moving his hand back and forth in front of the bulb in his reading light. The old man looked round.

'Er, popped by to say good night,' said the visitor.

'Thought you was Mrs Daventry.'

'Yes, the volunteer lady.'

'Smasher, she is,' said the old man. 'Funny habits, mind.'

The visitor stepped into the room. 'Such as?' he said, intrigued.

'Writes phone numbers on herself.'

Disappointed, the visitor said with a grudging laugh, 'But I do that sometimes!' And he mimed a quick scribble on the back of his left hand.

'That's never where she puts it,' said the old man. 'Good night.'

'The remarkable thing, Sister,' said Dr Murphy-Jones, the consultant, the next evening, 'is that the professor seems to have rallied, to be fighting tooth and nail to stay alive.'

She sighed. 'It often amazes me, the will to live.'

'Yet, when I saw him on admission, he appeared totally resigned. Has he had a visitor, someone who has – '

'No visitors, not one. The professor hasn't any kith and kin either, as you know.'

'And he hasn't been making any use of his pad to write on?'

'Hasn't touched it. We literally haven't had a word out of him.'

'Odd, very odd. And a bit of an embarrassment, between ourselves. I thought we'd have that bed free by the weekend.'

'His quality of life isn't . . .'

'Quite. Perhaps we could increase the dosage a fraction.'

You were so cold. Drenched in your sweat and shivering. As cold as a naked man left out in the snow on a stretcher.

You remembered the letter. 'I am very curious about the experiments with animal heat. Personally I believe these experiments may bring the best and most sustained results.'

You remembered the letter because you could feel the heat.

Seeping into you.

The visitor brought his wife, Chloe, his other aunt, and a distant cousin. They had been told by the hospice that a sudden relapse had occurred.

Sister Braithwaite, the one who moved like a nun and had peppermint on her breath, met them outside the lounge. 'It could be tonight,' she said. 'If anyone would like a bed, we do have a guest room – and more beds can be put up in the chapel.'

They nodded their thanks.

'Then if you'll come along with me,' said Sister Braithwaite.

The old man was watching them from in front of the tropical fish tank. He raised his scarred hand in greeting, and the visitor smiled. God knows why, but it was good to see him.

As the visitor reached his aunt's room, he glanced across into the room almost opposite it. A gaunt, bone-coloured man was shivering in his sleep and making movements that were shocking.

'It's going to be one of those nights, Pam,' said Sister Braithwaite, too much canteen food distending her again, making her silver buckle bite.

Staff Nurse Clement snorted. 'Christ, don't tell me! Mrs Grosvenor, the new admission, lung, has started deliriums.'

'I'd better get Dr Murphy-Jones down.'

'He'll have to be here sooner or later, so you might as well.'

'I've not had a moment since coming on to go through the Cardex properly – any special problems?'

'No, not really,' replied Staff Nurse Clement. 'That dozy OT has gone and upset old William. Thought Tess Wong's notes on the professor were a bit weird.'

'Yes, I talked to her about that last night.'

'Oh?'

'They were skimped.'

'No, *weird* weird, Sue.'

'In what way?'

'I've never – well, I don't know what to think.'

Aunt Judith, although greatly weakened, had adopted an imperious manner. With a limp wave of her hand, she dismissed the attention being paid her by close members of her family and demanded that Madge fetch Mrs Daventry.

'I've got a feeling she's probably off home by now, my duck,' said Madge. 'But I'll go and look in the changing room, see if we can catch her.'

Mrs Daventry came in, dressed in her street clothes and carrying her handbag. She nodded pleasantly, then went and took Aunt Judith's hand. Nothing was said, but the face of the dying woman became tranquil and she smiled. The visitor found Mrs Daventry a chair.

Then he studied her, covertly. The woman was probably in her mid-fifties, slightly-built, a little bowed in the legs like someone once poorly nourished, and had raven black hair that set off her pale, high-cheeked face. Her brown eyes, it was true, were remarkable; large and luminous, as deep as wells. Wells filled with tears, he added as an afterthought, before scorning such mawkish sentiment.

But he couldn't see where she wrote telephone numbers on herself, no matter how hard he looked.

Sister Braithwaite sat at her desk in the corridor and stared at the notes made on the professor by Staff Nurse Wong.

The notes were indeed far more comprehensive than those of the previous day. They gave a very good idea of how the professor had spent the last eight hours, both as a person and as an organism under attack. They said, in short, that he'd displayed signs of great agitation, but was physically no worse.

What Pam Clement had called the 'weird' part had been placed in brackets at the end:

(Observation: On looking in on the patient at 4.20 pm., I found him asleep on his right side, facing the door, and shivering. I felt his arm but it was not cold. I still took his temperature but it was normal. I noticed an indentation in his bed on the far side. The coverlet had been crushed and creased from the level of his shoulders to his feet. I smoothed out his coverlet and left.)

You were freezing.

You had been taken from the water with a rectal temperature of 86 degrees Fahrenheit.

You were on a wide bed.

Between two naked women.

And the crab was writing in the sand.

It wrote: 'Once the test persons regained consciousness, they never lost it again, quickly grasping their situation and nestling close to the naked bodies of the women. The rise of body temperature then proceeded at approximately the same speed as with test persons swathed in blankets.'

You read and approved what had been written, but pointed out certain exceptions to the rule.

'An exception,' scrawled the crab with its pincer, 'was formed by four test persons who practised sexual intercourse between 86 and 89.5 degrees. In these persons, after coitus, a very swift temperature rise ensued, comparable to that achieved by means of a hot-water bath.'

Ja, ja, you agreed, yet there was another exception more extraordinary than that, Dr Rascher – whereupon, a thousand fighter pilots, downed in the icy North Sea in special suits designed by you, applauded.

'Chloe, this is the old gentleman I've told you about,' said the visitor. 'Mr William – er, I'm sorry, I'm not sure I know your last name.'

'Atkins, son – same as Tommy, and no better off than 'e was at the Somme!'

'Pleased to meet you, Mr Atkins,' said the visitor's wife, pale behind the cosmetics on a plain, hard face. 'May I sit down?'

'Fancy plonking yourself in me lap, luv?'

But she declined with an awkward laugh, taking the seat opposite his wheelchair. 'I had to get out of there for a while,' she said, fanning herself with a copy of *Woman's Own*. 'It's so . . . well, depressing.'

'I see the others what come with you have hopped it already,' said the old man. 'Wasn't it that what the taxi came for?'

The visitor nodded. 'Even worse for them, the same generation,' he explained. 'Can I get you both a drink of some sort from the corner? Coffee, perhaps? Tea?'

'No, I'll see to that, Richard,' said Chloe. 'You'd better get back to poor Aunt Judith.'

'Mrs Daventry's with her, so I don't see –'

'Off you go, Richard,' she said softly in that special tone of hers.

He went. His aunt was alone.

'Mrs Daventry has gone to tell Sister I've asked her to spend the night,' said Aunt Judith. 'She's a widow, you see, so it won't make any difference.'

Close to wakening, your dreams changed.

You were in a snow-filled ditch with a dead horse and greasy black smoke was rising in the sky behind the barbed wire. It was the first time you had ever felt such cold. You were freezing.

Then fleeing.

Killing.

You had another man's clothes, another man's name.

Soon, if you were careful, only you would know the difference.

And you were careful, you were welcomed in, given another man's life to begin. Leicester University. Unbelievable.

Yet always fleeing.

Never far enough.

On second thoughts, Sister Braithwaite decided to ask Mrs Daventry if she really had the strength to make a night of it, having already spent much of the day in the hospice.

So she left her desk and hurried after her, seeing Mrs Daventry stop outside the professor's room, hesitate, and then go in. When she reached the room itself, Mrs Daventry was standing at the foot of the bed, rubbing her arm, and the professor was gazing at her, his eyes huge in their sunken sockets.

'So we're awake again?' said Sister Braithwaite, walking in. 'I suppose you've met Mrs Daventry before?'

To her surprise, he shook his head violently.

'Yes, wide awake,' said Mrs Daventry. 'It is what I noticed.'

'You've more than enough on your plate across the way,' said Sister Braithwaite. 'Are you sure that family isn't imposing on you too much? I'd pack anybody else off home, you know that!'

'No, I have the strength, Sister. If you will excuse me . . .'

Sister Braithwaite remarked to the patient when they were alone, 'She's a saint that woman – I never thought I'd live to say that of anyone.'

The professor turned his head away and stared out of his window at the night, so dark and empty out there.

'I'll close your curtains,' said Sister Braithwaite.

The visitor glanced up and was shaken to see the expression on his wife's face. 'Good God, Chloe,' he whispered, 'whatever's happened –?'

'Richard, take me home this instant.'

'But Aunt Ju–'

'Damn and blast Aunt Judith!' she hissed, her face very white. 'Get – me – out – of – here.'

So he scrambled to his feet in a fluster, to be calmed by Mrs Daventry laying a hand on his arm.

'You can return later,' Mrs Daventry said, 'or maybe not, as circumstances they are permitting. Your aunt will altogether be safe in my keeping.'

'Thank you,' he said, 'thank you very much.' And wanted to hug her, his emotions were in such a turmoil.

Chloe dug her long nails into his hand as he led her away up the short passage, to the right and then to the left, heading towards the lounge and the exit.

'No!' said Chloe, stopping. 'I won't go *near* there, not near that horrible old man again!'

'But I don't know another way out, so be sensible! And what

do you mean by –'

'Richard!'

He turned and hurried her in the opposite direction, still very confused. Then, passing two empty wheelchairs beside some other equipment, a sudden insight made him laugh. A cruel laugh, but what the hell, Chloe's cold blood had been a bitter disappointment to him.

You were awake and the crab had you by the throat and still the dreaming went on. But it wasn't dreaming, it was remembering.

That final, fascinating exception being, Dr Rascher, as you yourself wrote and I endorsed, one woman was able to warm a frozen man faster than two women. Your report read: 'I attribute this to the fact that in warming by means of one woman personal inhibitions are avoided and the woman clings more closely to the chilled person. Here, too, return of full consciousness was notably rapid.'

'There,' said the ward sister, 'all nice and clean again, and time for your medicine, professor.'

You shook your head.

The prick of a needle.

Bzzzzzzt – bzzzzzzt – bzzzzzzt . . .

Once a patient pressed the button, that heavy droning device buzzed and buzzed until someone had hurried in to switch it off and enquire what the matter was. Sometimes the matter was all too self-evident.

Sister Braithwaite, hastening in one direction, heard the sound stop and then begin again. This meant a second patient needed attention, so she spun on her heel and set off to see who this could be. She passed a doorway and saw Mrs Daventry sitting quietly, holding the old woman's hand.

No more than a quick glimpse, it left an odd impression: Mrs Daventry's face had seemed set very hard and those luminous eyes were as cold as ice. Some trick of the lighting.

The crab had made a quill of one of the eagle feathers. It started pricking out numbers. Blue numbers. Sets of numbers.

Then scurried across the beach, digging and scattering the pebbles to expose experimental bone grafts and gas gangrene wounds, all fascinating. In the rock pools, poison bullets grew in clusters, ready for testing, and here a sea anemone was swallowing a lethal dose of typhus. Down at the bright arc of sparkling surf, gypsies were being made to see how long they could live on salt water.

'Crab!' you cried. 'Crab, I never noticed you at Ravensbrück!'

Bzzzzzzzt – bzzzzzzzt – bzzzzzzzt . . .

There it was, going again!

'I'm dying for a quick puff,' muttered Staff Nurse Clement, over her shoulder.

'Not tonight, Josephine,' Sister Braithwaite muttered back, pushing the dressings trolley. 'How is Mrs Daventry faring over on the other side?'

'I've not had a moment.'

'She'll ring if she needs us.'

'Where *is* Dr Murphy-bloody-Jones?'

'Hush, Staff! That's no way to speak of God.'

'It is, when you're left to do his dirty work for him!'

Now the ravens were circling and the crab was lying low.

A winter landscape, with the snow outside striking a white light up through the barred windows and brightening the whole room, making it a bridal suite. On the bed, fresh from the snow, with a rectal temperature of 86 degrees Fahrenheit, a brutish young Pole. Pressed against him, a skinny female with black shining hair, naked and shivering, too. He warmed slowly. There was time to see the female was of poor background, a sufferer from rickets. There was time to study her face, and find in it evidence of the sub-human. There was even time to memorise its every line and hollow, if need be.

There was no need, but it must have happened.

'My God!' Dr Rascher exploded with a laugh. 'The animal thinks he's woken up in Heaven! Just look . . .'

Everyone was looking, smirking. The Pole, mumbling, had clutched the female to him, and now wept as he suckled at her flat breast, his loins already slowly heaving.

'Temperature reading?' said Dr Rascher.

You glanced at the dial, calling out: 'Eighty-eight and rising!'

'*And* rising . . .' echoed Dr Rascher, giggling.

The Last Place on Earth

The brute rolled over on to the female. She whispered softly, kissed his ear and opened her legs, welcoming him.

Dr Rascher gaped. 'What is this?' he said. 'Even here, she can enjoy it?'

'I think,' said the cameraman, 'she is sorry for him, that's all. She knows he gets his benzine injection when this is over.'

'Degenerate!' snapped Dr Rascher, then giggled again. 'These Poles ...! See this rabbit is kept for me, she excites certain possibilities.'

'Ninety degrees!' you reported.

'Yes, she must be kept and fed well,' declared Rascher. 'In 1946, I propose beginning a series of experiments which ...'

He talked on, but you were no longer listening. You were watching. As the Pole bucked harder and harder, moving to his climax, the female submitted herself totally to him, throwing back her arms and grasping the bedposts. Her limbs were thin but beautiful, marred only by her concentration camp number, tattooed in blue on the left inner arm.

Then they cried out together.

'What was that?' asked Sister Braithwaite, pausing with the flame an inch from her cigarette.

'Didn't hear a sound,' said Staff Nurse Clement.

Sister Braithwaite was trembling like on that night in Africa. 'It was –' she began, then swallowed. 'Look, I can't explain, I just think we'd better get back.'

They left the day wing and went first to the six-bed ward, found everyone asleep and started checking on the one-bed side wards.

'Funny smell down this way,' said Staff Nurse Clement.

'Oh, that's Staff Wong and her blessed greasy coat.'

'Pardon?'

'You're right, that was two days –'

'Oops!' said Staff Nurse Clement, coming to a sudden halt in a doorway. 'Guess who's ...' And she tiptoed in. 'Yes, he has – the professor's gone,' she said, reaching out to close an eyelid. 'A bit sudden.'

'And look at the way he's arched back, Pam! That really isn't natural.'

'What isn't natural?' asked Dr Murphy-Jones, wandering in

amiably. 'I say, quite a spasm. I hope you're not suggesting foul play, are you, Sister? This is surely the last place on – '

'No, no, it's simply I – '

'Excellent! You've someone you'd like me to take a look at?'

'Yer-yes, please,' said Sister Braithwaite, trying to get a grip on herself. 'If you'll just come this way, doctor.'

As she turned out into the corridor, she caught a glimpse of Mrs Daventry holding the old woman's hand, which was clenched tightly now. The light was playing another of its tricks, for when Mrs Daventry glanced round to give a quick, gentle smile, she looked absolutely beautiful, a young girl.

Both Dr Sigmund Rascher's own fate and his reports to Heinrich Himmler, the letter writer, are dealt with in detail in The Rise and Fall of the Third Reich *by William L. Shirer.*

Jennie Melville

CHICKEN FEED

Ellean Mills had in her life one short, alarming, revengeful burst.

Flipping through her newspaper as she drank her morning coffee where she stood in the kitchen before dashing out to work, Ellean saw a picture of a woman and a headline.

'Dead woman found in Minden Place Development.'

A few lines underneath said that in a show house in this new development of houses on the point of being completed had been found the dead body of a woman.

The face of the dead woman as caught in the photograph was blurred, not easily identifiable.

Ellean gave a little shudder. Her head ached already from the sleeping tablets she had taken. She was wondering about Rex but she wouldn't telephone him; she never telephoned him. He telephoned her, she didn't initiate a call. It was part of their relationship.

It had all begun yesterday.

She worked on the Minden Place estate as a kind of seller-cum-hostess, showing people around the furnished display houses, making viewers feel at home so that they wanted to buy. Ellean was good at making people feel at home. It might not be the sort of home they had expected to find themselves in, and one day they might turn around and say why ever did we buy it, but buy they did.

There was the scent of roses in Ellean's flat, you could smell it even in the kitchen where she drank her coffee.

Every week a bunch of roses was delivered, usually white but sometimes red. Perhaps it was a standing order with no very personal commitment behind it. She wondered about that; as a woman might when it grew dark, and night came in bringing with it sombre thoughts and self-doubt.

Ellean had driven to work speedily because she wanted to find out what was going on there. She was always anxious first thing. Transferred anxiety probably, moved over from Rex to her work, because she certainly had worries there. She drove well; everything she did with her body was well done. Occasionally her thought processes let her down, but her automatic physical responses never did. These she could count on. If you had a body like that who was going to worry about brains? Ellean had been a hairdresser before she got this job which paid well and kept the hands out of water; she had got it by, well, you had to call it influence.

At Minden Place everything looked normal, if not particularly active. Just a few brickies and plasterers working on an unfinished block of houses. No one was talking, no one was even moving fast. About as usual. Not the sort of day you expected anything much to happen in.

Ellean parked her car, opened her little office, hung up her fur coat on a hanger (you had to be careful, she might never get another one) then went out to ask some questions. She took a quick look at each show house as she passed, all neat and clear.

The site foreman, Steve Fisher, was walking around, carrying a file of papers and looking worried. He *was* worried, and was right to be worried. He was doing a job just beyond his capacity, and it took it out of him.

'So what's today's crisis?'

'Crisis?'

'There always is one here, Steve, and you know it. What's gone wrong today?'

Once someone had stolen the cement-mixer, another time a hammer had fallen on a passer-by's toe. Rex didn't like that sort of publicity or that sort of theft.

'Nothing much wrong. Someone's nicked a good chisel of mine.'

Steve had been a carpenter earlier in his career and always carried his tools. Like a baby might carry a reassuring rug or dummy, Ellean sometimes thought scornfully.

'I expect you've mislaid it yourself.'

'And one of my knives,' he grumbled. 'Gone, too. I had it yesterday. Lovely little blade.'

As the only woman on the site, Ellean expected, and got,

certain privileges: if something went wrong with the electricity or the plumbing in her flat someone would pop in and deal with it. She had had her front door repainted only this week. In return she dispensed tea and coffee in her office to a licensed few. Over coffee one day she had confided in Steve about the Game she played.

There were three types of dwelling on display: a one-bedroomed house, a two-bedroomed house, and another with three and an extra bathroom. To while away the inevitable moments of boredom she invented suitable families for all three.

Into the three-bedroomed house went a father, mother and adolescent son and daughter: she called them Mr and Mrs Sweet. Just a name. Sour would have been as good sometimes, but mostly they were amiable enough. If they bought, she liked them. No commission was involved but prestige was.

The two-bedroomed house was the slot for a newly married couple: John and Jemima Blissful. They didn't have to be married, but they usually were, with the confetti still in their hair, really. Once they'd brushed it out they might not stay, because there was no denying they were *tiny*, those houses. You would have to live close and love each other.

An ambitious young career woman (or man, Ellean was only minimally sexist) was the destined owner of the one-bedroomed house. It was amazing how people matched up to what she imagined. If she gave the Sweets a daughter called Fiona, then Fiona was bound to turn up next day to qualify. Equally if she gave the Blissfuls an imagined happy event then the next couple would turn up heavily pregnant, although where they would put the dear baby she could not say.

Armed with such secret pre-knowledge she scored well with Sweet and Blissful type buyers, but much less well with the Miss Career models. Perhaps they were too much like her so that she could not see them so clearly. Or perhaps they saw *her* too clearly. Anyway, they were not jokes to her, but real people.

There was one woman who kept coming back. Ellean called her Miss Lost Career, and suspected she was a secret Miss Lonelyhearts as well. A lot of bright girls grow into women like that. She knew the look well, had worn it herself for a time. It meant that you had had your heart broken not once but too often. When you got that look you either stayed that way for ever or got the killer instinct.

She wasn't sure if you could choose. Free-will might not come into it. You either had it in you or you didn't. Probably it wasn't till your teeth closed around your prey, or the knife went right into the flesh that you knew which you were. Until that incisive moment you probably thought you were a nice ordinary girl. But after that you *knew*.

'If I see anything I'll let you know. Or hear. But otherwise I'd say it was your own fault.'

Ellean took herself back to her office, brewed some coffee, then repaired her make-up while she waited for the coffee to drip through. It was a pleasure for her to attend to her appearance. She did it to soothe her nerves, as another type of woman might have weeded her garden or baked a cake. Ellean did not have a garden, only those roses and a windowbox full of plastic flowers. Still, they were the very best sort of plastic flowers with a claim to charm if not reality. She was looking forward to real flowers in a real garden; she felt there had been enough plastic ones in her life. That was why the roses were sent to her: as a promise. Some of her cynical women friends thought that Ellean sent the roses to herself, but this was not so. The flowers came from someone who claimed to love her.

Loving is never wise, the flowers were not wise. A standing order for flowers was most unwise. People, wives, get to know of standing orders. He ought to have plodded out and placed an order once a week himself and paid cash. But Rex was like that. Not prudent. Quick of temper, sometimes violent. You didn't create a building business like his by being a quiet man.

Every week Ellean brought one of the roses with her to work and placed it in a bud vase on her desk. That too was unwise.

She had brought the rose in as usual on Monday and it was there now on her desk. This was Wednesday. She added some water to the vase, drank her coffee and waited for it to be a busy day. Ellean was not exactly indispensable, the houses would have sold without her attention, but at this stage of her life she was never going to be out of a job.

There was the usual stream of viewers, all of whom fitted easily into her invented categories. They kept her on the run so that she forgot the dead woman. The most striking couple today had been two men, both interested in the middle-sized house, Mr Bright

Career, young and cheerful, and Mr Newly Divorced, older and depressed. No difficulty there in giving them names, indeed they had named themselves. They had passed each other on the way in looking like each other's past and future. If they became neighbours, as seemed probable, they might wonder what they had in common. To her surprise, both men put down a deposit at once.

She'd better stop this game. It was getting silly. They were all just people. Not specially happy or successful people, or they wouldn't be buying a piece of the Minden Development. She had no illusions about what Rex had created.

The woman she was sorry for was walking down the path: Miss Lonelyheart in person. Ellean, busy with the two men, waved her into the one-bedroom pad and let her get on with it. She did notice that the woman brandished a tape-measure as if she was measuring up for carpets or curtains. She usually made a pretence of some sort. What she really did in there was to pace around and stare. Ellean had seen her at it.

Looking at the little house never made her happier. Sometimes Ellean wanted to take her aside and say, 'Don't think of living here if it doesn't make you feel happier.'

In fact, she was pretty sure the woman did not mean to buy. It was a private rule of hers that those who came back and back never did buy. Those who bought did so on the day.

Ellean had seen the woman enter; she had to assume she had left because when Ellean went past the door with a young married couple she could see no sign of her. In the littlest house you could see the whole ground plan from the door, kitchen and bedroom included. Only the bathroom had any privacy and that minimal.

So the poor creature must have gone.

In a way Ellean was disappointed. It made a bit of excitement. At lunchtime Rex rang her up for the usual talk, and in the course of chatting she told him of it. He said thank God there was no woman hanging around, because she sounded neurotic and that could mean trouble. He had a lot of money tied up in the Minden Development and anything which slowed down the sale of the houses was out. She could tell he was not paying a lot of attention and what was more, might not even be alone. That was distinctly worrying.

In fact, a kind of a nightmare quality hung over that conversation. She felt as though something had disappeared into space, taking a bit of her with it.

She re-did her face carefully. There was a flaw in the mirror which slightly distorted one side of her mouth so that it twisted up in a half smile which Rex said he loved. He said it was the first thing about her he noticed. A lie, of course, she could always tell his lies which was why she had not asked him if he was alone.

At the end of the day she made her usual tidying-up round of the show houses. It was the part of the day she resented; not her job, she thought, to do housework, but Rex, usually so persuadable, was adamant she do it. It might be a way of keeping her in her place. In truth, it amounted to little more than making small adjustments to the pieces of furniture that had got moved out of position, and to checking the neatness of curtains and bed covers. It was work not entirely unpleasing to her, she was a tidy girl. Once a week a cleaning team came to vacuum-clean throughout and to polish.

She put on her cotton housework gloves and picked up a dustpan.

The largest houses were the untidiest today because a couple of family groups had gone through. Ellean had nothing against children, she rather liked them, but you could certainly see their tracks. Nothing much either in the sitting room of the two-bedroomed house either, only one other couple apart from the men had gone in today and both of them had come out quickly as if they didn't like the smell. She went in, locking the door behind her as usual. Once a cat had got in behind her, hid overnight and created a terrible mess. Now she always turned the key.

It did smell a bit. Nothing too unpleasant but a bit odd. Not a smell she could put a name to, she'd have to think about it. It was a person's smell, she could be sure of that, but not a dead smell. So she didn't have to start looking for a dead body.

She went into the bedroom, when at once she saw an indentation on the bed. The edge of the bed overlooking the window.

'Bed not dead,' she thought, the words coming into her mind unsolicited and unwanted. She sat down on the indentation. From it you could see right into her office.

Someone had sat there watching her. *Could* have been

watching, she told herself, don't be imaginative. Imaginative girls get lost, and Ellean did not mean to lose.

She locked up carefully then went on to the one-bedroomed house, which she always left till last because it was her favourite, and, in a way, the best.

Closing the door behind her and tossing the bundle of keys on the table, she stopped to sniff. Delicately, because Ellean did everything delicately. There was a faint scent in the air as if the presence that had caused the smell in the other house had been here too.

But for a shorter time, perhaps? Or left longer ago to go elsewhere?

The kitchen and the sitting room were tidy, except that someone had smoked a cigarette and dropped ash in the sink. And there was the knife Steve had complained of losing, on the counter. Trust him. Ellean tidied away the ash and stub, sweeping them into a plastic bag brought for the purpose. There was lipstick on the cigarette end so she blamed it on Miss Lonelyheart. The knife she left.

She went into the bathroom, where some unknown hand had written 'Bitch' in large letters with lipstick on the mirror.

She looked in the mirror and saw the word just below her reflection like a label.

Then she heard the door behind her open and close.

'Steve?' she called. 'Is that you?' She knew it was not Steve; he never came here. He'd gone home long since.

Silence. Forcing herself to move she went back into the sitting room.

A woman was sitting at the table; she had her back to Ellean as if Ellean was of no interest to her at all. But that could not be so.

Ellean knew it could not be so, and her voice when she spoke was hoarse. 'Hello. Were you looking for me?'

The woman did not turn round. But she spoke. Taking her time about it while Ellean found movement impossible. She knew now what frozen to the spot meant, only it was more like magnetism, she could feel the drag in her legs. It was how you felt in a nightmare.

'No. Not looking. Not exactly looking.'

There was a kind of harsh humour in the tone, although the

voice itself was sweet and low. An educated voice full of uneducated emotion was how it hit Ellean.

She knew the back, recognised the coat and black hair as belonging to the woman she called Miss Lonelyheart. What she didn't recognise was the hostility, the personal dislike.

The woman turned round.

The carelessly made-up face was more lined than she remembered. The skin was pale and clear, but all the colour had drained away so that the black hair looked too dramatic. It made Ellean uneasy.

'What do you want?' She advanced towards the table.

'You.'

'I think you'd better go.' Ellean walked towards the door to open it, but it was locked, it had a patent burglar-proof lock that required a key. She reached in her pocket for the bunch but she'd left them on the table and her visitor had her hand over them. 'Please. Let me have my keys.' The hand gripped the keys harder. 'Who are you?'

'Can't you guess? Nothing about me gives you pause for thought?' The voice was light and mocking. 'Don't you wonder how I got in? Where I got the keys? The keys I used.'

'You stole them.' Steve was notoriously casual. She'd got them from the row of keys above his desk.

'No. I came by them quite honestly. They were given to me. I could ask for them, you see.' She raised an eyebrow. 'No clue yet? – I'm Mrs Minden.'

Ellean opened her mouth, then shut it again without speaking.

'But of course you had guessed, hadn't you? You were just pretending not. What a game. You playing your game, me playing mine. Rex playing his. – Shut your mouth, dear, it's fallen open again. It doesn't look pretty open.'

'I thought,' began Ellean, then stopped. She ought to have seen, seen at once.

'That I would be a blonde? Rex always prefers blondes, doesn't he? Or so he says. If the girl he fancies happens to have blonde hair. Otherwise red, black or mouse will do.' The tone was self-lacerating now. 'No, maybe you didn't recognise me, maybe I didn't intend you to know me. But I needed to know you. To know your movements. Pattern of work, and all that. So I could plan. I'm a planner. Meticulous. Rex is going to miss that side of me. He's slapdash. But I expect you know that already.

'Rex and Jacqui. A very bright pair. Our friends loved our marriage. Envied us. So modern. So good. I contributed a lot to Minden Enterprises. Helped build it up. My baby too. We had no children as you must know.'

Ellean made a sort of noise.

'I expect you're thinking you'll remedy that. Don't fall into that trap. Whatever Rex says he doesn't want children. He's got a bastard son as it happens. Not much affection there as far as I noticed.'

Ellean said, 'I'm going. There's no future in this conversation.'

'You're right,' said Jacqui Minden. 'There is no future. For you.'

Ellean went to the door, banging and shouting. 'Steve, Steve, come and let me out.'

Jacqui let her bang and shout for a minute or two. 'There's no one there. They've all gone. You *know* they've all gone. Stop kidding yourself. It's just you and me.'

She got up, put her arm round the girl's shoulder. 'Come back. Sit down.' It was almost an affectionate gesture. 'Sit down and have a drink.'

'There's nothing to drink,' said Ellean shortly.

Jacqui laughed. 'Don't you believe it.' From her handbag came a beautifully polished silver flask. 'I borrowed this from Rex. Vulgar, I think, but then some little blonde gave it to him, I expect. He won't notice. Never uses it.' Ellean flinched. Jacqui poured out some whisky into the silver cup which screwed into the top. 'Have a drink from the poisoned chalice.'

'I'm not going to touch it.'

'Not poisoned really. I'll drink it. Look, watch me.' Jacqui drained the whisky at a gulp. Then she poured another silver noggin. 'Have some.'

Ellean shook her head. For an answer Jacqui produced a small revolver and laid it silently but significantly by her hand.

'That's a toy,' said Ellean. 'And if it wasn't, you'd never use it.'

'Try me.' Jacqui gave the drink a little push towards her prey. 'Drink up.'

Ellean drank. As far as she could tell it was neat spirit, she felt it track down her throat then hit her stomach like a small, hot missile. Almost at once the alcohol loosened her tongue.

'I know about you now. I know what that smell was: it was anger.'

Jacqui brushed her aside with contempt. 'I don't go around spraying a smell like a cat.'

'You're exuding it,' said Ellean with conviction, her eyes wide so that the white showed all round the iris. It was a panic signal that displayed itself to Jacqui. Ellean was very frightened. A smell like that (she had just got a whiff of it again) carried conviction, but she tried to bluff it out. 'If you want me to give Rex up, you won't do it by threatening me. Besides, it would be no good. He loves me. He's going to divorce you and marry me.'

'I'm not threatening you. You've got me all wrong, if you think that. Stay sitting down, dear: you worry me when you start to move around, and the doctor says I mustn't be worried, I might blow up. No, I'm not threatening you. To threaten suggests there won't be a performance. I'm promising.'

'You couldn't kill me. Not here.'

'Who said anything about killing you?' Jacqui smiled. A waft of anger came Ellean's way. 'No, I'm just going to give you a chance to die.'

Once again she reached into her handbag, this time to produce a small bottle, out of which she tipped a heap of blue capsules, then with delicate forefingers arranged them in a row.

'Sleepers. Little blue babies. A dozen of these in a nip like that one there will see you well away.'

Ellean shoved the capsules back into disorder. 'I won't take them. You can't make me.' Jacqui held up the gun. To the frightened girl it looked very real now. 'And you wouldn't dare use that. If I'm shot here, then it won't be long before they come for you.'

'You won't die here. You are just going to disappear. Soon it will be dark. I've got my car parked very close. I'm a bigger woman than you. I'll get you into it. A fireman's lift, you know. Or I might walk you into it when you are all woozy. Off and away.' She fixed her shadowy blue eyes on Ellean, so that the girl could not move her eyes away. She was sinking deeper and deeper into this nightmare. There was a hook in each eye which seemed attached to each of Jacqui's. 'And don't worry about your flat,' went on Jacqui. 'I'll have the keys, remember, from your bag. I'll tidy it up, pack your bags and move you out. Gone.'

She made it sound feasible.

'My body,' gasped Ellean. 'That'll be found.'

'What makes you think there will be a body? I've got a very powerful machine down at my little place in the country. My chickens will eat you up.'

'Chickens aren't meat eaters. Chickens eat grain.' Did she really manage to gasp that out?

'Want to bet? My chickens will eat anything. And then there are the sea-gulls. I get them in bad weather. Closely related to vultures, they are.'

Ellean reached out a hand and took a capsule. She swallowed one, only one. Then she had an idea. 'I want water. I must have water.' She knocked the drink away. 'I can't take that . . . Water in the kitchen.'

She stumbled off in her nightmare; Jacqui in her own private nightmare let her go.

Out in the kitchen the outline of sink and cupboards wavered, were not there when Ellean tried to lean on them to steady herself, they were suddenly papery thin and insubstantial to her gaze. The knife was still there, though, solid and gleaming, less like a carpenter's knife than a butcher's. She got her hand on it.

Then Jacqui, a huge wavering form, loomed up behind her like a monster; she could smell that smell again.

In Jacqui's nightmare, private and personal to her, she was feeling the betrayal of hands she had once loved. Rage beyond anything she had known before rose in her like a silent shout.

She put out hands to seize, to strangle the throat in front of her. Her own nightmare was taking over now.

Ellean felt the hands throttling her, she brought the knife up, making jabbing movements. She felt the knife go through flesh.

Suddenly the body that was Jacqui's fell away from her to the ground.

'I've killed her,' thought Ellean. Oddly there didn't seem to be much blood, not even on her gloves.

Jacqui's face seemed veiled, a blur, as if the skull and flesh were fading.

In her fall her hair had become disarranged.

The black curls had tumbled off. Underneath was greying, fair hair which had been dyed a pale yellow, and the dye had not been a success. Ellean saw that. Some hair would just *not* take dye, she knew that from her hairdressing days.

Poor cow, she thought. 'She put that wig on so I wouldn't know her. But I didn't anyway.'

For a moment she closed her eyes. Sleep seemed to be overtaking her. Those bloody sleeping capsules.

She had to get home. Grabbing her keys and bag, she stepped around Jacqui's body and fled. The drive home seemed to disappear. She might have been driving in her sleep. Probably she was.

All the same, she managed to get into her flat and on to the bed before the hypnotic and drink overcame her.

Blackness.

A bell ringing roused her. She stirred. Awoke to terrible memories of Jacqui. She came back to a crushing sense of fear; she didn't want to wake up. Her eyes closed.

But the telephone was ringing, going right through her head, hardly a bell at all, just pure sound. She reached out a hand, trying to get her eyes open.

'Rex here. Ellie? You there?' He hurried on without waiting. 'Something terrible's happened. I've had the police here. Jacqui's been killed. They said she'd been stabbed. In one of the Minden Place houses. She had my flask with her. Got my finger-prints on it. I think, I think the police believe I stabbed her. Say I was with you, will you, Ellie?' His voice was rough, thick, as if the throat was constricted. 'I think they may be on their way to you now. Will you, Ellie?'

'Yes,' she agreed sleepily. 'But where were you, Rex?'

'Here. On my own,' he said at once.

His voice sounded tiny, and very very far away. Not a voice to believe in.

'Have you got a cold?' Where *had* he been? Not with her, anyway.

'No, just hurt my throat a bit. You're going to be all right, Ellie?'

'Yes.' She put up a hand to her own throat, where Jacqui had gripped, but it felt fine. 'I think I hear the door bell now.'

She put the receiver down and lay back a moment with closed eyes. The door bell had stopped ringing. There was absolute silence, as if it had never rung.

A blackness closed over her. Fear.

In a minute, she got up, put on her dressing-gown and went to open the door.

The newspaper was on the mat, and a policeman was picking it up to hand to her.

She knew what she had to do. She had a duty to herself and to Jacqui who had been a decent sort in her way. She knew Jacqui would have said: 'Save yourself, my girl, and let Rex take whatever's coming to him. His share of the pains of life: he's had the pleasures.'

Yes, he deserved it.

She looked surprised at the police being there at all, surprised at the questions. No, Rex Minden had *not* been with her. No, she had been alone all night. That was true enough.

She saw them go away satisfied.

Then she went into the kitchen to make her coffee; she stood there drinking it, and reading the newspaper.

'Dead woman found in Minden Place Development,' she read.

Husband detained. No, that would be in tomorrow's press. You couldn't call it revenge, could you? Ellean couldn't. To her it was a kind of natural justice. Jacqui's death had been an accident, but one caused by the behaviour of Rex. All right, yes, so it was revenge for the way he had treated her and was about to treat her. Because Ellean knew in her heart that although poor Jacqui had thought her worth killing, Rex wasn't going to marry Ellean.

So a girl had to look after herself.

Ellis Peters

A LIGHT ON THE ROAD TO WOODSTOCK

The King's court was in no hurry to return to England, that late autumn of 1120, even though the fighting, somewhat desultory in these last stages, was long over, and the enforced peace sealed by a royal marriage. King Henry had brought to a successful conclusion his sixteen years of patient, cunning, relentless plotting, fighting and manipulating, and could now sit back in high content, master not only of England but of Normandy, too. What the Conqueror had misguidedly dealt out in two separate parcels to his two elder sons, his youngest son had now put together again and clamped into one. Not without a hand in removing from the light of day, some said, both of his brothers, one of whom had been shovelled into a hasty grave under the tower at Winchester, while the other was now a prisoner in Devizes, and unlikely ever to be seen again by the outer world.

The court could well afford to linger to enjoy victory, while Henry trimmed into neatness the last loose edges still to be made secure. But his fleet was already preparing at Barfleur for the voyage back to England, and he would be home before the month ended. Meantime, many of his barons and knights who had fought his battles were withdrawing their contingents and making for home, among them one Roger Mauduit, who had a young and handsome wife waiting for him, certain legal business on his mind, and twenty-five men to ship back to England, most of them to be paid off on landing.

There were one or two among the miscellaneous riff-raff he had recruited here in Normandy on his lord's behalf whom it might be worth keeping on in his own service, along with the few men of his household, at least until he was safely home. The vagabond clerk turned soldier, let him be unfrocked priest or what he might, was an excellent copyist and a sound Latin scholar, and could put legal documents in their best and most presentable form, in good time for the King's court at Woodstock. And the Welsh man-at-arms, blunt and insubordinate as he was, was also experienced and accomplished in arms, a man of his word, once given, and utterly reliable in whatever situation on land or sea, for in both elements he had long practice behind him. Roger was well aware that he was not greatly loved, and had little faith in either the valour or the loyalty of his own men. But this Welshman from Gwynedd, by way of Antioch and Jerusalem and only God knew where else, had imbibed the code of arms and wore it as a second nature. With or without love, such service as he pledged, that he would provide.

Roger put it to them both as his men were embarking at Barfleur, in the middle of a deceptively placid November, and upon a calm sea.

'I would have you two accompany me to my manor of Sutton Mauduit by Northampton, when we disembark, and stay in my pay until a certain lawsuit I have against the abbey of Shrewsbury is resolved. The King intends to come to Woodstock when he arrives in England, and will be there to preside over my case on the twenty-third day of this month. Will you remain in my service until that day?'

The Welshman said that he would, until that day or until the case was resolved. He said it indifferently, as one who has no business of any importance anywhere in the world to pull him in another direction. As well Northampton as anywhere else. As well Woodstock. And after Woodstock? Why anywhere in particular? There was no identifiable light beckoning him anywhere, along any road. The world was wide, fair and full of savour, but without signposts.

Alard, the tatterdemalion clerk, hesitated, scratched his thick thatch of grizzled red hair, and finally also said yes, but as if some vague regret drew him in another direction. It meant pay for some days more, he could not afford to say no.

'I would have gone with him with better heart,' he said later, when they were leaning on the rail together, watching the low blue line of the English shore rise out of a placid sea, 'if he had been taking a more westerly road.'

'Why that?' asked Cadfael ap Meilyr ap Dafydd. 'Have you kin in the west?'

'I had once. I have not now.'

'Dead?'

'I am the one who died.' Alard heaved lean shoulders in a helpless shrug, and grinned. 'Fifty-seven brothers I had, and now I'm brotherless. I begin to miss my kin, now I'm past forty. I never valued them when I was young.' He slanted a rueful glance at his companion and shook his head. 'I was a monk of Evesham, an *oblatus*, given to God by my father when I was five years old. When I was fifteen I could no longer abide to live my life in one place, and I ran. Stability is one of the vows we take – to be content in one stay, and go abroad only when ordered. That was not for me, not then. My sort they call *vagus* – frivolous minds that must wander. Well, I've wandered far enough, God knows, in my time. I begin to fear I can never stand still again.'

The Welshman drew his cloak about him against the chill of the wind. 'Are you hankering for a return?'

'Even you seamen must drop anchor somewhere at last,' said Alard. 'They'd have my hide if I went back, that I know. But there's this about penance, it pays all debts, and leaves the record clear. They'd find a place for me, once I'd paid. But I don't know . . . I don't know . . . The *vagus* is still in me. I'm torn two ways.'

'After twenty-five years,' said Cadfael, 'a month or two more for quiet thinking can do no harm. Copy his papers for him and take your ease until his business is settled.'

They were much of an age, though the renegade monk looked the elder by ten years, and much knocked about by the world he had coveted from within the cloister. It had never paid him well in goods or gear, for he went threadbare and thin, but in wisdom he might have got his fair wages. A little soldiering, a little clerking, some horse-tending, any labour that came to hand, until he could turn his hand to almost anything a hale man can do. He had seen, he said, Italy as far south as Rome, served once for a time under the Count of Flanders, crossed the mountains into Spain, never abiding anywhere for long. His feet still served him, but his mind grew weary of the road.

'And you?' he said, eyeing his companion, whom he had known now for a year in this last campaign. 'You're something of a *vagus* yourself, by your own account. All those years crusading and battling corsairs in the midland sea, and still you have not enough of it, but must cross the sea again to get buffeted about

Normandy. Had you no better business of your own, once you got back to England, but you must enlist again in this muddled mêlée of a war? No woman to take your mind off fighting?'

'What of yourself? Free of the cloister, free of the vows!'

'Somehow,' said Alard, himself puzzled, 'I never saw it so. A woman here and there, yes, when the heat was on me, and there was a woman by and willing, but marriage and wiving . . . it never seemed to me I had the right.'

The Welshman braced his feet on the gently swaying deck and watched the distant shore draw nearer. A broad-set, sturdy, muscular man in his healthy prime, brown-haired and brown-skinned from eastern suns and outdoor living, well-provided in leather coat and good cloth, and well-armed with sword and dagger. A comely enough face, strongly featured, with the bold bones of his race – there had been women, in his time, who had found him handsome.

'I had a girl,' he said meditatively, 'years back, before ever I went crusading. But I left her when I took the Cross, left her for three years and stayed away seventeen. The truth is, in the east I forgot her, and in the west she, thanks be to God, had forgotten me. I did enquire, when I got back. She'd made a better bargain, and married a decent, solid man who had nothing of the *vagus* in him. A guildsman and counsellor of the town of Shrewsbury, no less. So I shed the load from my conscience and went back to what I knew, soldiering. With no regrets,' he said simply. 'It was all over and done, years since. I doubt if I should have known her again, or she me.' There had been other women's faces in the years between, still vivid in his memory, while hers had faded into mist.

'And what will you do,' asked Alard, 'now the King's got everything he wanted, married his son to Anjou and Maine, and made an end of fighting? Go back to the east? There's never any want of squabbles there to keep a man busy.'

'No,' said Cadfael, eyes fixed on the shore that began to show the solidity of land and the undulations of cliff and down. For that, too, was over and done, years since, and not as well done as once he had hoped. This desultory campaigning in Normandy was little more than a postscriptum, an afterthought, a means of filling in the interim between what was past and what was to come, and as yet unrevealed. All he knew of it was that it must be something new and momentous, a door opening into another room. 'It seems we have both a few days' grace, you and I, to find out where we are going. We'd best make good use of the time.'

There was stir enough before night to keep them from wondering beyond the next moment, or troubling their minds about what was past or what was to come. Their ship put into the roads with a steady and favourable wind, and made course into Southampton before the light faded, and there was work for Alard checking the gear as it was unloaded, and for Cadfael disembarking the horses. A night's sleep in lodgings and stables in the town, and they would be on their way with the dawn.

'So the King's due in Woodstock,' said Alard, rustling sleepily in his straw in a warm loft over the horses, 'in time to sit in judgement on the twenty-third of the month. He makes his forest lodges the hub of his kingdom, there's more statecraft talked at Woodstock, so they say, than ever at Westminster. And he keeps his beasts there – lions and leopards – even camels. Did you ever see camels, Cadfael? There in the east?'

'Saw them and rode them. Common as horses there, hardworking and serviceable, but uncomfortable riding, and foul-tempered. Thank God it's horses we'll be mounting in the morning.' And after a long silence, on the edge of sleep, he asked curiously into the straw-scented darkness: 'If ever you do go back, what is it you want of Evesham?'

'Do I know?' responded Alard drowsily, and followed that with a sudden sharpening sigh, again fully awake. 'The silence, it might be . . . or the stillness. To have no more running to do . . . to have arrived, and have no more need to run. The appetite changes. Now I think it would be a beautiful thing to be still.'

The manor which was the head of Roger Mauduit's scattered and substantial honour lay somewhat south-east of Northampton, comfortably under the lee of the long ridge of wooded hills where the king had a chase, and spreading its extensive fields over the rich lowland between. The house was of stone, and ample, over a deep undercroft, and with a low tower providing two small chambers at the eastern end, and the array of sturdy byres, barns and stables that lined the containing walls was impressive. Someone had proved a good steward while the lord was away about King Henry's business.

The furnishings of the hall were no less eloquent of good management, and the men and maids of the household went about their work with a brisk wariness that showed they went in some awe of whoever presided over their labours. It needed only a single day of watching the Lady Eadwina in action to show who ruled the roost here. Roger Mauduit had married a wife not only handsome, but also efficient and masterful. She had had her own way here for three years, and by all the signs had enjoyed her dominance. She might, even, be none too glad to resign her charge now, however glad she might be to have her lord home again.

She was a tall, graceful woman, ten years younger than Roger, with an abundance of fair hair, and large blue eyes that went discreetly half-veiled by absurdly long lashes most of the time, but flashed a bright and steely challenge when she opened them fully. Her smile was likewise discreet and almost constant, concealing rather than revealing whatever went on in her mind; and though her welcome to her returning lord left nothing to be desired, but lavished on him every possible tribute of ceremony and affection from the moment his horse entered at the gate, Cadfael could not but wonder whether she was not, at the same time, taking stock of every man he brought in with him, and every article of gear or harness or weaponry in their equipment, as one taking jealous inventory of his goods and reserves to make sure nothing was lacking.

She had her little son by the hand, a boy of about seven years old, and the child had the same fair colouring, the same contained and almost supercilious smile, and was as spruce and fine as his mother.

The lady received Alard with a sweeping glance that deprecated his tatterdemalion appearance and doubted his morality, but nevertheless was willing to accept and make use of his abilities. The clerk who kept the manor roll and the accounts was efficient enough, but had no Latin, and could not write a good court hand. Alard was whisked away to a small table set in the angle of the great hearth, and kept hard at work copying certain charters and letters, and preparing them for presentation.

'This suit of his is against the abbey of Shrewsbury,' said Alard, freed of his labours after supper in hall. 'I recall you said that girl of yours had married a merchant in that town.

Shrewsbury is a Benedictine house, like mine of Evesham.' His, he called it still, after so many years of abandoning it; or his again, after time had brushed away whatever division there had ever been. 'You must know it, if you come from there.'

'I was born in Trefriw, in Gwynedd,' said Cadfael, 'but I took service early with an English wool-merchant, and came to Shrewsbury with his household. Fourteen, I was then – in Wales fourteen is manhood, and as I was a good lad with the short bow, and took kindly to the sword, I suppose I was worth my keep. The best of my following years were spent in Shrewsbury, I know it like my own palm, abbey and all. My master sent me there a year and more, to get my letters. But I quit that service when he died. I'd pledged nothing to the son, and he was a poor shadow of his father. That was when I took the Cross. So did many like me, all afire. I won't say what followed was all ash, but it burned very low at times.'

'It's Mauduit who holds this disputed land,' said Alard, 'and the abbey that sues to recover it, and the thing's been going on four years without a settlement, ever since the old man here died. From what I know of the Benedictines, I'd rate their honesty above our Roger's, I tell you straight. And yet his charters seem to be genuine, as far as I can tell.'

'Where is this land they're fighting over?' asked Cadfael.

'It's a manor by the name of Rotesley, near Stretton, demesne, village, advowson of the church and all. It seems when the great earl was just dead and his abbey still building, Roger's father gave Rotesley to the abbey. No dispute about that, the charter's there to show it. But the abbey granted it back to him as tenant for life, to live out his latter years there undisturbed, Roger being then married and installed here at Sutton. That's where the dispute starts. The abbey claims it was clearly agreed the tenancy ended with the old man's death, that he himself understood it so, and intended it should be restored to the abbey as soon as he was out of it. While Roger says there was no such agreement to restore it unconditionally, but the tenancy was granted to the Mauduits, and ought to be hereditary. And so far he's hung on to it tooth and claw. After several hearings they remitted it to the King himself. And that's why you and I, my friend, will be off with his lordship to Woodstock the day after tomorrow.'

'And how do you rate his chances of success? He seems none

too sure himself,' said Cadfael, 'to judge by his short temper and nail-biting this last day or so.'

'Why, the charter could have been worded better. It says simply that the village is granted back in tenancy during the old man's lifetime, but fails to say anything about what shall happen afterwards, whatever may have been intended. From what I hear, they were on very good terms, Abbot Fulchered and the old lord, agreements between them on other matters in the manor book are worded as between men who trusted each other. The witnesses are all of them dead, as Abbot Fulchered is dead. It's one Godefrid now. But for all I know the abbey may hold letters that have passed between the two, and a letter is witness of intent, no less than a formal charter. All in good time we shall see.'

The nobility still sat at the high table, in no haste to retire, Roger brooding over his wine, of which he had already drunk his fair share and more. Cadfael eyed them with interest, seen thus in a family setting. The boy had gone to his bed, hauled away by an elderly nurse, but the Lady Eadwina sat in close attendance at her lord's left hand, and kept his cup well filled, smiling her faint, demure smile. On her left sat a very fine young squire of about twenty-five years, deferential and discreet, with a smile somehow the male reflection of her own. The source of both was secret, the spring of their pleasure or amusement, or whatever caused them so to smile, remained private and slightly unnerving, like the carved stone smiles of certain very old statues Cadfael had seen in Greece, long ago. For all his mild, amiable and ornamental appearance, combed and curled and courtly, he was a big, well-set-up young fellow, with a set to his smooth jaw. Cadfael studied him with interest, for he was plainly privileged here.

'Goscelin,' said Alard by way of explanation, following his friend's glance. 'Her right-hand man while Roger was away.'

Her left-hand man now, by the look of it, thought Cadfael. For her left hand and Goscelin's right were private under the table, while she spoke winningly into her husband's ear; and if those two hands were not paddling palms at this moment Cadfael was very much deceived. Above and below the drapings of the board were two different worlds. 'I wonder,' he said thoughtfully, 'what she's breathing into Roger's ear now.'

What the lady was breathing into her husband's ear was, in fact: 'You fret over nothing, my lord. What does it matter how strong his proofs, if he never reaches Woodstock in time to present them? You know the law: if one party fails to appear, judgement is given for the other. The assize judges may allow more than one default if they please, but do you think King Henry will? Whoever fails of keeping tryst with him will be felled on the spot. And you know the road by which Prior Heribert must come.' Her voice was a silken purr in his ear. 'And have you not a hunting-lodge in the forest north of Woodstock, through which that road passes?'

Roger's hand had stiffened round the stem of his wine cup. He was not so drunk but he was listening intently.

'Shrewsbury to Woodstock will be a two- or three-day journey to such a rider. All you need do is have a watcher on the road north of you, to give warning. The woods are thick enough, masterless men have been known to haunt there. Even if he comes by daylight, your part need never be known. Hide him but a few days, it will be long enough. Then turn him loose by night, and who's ever to know what footpads held and robbed him? You need not even touch his parchments – robbers would count them worthless. Take what common thieves would take, and theirs will be the blame.'

Roger opened his tight-shut mouth to say in a doubtful growl: 'He'll not be travelling alone.'

'Hah! Two or three abbey servants – they'll run like hares. You need not trouble yourself over them. Three stout, silent men of your own will be more than enough.'

He brooded, and began to think so, too, and to review in his mind the men of his household, seeking the right hands for such work. Not the Welshman and the clerk, the strangers here; their part was to be the honest onlookers, in case there should ever be questions asked.

They left Sutton Mauduit on the twentieth day of November, which seemed unnecessarily early, though as Roger had decreed that they should settle in his hunting-lodge in the forest close by Woodstock, which meant conveying stores with them to make the house habitable and provision it for a party for, presumably, a stay of three nights at least, it was perhaps a wise precaution. Roger was taking no chances in his suit, he said; he meant to be established on the ground in good time, and have all his proofs in order.

'But so he has,' said Alard, pricked in his professional pride, 'for I've gone over everything with him, and the case, if open in default of specific instructions, is plain enough and will stand up. What the abbey can muster, who knows? They say the abbot is not well, which is why his prior comes in his place. My work is done.'

He had the faraway look in his eye, as the party rode out and faced westward, of one either penned and longing to be where he could but see, or loose and weary and being drawn home. Either a *vagus* escaping outward, or a penitent flying back in haste before the doors should close against him. There must indeed be something desirable and lovely to cause a man to look towards it with that look on his face.

Three men-at-arms and two grooms accompanied Roger, in addition to Alard and Cadfael, whose term of service would end with the session in court, after which they might go where they would, Cadfael horsed, since he owned his own mount, Alard afoot, since the pony he rode belonged to Roger. It came as something of a surprise to Cadfael that the squire Goscelin should also saddle up and ride with the party, very debonair and well-armed with sword and dagger.

'I marvel,' said Cadfael drily, 'that the lady doesn't need him at home for her own protection, while her lord's absent.'

The Lady Eadwina, however, bade farewell to the whole party with the greatest serenity, and to her husband with demonstrative affection, putting forward her little son to be embraced and kissed. Perhaps, thought Cadfael, relenting, I do her wrong, simply because I feel chilled by that smile of hers. For all I know she may be the truest wife living.

They set out early, and before Buckingham made a halt at the small and penurious priory of Bradwell, where Roger elected to spend the night, keeping his three men-at-arms with him, while Goscelin with the rest of the party rode on to the hunting-lodge to make all ready for their lord's reception the following day. It was growing dark by the time they arrived, and the bustle of kindling fire and torches, and unloading the bed-linen and stores from the sumpter ponies went on into the night. The lodge was small, stockaded, well-furnished with stabling and mews, and in thick woodland, a place comfortable enough once they had a roaring fire on the hearth and food on the table.

A Light on the Road to Woodstock

'The road the prior of Shrewsbury will be coming by,' said Alard, warming himself by the fire after supper, 'passes through Evesham. As like as not they'll stay the last night there.' With every mile west Cadfael had seen him straining forward with mounting eagerness. 'The road cannot be far away from us here, it passes through this forest.'

'It must be nearly thirty miles to Evesham,' said Cadfael. 'A long day's riding for a clerical party. It will be night by the time they ride past into Woodstock. If you're set on going, stay at least to get your pay, for you'll need it before the thirty miles is done.'

They went to their slumber in the warmth of the hall without a word more said. But he would go, Alard, whether he himself knew it yet or not. Cadfael knew it. His friend was a tired horse with the scent of the stable in his nostrils; nothing would stop him now until he reached it.

It was well into the middle of the day when Roger and his escort arrived, and they approached not directly, as the advance party had done, but from the woods to the north, as though they had been indulging in a little hunting or hawking by the way, except that they had neither hawk nor hound with them. A fine, clear, cool day for riding, there was no reason in the world why they should not go roundabout for the pure pleasure of it – and indeed, they seemed to come in high content! – but that Roger's mind had been so preoccupied and so anxious concerning his lawsuit that distractions seemed unlikely. Cadfael was given to thinking about unlikely developments, which from old campaigns he knew to prove significant in most cases. Goscelin, who was out at the gate to welcome them in, was apparently oblivious to the direction from which they came. That way lay Alard's highway to his rest. But what meaning ought it to have for Roger Mauduit?

The table was lavish that night, and lord and squire drank well and ate well, and gave no sign of any care, though they might, Cadfael thought, watching them from his lower place, seem a little tight and knife-edged. Well, the King's court could account for that. Shrewsbury's prior was drawing steadily nearer, with whatever weapons he had for the battle. But it seemed rather an exultant tension than an anxious one. Was Roger counting his chickens already?

The morning of the twenty-second of November dawned, and the noon passed, and with every moment Alard's restlessness and abstraction grew, until with evening it possessed him utterly, and he could no longer resist. He presented himself before Roger after supper, when his mood might be mellow from good food and wine.

'My lord, with the morrow my service to you is completed. You need me no longer, and with your goodwill I would set forth now for where I am going. I go afoot and need provision for the road. If you have been content with my work, pay me what is due, and let me go.'

It seemed that Roger had been startled out of some equally absorbing preoccupation of his own, and was in haste to return to it, for he made no demur, but paid at once. To do him justice, he had never been a grudging paymaster. He drove as hard a bargain as he could at the outset, but once the agreement was made, he kept it.

'Go when you please,' he said. 'Fill your bag from the kitchen for the journey when you leave. You did good work, I give you that.'

And he returned to whatever it was that so engrossed his thoughts, and Alard went to collect the proffered largesse and his own meagre possessions.

'I am going,' he said, meeting Cadfael in the hall doorway. 'I must go.' There was no more doubt in voice or face. 'They will take me back, though in the lowest place. From that there's no falling. The blessed Benedict wrote in the Rule that even to the third time of straying a man may be received again if he promise full amendment.'

It was a dark night, without moon or stars but in fleeting moments when the wind ripped apart the cloud covering to let through a brief gleam of moonlight. The weather had grown gusty and wild in the last two days, the King's fleet must have had a rough crossing from Barfleur.

'You'd do better,' urged Cadfael, 'to wait for morning, and go by daylight. Here's a safe bed, and the King's peace, however well enforced, hardly covers every mile of the King's highroads.'

But Alard would not wait. The yearning was on him too strongly, and a penniless vagabond who had ventured all the roads of Christendom by day or night was hardly likely to flinch from the last thirty miles of his wanderings.

'Then I'll go with you as far as the road, and see you on your way,' said Cadfael.

There was a mile or so of track through thick forest between them and the highroad that bore away west-north-west on the upland journey to Evesham. The ribbon of open highway, hemmed on both sides by trees, was hardly less dark than the forest itself. King Henry had fenced in his private park at Woodstock to house his wild beasts, but maintained also his hunting chase here, many miles in extent. At the road they parted, and Cadfael stood to watch his friend march steadily away towards the west, eyes fixed ahead, upon his penance and his absolution, a tired man with a rest assured.

Cadfael turned back towards the lodge as soon as the receding shadow had melted into the night. He was in no haste to go in, for the night, though blustery, was not cold, and he was in no mind to seek the company of others of the party now that the one best known to him was gone, and gone in so mysterioulsy rapt a fashion. He walked on among the trees, turning his back on his bed for a while.

The constant thrashing of branches in the wind all but drowned the scuffling and shouting that suddenly broke out behind him, at some distance among the trees, until a horse's shrill whinny brought him about with a jerk, and set him running through the underbrush towards the spot where confused voices yelled alarm and broken bushes thrashed. The clamour seemed some little way off, and he was startled as he shouldered his way headlong through a thicket to collide heavily with two entangled bodies, send them spinning apart, and himself fall a-sprawl upon one of them in the flattened grass. The man under him uttered a scared and angry cry, and the voice was Roger's. The other man had made no sound at all, but slid away very rapidly and lightly to vanish among the trees, a tall shadow swallowed in shadows.

Cadfael drew off in haste, reaching an arm to hoist the winded man. 'My lord, are you hurt? What, in God's name, is to do here?' The sleeve he clutched slid warm and wet under his hand. 'You're injured! Hold fast, let's see what harm's done before you move . . .'

Then there was the voice of Goscelin, for once loud and vehement in alarm, shouting for his lord and crashing headlong through bush and brake to fall on his knees beside Roger, lamenting and raging.

'My lord, my lord, what happened here? What rogues were those, loose in the woods? Dared they waylay travellers so close to the King's highway? You're hurt – here's blood . . .'

Roger got his breath back and sat up, feeling at his left arm below the shoulder, and wincing. 'A scratch. My arm . . . God curse him, whoever he may be, the fellow struck for my heart. Man, if you had not come charging like a bull, I might have been dead. You hurled me off the point of his dagger. Thank God, there's no great harm, but I bleed . . . Help me back home!'

'That a man may not walk by night in his own woods,' fumed Goscelin, hoisting his lord carefully to his feet, 'without being set upon by outlaws! Help here, you, Cadfael, take his other arm . . . Footpads so close to Woodstock! Tomorrow we must turn out the watch to comb these tracks and hunt them out of cover, before they kill . . .'

'Get me withindoors,' snapped Roger, 'and have this coat and shirt off me, and let's staunch this bleeding. I'm alive, that's the main!'

They helped him back between them, through the more open ways towards the lodge. It dawned on Cadfael, as they went, that the clamour of furtive battle had ceased completely, even the wind had abated, and somewhere on the road, distantly, he caught the rhythm of galloping hooves, very fast and light, as of a riderless horse in panic flight.

The gash in Roger Mauduit's left arm, just below the shoulder, was long but not deep, and grew shallower as it descended. The stroke that marked him thus could well have been meant for his heart. Cadfael's hurtling impact, at the very moment the attack was launched, had been the means of averting murder. The shadow that had melted into the night had no form, nothing about it rendered it human or recognisable. He had heard an outcry and run towards it, a projectile to strike attacked and attacker apart; questioned, that was all he could say.

For which, said Roger, bandaged and resting and warmed with mulled wine, he was heartily thankful. And indeed, Roger was behaving with remarkable fortitude and calm for a man who had just escaped death. By the time he had demonstrated to his dismayed grooms and men-at-arms that he was alive and not much the worse, appointed the hour when they should set out

A Light on the Road to Woodstock

for Woodstock in the morning, and been helped to his bed by Goscelin, there was even a suggestion of complacency about him, as though a gash in the arm was a small price to pay for the successful retention of a valuable property and the defeat of his clerical opponents.

In the court of the palace of Woodstock the King's chamberlains, clerks and judges were fluttering about in a curiously distracted manner, or so it seemed to Cadfael, standing apart among the commoners to observe their antics. They gathered in small groups, conversing in low voices and with anxious faces, broke apart to regroup with others of their kind, hurried in and out among the litigants, avoiding or brushing off all questions, exchanged documents, hurried to the door to peer out, as if looking for some late arrival. And there was indeed one litigant who had not kept to his time, for there was no sign of a Benedictine prior among those assembled, nor had anyone appeared to explain or justify his absence. And Roger Mauduit, in spite of his stiff and painful arm, continued to relax, with ever-increasing assurance, into shining complacency.

The appointed hour was already some minutes past when four agitated fellows, two of them Benedictine brothers, made a hasty entrance, and accosted the presiding clerk.

'Sir,' bleated the leader, loud in nervous dismay, 'we here are come from the abbey of Shrewsbury, escort to our prior, who was on his way to plead a case at law here. Sir, you must hold him excused, for it is not his blame nor ours that he cannot appear. In the forest some two miles north, as we rode hither last night in the dark, we were attacked by a band of lawless robbers, and they have seized our prior and dragged him away . . .'

The spokesman's voice had risen shrilly in his agitation, he had the attention of every man in the hall by this time. Certainly he had Cadfael's. Masterless men some two miles out of Woodstock, plying their trade last night, could only be the same who had happened upon Roger Mauduit and all but been the death of him. Any such gang, so close to the court, was astonishing enough, there could hardly be two. The clerk was outraged at the very idea.

'Seized and captured him? And you four were with him? Can this be true? How many were they who attacked you?'

'We could not tell for certain. Three at least – but they were lying in ambush, we had no chance to stand them off. They pulled him from his horse and were off into the trees with him. They knew the woods, and we did not. Sir, we did go after them, but they beat us off.'

It was evident they had done their best, for two of them showed bruises and scratched, and all were soiled and torn as to their clothing.

'We have hunted through the night, but found no trace, only we caught his horse a mile down the highway as we came hither. So we plead here that our prior's absence be not seen as a default, for indeed he would have been here in the town last night if all had gone as it should.'

'Hush, wait!' said the clerk peremptorily.

All heads had turned towards the door of the hall, where a great flurry of officials had suddenly surged into view, cleaving through the press with fixed and ominous haste, to take the centre of the floor below the King's empty dais. A chamberlain, elderly and authoritative, struck the floor loudly with his staff and commanded silence. And at sight of his face silence fell like a stone.

'My lords, gentlemen, all who have pleas here this day, and all others present, you are bidden to disperse, for there will be no hearings today. All suits that should be heard here must be postponed three days, and will be heard by his Grace's judges. His Grace the King cannot appear.'

This time the silence fell again like a heavy curtain, muffling even thought or conjecture.

'The court is in mourning from this hour. We have received news of desolating import. His Grace with the greater part of his fleet made the crossing to England safely, as is known, but the *Blanche Nef*, in which his Grace's son and heir, Prince William, with all his companions and many other noble souls were embarked, put to sea late, and was caught in gales before ever clearing Barfleur. The ship is lost, split upon a rock, foundered with all hands, not a soul is come safe to land. Go hence quietly, and pray for the souls of the flower of this realm.'

So that was the end of one man's year of triumph, an empty achievement, a ruinous victory, Normandy won, his enemies routed, and now everything swept aside, broken apart upon an

A Light on the Road to Woodstock

obstinate rock, washed away in a malicious sea. His only lawful son, recently married in splendour, now denied even a coffin and a grave, for if ever they found those royal bodies it would be by the relenting grace of God, for the sea seldom put its winnings ashore by Barfleur. Even some of his unlawful sons, of whom there were many, gone down with their royal brother, no one left but the one legal daughter to inherit a barren empire.

Cadfael walked alone in a corner of the King's park and considered the foolishness of mortal vainglory, that was paid for with such a bitter price. But also he thought of the affairs of little men, to whom even a luckless King owed justice. For somewhere there was still to be sought the lost prior of Shrewsbury, carried off by masterless men in the forest, a litigant who might still be lost three days hence, when his suit came up again for hearing, unless someone in the meantime knew where to look for him.

He was in little doubt now. A lawless gang at liberty so close to a royal palace was in any case unlikely enough, and Cadfael was liable to brood on the unlikely. But that there should be two – no, that was impossible. And if one only, then that same one whose ambush he had overheard at some distance, yet close enough, too close for comfort, to Roger Mauduit's hunting-lodge.

Probably the unhappy brothers from Shrewsbury were off beating the wilds of the forest afresh. Cadfael knew better where to look. No doubt Roger was biting his nails in some anxiety over the delay, but he had no reason to suppose that three days would release the captive to appear against him, nor was he paying much attention to what his Welsh man-at-arms was doing with his time.

Cadfael took his horse and rode back without haste towards the hunting-lodge. He left in the early dusk, as soon as the evening meal was over in Mauduit's lodging. No one was paying any heed to him by that time of day. All Roger had to do was hold his tongue and keep his wits about him for three days, and the disputed manor would still be adjudged to him. Everything was beautifully in hand, after all.

Two of the men-at-arms and one groom had been left behind at the hunting-lodge. Cadfael doubted if the man they guarded was to be found in the house itself, for unless he was blindfolded he would be able to gather far too much knowledge of his surroundings, and the fable of the masterless men would be tossed into the rubbish-heap. No, he would be held in darkness, or dim light at best, even during the day, in straw or the rush flooring of a common hut, fed adequately but plainly and roughly, as wild men might keep a prisoner they were too cautious to kill, or too superstitious, until they turned him loose in some remote place, stripped of everything he had of value. On the other hand, he must be somewhere securely inside the boundary fence, otherwise there would be too high a risk of his being found. Between the gate and the house there were trees enough to obscure the large holding of a man of consequence. Somewhere among the stables and barns, or the now empty kennels, there he must be held.

Cadfael tethered his horse in cover well aside from the lodge and found himself a perch in a tall oak tree, from which vantage point he could see over the fence into the courtyard.

He was in luck. The three within fed themselves at leisure before they fed their prisoner, preferring to wait for dark. By the time the groom emerged from the hall with a pitcher and a bowl in his hands, Cadfael had his night eyes. They were quite easy about their charge, expecting no interference from any man. The groom vanished momentarily between the trees within the enclosure, but appeared again at one of the low buildings tucked under the fence, set down his pitcher for a moment while he hoisted clear a heavy wooden bar that held the door fast shut, and vanished within. The door thudded to after him, as though he had slammed it shut with his back braced against it, taking no chances even with an elderly monastic. In a few minutes he emerged again empty-handed, hauled the bar into place again, and returned, whistling, to the hall and the enjoyment of Mauduit's ale.

Not the stables nor the kennels, but a small, stout hay-store built on short wooden piles raised from the ground. At least the prior would have fairly snug lying.

Cadfael let the last of the light fade before he made a move. The wooden wall was stout and high, but more than one of the old trees outside leaned a branch over it, and it was no great labour to climb without and drop into the deep grass within. He made first for the gate, and quietly unbarred the narrow wicket set into it. Faint threads of torchlight filtered through the chinks in the hall shutters, but nothing else stirred. Cadfael laid hold of the heavy bar of the storehouse door, and eased it silently out of its socket, opening the door by cautious inches, and whispering through the chink: 'Father . . . ?'

There was a sharp rustling of hay within, but no immediate reply.

'Father Prior, is it you? Softly . . . Are you bound?'

A hesitant and slightly timorous voice said; 'No.' And in a moment, with better assurance: 'My son, you are not one of these sinful men?'

'Sinful man I am, but not of their company. Hush, quietly now! I have a horse close by. I came from Woodstock to find you. Reach me your hand, Father, and come forth.'

A hand came wavering out of the hay-scented darkness to clutch convulsively at Cadfael's hand. The pale patch of a tonsured crown gleamed faintly, and a small, rounded figure crept forth and stepped into the thick grass. He had the wit to waste no breath then on questions, but stood docile and silent while Cadfael re-barred the door on emptiness, and, taking him by the hand, led him softly along the fence to the unfastened wicket in the great gate. Only when the door was closed as softly behind them did he heave a great, thankful sigh.

They were out, it was done, and no one would be likely to learn of the escape until morning. Cadfael led the way to where he had left his horse tethered. The forest lay serene and quiet about them.

'You ride, Father, and I'll walk with you. It's no more than two miles into Woodstock. We're safe enough now.'

Bewildered and confused by so sudden a reversal, the prior confided and obeyed like a child. Not until they were out on the silent highroad did he say sadly 'I have failed of my mission. Son, may God bless you for this kindness which is beyond my understanding. For how did you know of me, and how could you divine where to find me? I understand nothing of what has been happening to me. And I am not a very brave man . . . But my failure is no fault of yours, and my blessing I owe you without stint.'

'You have not failed, Father,' said Cadfael simply. 'The suit is still unheard, and will be for three days more. All your companions are safe in Woodstock, except that they fret and search for you. And if you know where they will be lodging, I would recommend that you join them now, by night, and stay well out of sight until the day the case is heard. For if this trap was designed to keep you from appearing in the King's court, some further attempt might yet be made. Have you your evidences safe? They did not take them?'

'Brother Orderic, my clerk, was carrying the documents, but he could not conduct the case in court. I only am accredited to represent my abbot. But, my son, how is it that the case still goes unheard? The King keeps strict day and time, it's well known. How comes it that God and you have saved me from disgrace and loss?'

'Father, for all too bitter reason the King could not be present.'

Cadfael told him the whole of it, how half the young chivalry of England had been wiped out in one blow, and the King left without an heir. Prior Heribert, shocked and dismayed, fell to praying in a grieving whisper for both dead and living, and Cadfael walked beside the horse in silence, for what more was there to be said? Except that King Henry, even in this shattering hour, willed that his justice should still prevail, and that was virtue in any monarch. Only when they came into the sleeping town did Cadfael again interrupt the prior's fervent prayers with a strange question.

'Father, was any man of your escort carrying steel? A dagger, or any such weapon?'

'No, no, God forbid!' said the prior, shocked. 'We have no use for arms. We trust in God's peace, and after it in the King's.'

'So I thought,' said Cadfael, nodding. 'It is another discipline, for another venture.'

By the change in Mauduit's countenance Cadfael knew the hour of the following day when the news reached him that his prisoner was flown. All the rest of that day he went about with nerves at stretch and ears pricked for any sensational rumours being bandied around the town, and eyes roving anxiously in dread of the sight of Prior Heribert in court or street, braced to pour out his complaint to the King's officers. But as the hours passed and still there was no sign, he began to be a little eased in his mind, and to hope still for a miraculous deliverance. The Benedictine brothers were seen here and there, mute and sombre-faced; surely they could have had no word of their superior. There was nothing to be done but set his teeth, keep his countenance, wait and hope.

The second day passed, and the third day came, and Mauduit's hopes had soared again, for still there was no word. He made his appearance before the King's judge confidently, his charters in hand. The abbey was the suitor. If all went well, Roger would not even have to state his case, for the plea would fail of itself when the pleader failed to appear.

It came as a shattering shock when a sudden stir at the door, prompt to the hour appointed, blew into the hall a small, round, unimpressive person in the Benedictine habit, hugging to him an armful of vellum rolls, and followed by his black-gowned brothers in close attendance. Cadfael, too, was observing him with interest, for it was the first time he had seen him clearly. A modest man of comfortable figure and amiable countenance, rosy and mild. Not so old as that night journey had suggested, perhaps forty-five, with a shining innocence about him. But to Roger Mauduit it might have been a fire-breathing dragon entering the hall.

And who would have expected, from that gentle, even deprecating presence, the clarity and expertise with which that small man deployed his original charter, punctiliously identical to Roger's, according to the account Alard had given, and omitting any specific mention of what should follow Arnulf Mauduit's death – how scrupulously he pointed out the omission and the arguments to which it might give rise, and followed it up with two letters written by that same Arnulf Mauduit to Abbot Fulchered, referring in plain terms to the obligatory return of the manor and village after his death, and pledging his son's loyal observance of the obligation.

It might have been want of proofs that caused Roger to make so poor a job of refuting the evidence, or it might have been craven conscience. Whatever the cause, judgement was given for the abbey.

Cadfael presented himself before the lord he was leaving barely an hour after the verdict was given.

'My lord, your suit is concluded, and my service with it. I have done what I pledged, here I part from you.'

Roger sat sunk in gloom and rage, and lifted upon him a glare that should have felled him, but failed of its impact.

'I misdoubt me,' said Roger, smouldering, 'how you have observed your loyalty to me. Who else could know . . .' He bit his tongue in time, for as long as it remained unsaid no accusation had been made, and no rebuttal was needed. He would have liked to ask: How *did* you know? But he thought better of it. 'Go, then, if you have nothing more to say.'

'As to that,' said Cadfael meaningly, 'nothing more need be said. It's over.' And that was recognisable as a promise, but with uneasy implications, for plainly on some other matter he still had a thing to say.

'My lord, give some thought to this, for I was until now in your service, and wish you no harm. Of those four who attended Prior Heribert on his way here, not one carried arms. There was neither sword nor dagger nor knife of any kind among the five of them.'

He saw the significance of that go home, slowly but with bitter force. The masterless men had been nothing but a children's tale, but until now Roger had thought, as he had been meant to think, that that dagger-stroke in the forest had been a bold attempt by an abbey servant to defend his prior. He blinked and swallowed and stared, and began to sweat, beholding a perilous gulf into which he had all but stumbled.

'There were none there who bore arms,' said Cadfael, 'but your own.'

A double-edged ambush that had been, to have him out in the forest by night, all unsuspecting. And there were as many miles between Woodstock and Sutton Mauduit returning as coming, and there would be other nights as dark on the way.

'Who?' asked Roger in a grating whisper. 'Which of them? Give him a name!'

'No,' said Cadfael simply. 'Do your own divining. I am no longer in your service, I have said all I mean to say.'

Roger's face had turned grey. He was hearing again the plan unfolded so seductively in his ear. 'You cannot leave me so! If you know so much, for God's sake return with me, see me safely home, at least. You I could trust!'

'No,' said Cadfael again. 'You are warned, now guard yourself.'

It was fair, he considered; it was enough. He turned and went away without another word. He went, just as he was, to Vespers in the parish church, for no better reason – or so he thought then – than that the dimness within the open doorway beckoned him as he turned his back on a duty completed, inviting him to quietness and thought, and the bell was just sounding. The little prior was there, ardent in thanksgiving, one more creature who had fumbled his way to the completion of a task, and the turning of a leaf in the book of his life.

Cadfael watched out the office, and stood mute and still for some time after priest and worshippers had departed. The silence after their going was deeper than the ocean and more secure than the earth. Cadfael breathed and consumed it like new bread. It was the light touch of a small hand on the hilt of his sword that startled him out of that profound isolation. He looked down to see a little acolyte, no higher than his elbow, regarding him gravely from great round eyes of blinding blue, intent and challenging, as solemn as ever was angelic messenger.

'Sir,' said the child in stern treble reproof, tapping the hilt with an infant finger, 'should not all weapons of war be laid aside here?'

'Sir,' said Cadfael hardly less gravely, though he was smiling, 'you may very well be right.' And slowly he unbuckled the sword from his belt, and went and laid it down, flatlings, on the lowest step under the altar. It looked strangely appropriate and at peace there. The hilt, after all, was a cross.

Prior Heribert was at a frugal supper with his happy brothers in the parish priest's house when Cadfael asked audience with him. The little man came out graciously to welcome a stranger, and knew him for an acquaintance at least, and now at a breath certainly a friend.

'You, my son! And surely it was you at Vespers? I felt that I should know the shape of you. You are the most welcome of guests here, and if there is anything I and mine can do to repay you for what you did for us, you need but name it.'

'Father,' said Cadfael, briskly Welsh in his asking, 'do you ride for home tomorrow?'

'Surely, my son, we leave after Prime. Abbot Godefrid will be waiting to hear how we have fared.'

'Then, Father, here am I at the turning of my life, free of one master's service, and finished with arms. Take me with you!'

Julian Symons

THE BIRTHMARK

It is often said that doctors know of several undetectable poisons which they never mention in the presence of patients, but in truth these reports are much exaggerated, for they generally refer to beneficial medicines that may have a deadly effect if wrongly used. Insulin injections, for instance, are vital for diabetics but can cause death through hypoglycemia if injected into a perfectly healthy person. The truly undetectable poisons are discovered by research chemists, and the secrets of them remain buried in their laboratories. Or at least, that is where they should remain.

The use of such a poison was the undoing of Courtney Vance. After the trial and sentence he freely admitted his guilt, complaining to prisoners and warders alike about his bad luck. 'It was perfect, really perfect,' he would say. 'Nothing could possibly go wrong.' Then he would launch into a lengthy account of the affair and just what did, unbelievably, go wrong. Courtney got a life sentence, which with remission generally means nine years in Britain, but he served only three of them. Another prisoner, who had slaughtered his wife and three children with an axe and suffered agonies of remorse ever since, was enraged by the endless repetition of the tale, and Courtney's callousness about the crime. He stabbed Courtney fatally with a shiv made in the prison craft shop where they worked side by side. The axe murderer was sent to Broadmoor, where he in turn bored his doctors with an endless recital of grief about his lost family.

Courtney Vance was in his late thirties at the time of the murder, a senior sales representative for DPN Medical Supplies. The term *salesman* was deprecated, but he was in fact a salesman and a very good one. His manner with the wholesale chemists on whom he called was confident but deferential, impressive both through his grasp of medical detail and his refusal to oversell any product. 'This is something that our wise men think may be helpful in certain arthritic cases,' he would say. 'But they do acknowledge it has limitations, and frankly my own feeling is that there *may* be side effects in certain conditions, although of course I'm not a doctor.'

His smile conveyed, what was already known to many of his customers, that he might have been – could have been – a doctor if mysterious family troubles had not prevented him from taking the final examinations. In fact he had failed his prelims twice, and then given up. Or rather his father, an assistant bank manager, had been told that it would be a waste of money for him to continue.

'They say you've got no application. "Not too bright and lacks application", that was the story at school, and it's the same now. I don't know what you're fitted for, Bill, except to sweep the streets.'

Courtney said truthfully that it had been his father who wanted him to be a doctor, and he hoped it would not come to sweeping the streets. What did he feel inclined for? Some kind of journalism perhaps, certainly something that wasn't tied down to regular hours in an office or a doctor's surgery. He had half-a-dozen jobs in as many years after giving up medicine, and left or failed at all of them, before being taken on for a trial period by DPN. There he was a success from the start, and at the time of the murder had been with them for ten years. He worked from home, which was an outer suburb of London called Warners Green, although he was required to spend four weeks each year at the laboratories outside Northampton where new products were tested, and another four at conferences where selling points were emphasised. He much enjoyed these occasions, when he impressed everybody by his authoritative manner, which was combined always with deference to superiors.

It was shortly after he got the DPN job that he married Evelyn Bridges, whom he had known at school. Her father was understood to be something influential in the City. Certainly he always wore a bowler hat when he drove up every day from Warners Green to town in his Mercedes, except on days when the Mercedes was to be seen outside the local golf club. His wife drove a small Lancia. 'They're a two-car family,' Mr Vance senior said when his son told him he had been accepted by Evelyn. 'It's a good marriage, son.' His wife wiped her eye, and

The Birthmark

said it seemed like fate that they should have met again. Evelyn, like Courtney (who had by now discarded his first name of William, always detestably abbreviated to Bill) was an only child.

In fact fate had received some assistance from Courtney. After that first chance renewal of acquaintance at a local Conservative Club dance he had sensed that Evelyn was his for the taking, and had courted her assiduously. He was in his late twenties, and had been thinking that it was time for marriage. This was even truer of Evelyn, who was a couple of years older, plump, placid and plain. In a physical sense she was hardly a catch, but there was the Mercedes, the Lancia, that 'something in the City' aura of money. It was a church wedding, the reception for a hundred and fifty people was held at the best local hotel, Mr Bridges paid for a honeymoon in Paris. He waved aside Courtney's thanks. 'You're one of the family now, m'boy.'

Being one of the family, however, did not bring the benefits Courtney had hoped for, even expected. When Mr Bridges had a heart attack and died on the golf course a couple of years later, the bowler hat proved to have been, as one might say, a deception. Whatever Mr Bridges had been in the City it was something not very important, or not very profitable. He had lived consistently above his income. The house had to be sold, the Mercedes went of course, the Lancia was replaced by a Mini, the widow settled down in a small flat. For Courtney and Evelyn there was nothing at all.

It was true, as she said, that they had each other, and by now Courtney had received promotion at DPN. They lived in a neat little semi-detached house in a row of almost exactly similar houses, with a pocket handkerchief garden in front and a bigger patch behind. There were in the first years no children, something which Evelyn regretted but which secretly pleased Courtney. He was a careful, cautious man, and regarded a child as an expense which they really could not afford. This was something Evelyn knew, as she seemed mysteriously to know everything about him. He realised the depth of her understanding when she suggested he should have a vasectomy.

'You know you don't want children,' she said. 'Admit it.'

He found that difficult. 'It isn't exactly that I don't want them, it's what they cost. I've worked it out, and the annual expense when you take everything into account –'

'It doesn't matter. I want us to be happy, Court, that's all.'

'I should like you just to look at these figures, they show the situation so clearly . . .'

Evelyn looked at the figures and said yes, he had the vasectomy, and felt distinctly relieved. They had quite a busy social life. The senior Vances and Mrs Bridges came round to Sunday lunch or supper at regular intervals, and both Courtney and Evelyn were pillars of the local Conservatives. There were socials and bazaars, at homes, tea and supper parties. Evelyn made little scones and cakes and home-made jams, and was an excellent housekeeper, working always within the agreed sum he gave her each month. 'She's just a wonderful little wife, son,' the now retired Mr Vance senior said after a supper party of beef olives, potatoes done in some French manner with cream or butter, and a green salad, all washed down with cheap but flavoursome supermarket wine. Courtney did not dissent, although 'little' was by now a misnomer, for Evelyn enjoyed her own cooking and was distinctly big.

It was because of her size, Courtney told himself, that he indulged in occasional peccadilloes. His success as a salesman for DPN products had led to an extension of his territory, so that he often spent a night or two away from home. On these occasions he looked deliberately for one-night stands, and often found them. These peccadilloes – which was the word he always used to himself about them – did not, he felt sure, affect his marriage. Even so, it was disconcerting to find that Evelyn's ability to understand him extended to them.

'Would you say you married me for my money, Court?' she asked one evening. That was ridiculous, he said, he hadn't had a penny from her family. 'Correction, I should have said in hope of making useful contacts, perhaps daddy getting you into some glamorous job, and finally inheriting a nice little packet when he died.'

'If you put it that way – well, not exactly, but some of those thoughts might have been in my mind.'

'Still, it hasn't worked out badly, has it?' He kissed her and said it had been marvellous. 'No, marvellous isn't the word, but it's been all right. You're doing well, we have a lot of friends, I'm good at running the house –' He interrupted her to say truthfully

The Birthmark

that she was a wonderful manager. 'Only trouble is, you don't like fat women. Don't interrupt, you know it's true. And I'm fat, can't be helped, something to do with metabolism, I've read it all up. You go on doing your duty, but I know it is a duty. Remember when you used to bring me flowers, give me scent? Not any more. And you're working off some of that surplus energy when you're away for the night. No need to worry about it. I just want you to know that I know, and don't mind, that's all.'

There was something uncomfortable about being so thoroughly understood, but he did not deny what she had said. Instead, he asked how she could put up with him. She said, with a sparkle in her eye, 'Because you're just about the handsomest man I ever saw, that's why.'

At this time Courtney Vance was certainly handsome. In youth he had looked immature and uncertain, but success, confidence, and the passing years had greatly improved his appearance. He looked, he thought himself, like a film star in the days when they dressed well, bathed and shaved often, had hair that was properly brushed and combed – Cary Grant perhaps, with a touch of David Niven. An old-fashioned look? Well, he didn't pretend or wish to be one of your long-haired teenagers in jeans. His thick dark hair was becomingly flecked with grey at the sides, his figure as slim now as it had been when he married, his profile as clear-cut. There was a suggestion of weakness in the wobbly, shapeless mouth, and of self-satisfaction in the way he smoothed his little moustache, but taken all round Courtney Vance was undoubtedly a handsome man, and for many women an attractive one.

A day or two after that conversation Courtney bought Evelyn flowers, and a week later a bottle of 'Magical Night', the tangy fragrance of which had enlivened their honeymoon. Evelyn smiled, thanked him, patted his cheek. He was pleased, but also a little resentful. Did one bring home a bottle of sexy perfume to be patted on the cheek like a child? But he enjoyed his job, admired his wife even though he did not love her passionately. If he had been asked whether he was a contented man he would have said *yes*.

Then, a year before the murder, he acquired a mistress.

Thelma was the American-born wife of a local building

contractor named George Hartley, a great bull-necked man with a voice which seemed always to be issuing through a megaphone. Courtney had found himself sitting next to her at a Conservative Club dinner, and they had got on wonderfully well from the start. Not surprisingly perhaps, since almost her first words were: 'I've seen you at meetings often enough, and you know what I've always thought? One day I'm going to be sitting next to that man, and then I'll say it straight out to him.'

'Say what?'

'Tell him he's the most attractive man in the room. There, I've said it.' Dark eyes flashed at him. 'I know Evelyn already, we're on a couple of committees together, she's a honey. But you've got no time for that sort of stuff, I know. Evelyn says you're a busy man.'

He told her what he did, implying that it was only a matter of time before he was invited to join the DPN board. 'And your husband is –'

'Over on the next table. The man with the thickest neck in the room. And the thickest skin. He only thinks about one thing.' There was a pause before she said, 'Money. He's away a lot too.' She turned and faced him directly. She had a high colour, strong features, flaring nostrils. The side of her face that had been turned away from him was marred by a birthmark, going from cheekbone to temple, purplish and menacing. A smile touched her lips, then she turned away abruptly, spoke to her neighbour on the other side. What had she been hinting?

He asked Evelyn about her, casually, tactfully, and learned that Hartley had met her at some convention where she was handling public relations for the English end of an American firm. They had been married within a few months, both for the second time.

'Some of the Tory ladies don't like her. Think she married George Hartley for his money, and that might be true – she's years younger than he is. Then she offers to do this and that, and they think she's pushy. If you ask me they're just jealous, I like her. How old do you suppose she is, thirty?'

'I really hadn't thought.'

'She *is* very direct, says what she thinks. How did you get on?'

'Well enough. She's rather aggressive for my taste.'

'You like everything to run smoothly, no rows, I know that.'

The Birthmark

She smiled at him. It was true, but he slightly resented her knowing it, and saying so. Indeed he found himself more and more irritated by the way in which Evelyn seemed always to know what he thought in advance.

It has been said that Courtney Vance was a cautious man. He had no wish to do anything that might affect his marriage, his work, or what he thought of as his social position. All the peccadilloes had taken place well away from home, and although he thought about Thelma Hartley and the look she had given him, it was not until she came in to the local pub where he was having lunch that he did anything about it. It would have been absurd not to eat their sandwiches and drink their beer together. He asked what she was doing there.

'When George is on a trip and I can't be bothered to cook for one, I often go to a pub. What about you? I thought you were always away.'

'Doing a round of local calls. I'm off on a little tour tomorrow, Surrey and Sussex. I'll be away two or three days.' She said he was lucky. He thought quickly. On the following day his calls would, or could, take him within a few miles of Warners Green. He asked if she would have dinner with him, naming a hotel near enough for her to drive to it, far enough away to make it unlikely that any Warners Green resident would be there.

She drained her beer and said, 'I thought you'd never ask.' The birthmark glowed a fiery red. In some curious way he found this flaw on her otherwise perfect skin attractive.

In the hotel on the following night they did not eat dinner, but went straight up to the room he had booked in the traditional name of Smith. Before the act and after it, Thelma talked. She said that she was bored with the bull, which was what she called her husband, bored with Warners Green, bored with the stuffiness and pettiness of local politics. Courtney said he was bored too, although that was not true.

She walked out naked to the bathroom, showered, came back. 'You've done this kind of thing before.'

'Not *this* kind of thing,' he said, and meant it. Her passion and eagerness was strange to him. Afterwards she had been dripping with sweat. He did not ask about her own experiences, afraid of what he might hear. What followed was not exactly a night of bliss, for Courtney was nervous of such raw excitement as she displayed, but it was certainly a night of a kind outside his knowledge, one he wanted to repeat. At one moment she said, 'What about Evelyn? You going to tell her?'

He was shocked. 'Good heavens, no. Certainly not. You surely don't intend – '

'To tell the bull? No, he might fly off the handle, though let me tell you, he's no reason to complain. He's got a string of floozies, I've found letters in his pockets. If I wanted to I could take George for half the money he's got.' Her mouth shut like a trap, her natural colour was heightened, the birthmark glowed.

Over the next months there were a dozen occasions when she stayed at hotels with him. Sometimes Hartley was at home, and she had to say no. Courtney then felt deeply frustrated, but he did not seek out other girls in her absence. They had been peccadilloes, this was the real thing, a grand passion.

He was slightly embarrassed by the fact that Thelma and Evelyn became very friendly. Twice he came home from trips during which Thelma had spent a night with him to find her in the living room.

'She's really interesting,' Evelyn said. 'Got quite a different slant on things. Perhaps it's because she's American.'

'I shouldn't see too much of her if I were you.' He added rather feebly and absurdly that she had a doubtful reputation. He never had a real row with Evelyn – as she had said, he did not care for raised voices – but some acrimonious words passed, and he brought her flowers on the following day. She accepted them with a smile, and patted his cheek.

One night, at a hotel in Brighton, Thelma told him that she and George Hartley had parted. She laughed at his look of shocked surprise.

'Don't look so amazed, these things happen. No need to look worried either, your name hasn't been mentioned. I told you I had the goods on George, it's separation by mutual consent, with what you might call a truly handsome settlement. He wants to marry one of the floozies after the divorce, which won't be yet awhile. Do you know you've got the finest body of any man I've ever seen? Come here and let me make a spot check.'

A little later he said, 'You'll be leaving Warners Green.'

'Right. I've got my eye on a flat in Kensington.'

'That means the end for us.'

The Birthmark

'I don't see why.'

But he knew it did. In Kensington, meeting again her sophisticated London friends, public relations people and the like, she would soon forget him. He found the thought of life without her dismaying, and said so. Indeed, he used the word unbearable. She looked at him consideringly.

'We do seem to suit each other, don't we? Much better than most. Be a pity to lose it. But you'll come up to town and see me. And I'll still make little trips out to hotels, I quite enjoy the sordidness.'

They didn't have to lose it at all, he said wildly, they could live together.

'What about Evelyn? I couldn't do that to her, break up her life. She's my friend.'

'I could talk to her, make her understand. She wouldn't want to stand in my way.'

'You're talking rubbish and you know it, Courtney Vance. For me you're a playmate, for Evelyn you're a husband. I don't even know that I like you, I just like what we do. And you might find that this put you off, when you saw it every day.' She took his hand and put it on the birthmark. He protested that he hardly noticed it. 'Mind you, you're such a pretty playmate that if Evelyn weren't there I might want to have you for keeps. But she is.'

He knew that what she said was true, and went home dejected. Evelyn said, 'It's Thelma, isn't it? I shall miss her too.'

'What do you mean?'

'I know about the two of you, of course I do. Oh, not from Thelma, she's said nothing. I knew what was going to happen when you asked those questions after the dinner.'

'But didn't you *mind*?'

'Oh yes, I minded.' Her placid moon face, a double chin now distinctly visible, smiled at him. 'But it seemed to make you happy in ways I couldn't, so I put up with it. A lot of marriage consists of that, putting up with things.'

When Courtney paid his quarterly visit to the laboratories outside Northampton, Thelma was still living in Warners Green. She had moved out of her husband's pretentious neo-Gothic house, but the Kensington flat was still the subject of argument about the lease. Evelyn had suggested that she should move into their spare bedroom, but the idea shocked Courtney, and he rejected it out of hand. So Thelma was staying with a niece of her husband's, but she saw Evelyn almost every day.

On the drive up to Northampton Courtney felt he was escaping from an awkward and slightly ridiculous situation. He had been altogether bowled over by Thelma, but could see no chance of a permanent relationship with her while Evelyn was there, and he quite accepted that Evelyn would always be there. The thought of Evelyn's death, and the possibility that he might cause it, never entered his mind. If he had ever considered such a thing he would have rejected the idea as far too dangerous. It might rather fancifully be said – and afterwards Courtney often and tediously said it – that Heinz Muller turned Courtney Vance into a murderer.

Heinz was an experimental research chemist, who was allowed to be a law unto himself within the firm. He was the chief of something called the Possibilities Ambit Laboratory, called Pal for short, where ideas derived from articles in scientific papers all over the world were tried out. Most of them never got beyond the testing stage, but every so often Heinz came up with a winner, something that could plausibly be called a variant on an existing product or technique, and was marketed successfully. He was unmarried, a Pickwickian little man with merry eyes behind gold-rimmed glasses, a hard drinker and inveterate womaniser. He and Courtney had got along well from the first time they met, and had done some peccadilloing together.

On this visit Courtney went as usual round the various labs, including Pal, talking to the scientists and technicians about what was in the pipeline. In Pal he was greeted warmly. Heinz showed him blends of this or that bubbling in retorts, rats and mice injected with various serums that made their behaviour depressed or manic, caused or were meant to cure skin infections and various diseases. At one end of the lab were little jars and bottles of possibilities promising enough for full-scale testing. Most would be found to have undesirable side effects, with luck one or two might be considered for marketing. Heinz talked about them all with enthusiasm, little eyes gleaming. Courtney knew enough to ask informed questions, and he was genuinely interested. Heinz picked up two bottles, one large containing a cloudy liquid, the other small with liquid of a clear yellow colour. He held up the large bottle, which was labelled *Noscan*.

'*Very* promising, *quite* revolutionary, amazing. You know pregnant women now all have the maternity scan to see where the baby is positioned, and so on? But it can have bad effects if repeated, so some doctors say. You take Noscan, and you can forget the scan. After a dose of it everything shows as clear as if it were an etching.'

'What's the snag?'

Heinz looked comically offended. 'I do not say there is any snag. There is perhaps a little local difficulty, a matter of adjustment.'

'How do you mean? What's in the other bottle?' The small bottle was labelled simply NX.

Heinz chuckled. 'Pure poison.' He might have been Mr Pickwick enjoying a Christmas game at Dingley Dell. 'I read an article by a German scientist about the properties of the juice of the beloa shrub which grows in the Brazilian rain forests. The Indians there use it mixed with mud to heal wounds and sores, and they think it is magical, a cure for everything under the sun. I don't tell you how I get it, but this is pure beloa juice. No colour, no taste, but pure poison. You handle it with kid gloves, as they say. Spread a little on your handkerchief and inhale it, let a few drops go on the skin, and – phut, you are dead. No pain, no symptoms, no traces, just dead.' He laughed heartily.

'Then it's surely no use.'

'Ah, that is the local difficulty, the adjustment needed. It is the beloa juice that makes the etching, you understand. We have to find out how to counteract its poisonous effects, yet it must remain effective. We cannot be like the Indians and mix it with mud, it has to be a liquid. So we tried different mixtures. This is Noscan 7, the seventh mixture. We tried the first six on mice, rabbits, guinea pigs.'

'With what effect?'

'They all died. That is our local difficulty. But enough of Noscan; shall we see each other this evening? Go out on the town? I have arranged a little something.'

Heinz came round to Courtney's hotel after dinner, they had drinks and talked. Then they met two of what Heinz called his professional amateurs, housewives ready to make a little extra money, but in the end Courtney declined the chance of a peccadillo, feeling a guilt about being unfaithful to Thelma which had never touched him in relation to Evelyn. Muller took one of the professional amateurs back to his apartment, but Courtney gave money to his and apologised for not being in the mood.

He spent a sleepless night. It was true he had accepted that Evelyn would always be there, but that was based on the belief that anything else was impossible. She had known about and tolerated the peccadilloes, known about and tolerated Thelma, what was it she had said? 'Marriage consists of putting up with things.' He saw years and years of toleration ahead, years in which she would get monstrously fat, plumping up like a giant cushion. And she would know always, as she seemed to, just what he was thinking and doing, and would put up with it. The prospect appalled him. And in the back of his mind there echoed those words of Thelma's: 'If Evelyn weren't there I might want to have you for keeps.' He changed it mentally to *I long to have you for keeps*.

All this – he had to be honest with himself and admit it – would never have come to the front of his mind but for Heinz's talk about Noscan and the little bottle of NX. He had asked one or two questions – casually, quite casually – while they waited for the professional amateurs, and Heinz had been delighted to expand on his discovery. The poison worked by inhalation, by drinking, by contact with the skin. It caused no pain (very important, Courtney thought, he would never have considered anything painful), and left no traces (equally important). Rabbits and guinea pigs just keeled over, suffering heart failure. (Evelyn was overweight.)

Courtney thought and thought about it. He was a cautious man, and if there had been the smallest possibility of detection he would never have considered the idea. But there was no such possibility. If Heinz had exaggerated and the whole thing failed, nobody would know.

The problem, then, was to get access to the bottle without being seen by Heinz. But there again, he told himself, if no opportunity arose he would take it as a sign that he should leave the whole thing alone, having nothing to do with it. Nonetheless he prepared himself by buying a tiny phial, a little pipette, a pair of rubber gloves.

The Birthmark

In the end that particular problem was solved with absurd ease, as if by destiny. He always stayed three days at the laboratories, and on each day visited Pal to chat with Heinz. On the last day Heinz's assistant was on the next floor searching for some records in the library, and Heinz was called to the telephone so that he was alone in the laboratory. The little bottle was three-quarters full. He put on the rubber gloves, poured no more than half an inch of liquid into his phial, stoppered it. The operation took no more than a few seconds. He was pleased to see the total steadiness of his hand.

After that, the car of destiny bore him onwards. If he had any doubts about the need for action they were removed when, on his return, he found Thelma installed in the spare bedroom. The Kensington lease was still presenting problems, Thelma had had a row with the niece, Evelyn thought it only right that she should come and stay.

'After all, Thelma's almost one of the family,' Evelyn said in the placid unshockable way that succeeded in shocking, and even disgusting him. Thelma looked at him with sparkling dark eyes, and seemed amused by his reaction. The limit came when, a couple of nights after his return, Evelyn said, 'If you want to go in to Thelma tonight, I shall understand.'

He was horrified. 'Certainly not. Under our roof, how can you suggest such a thing?'

'What does it matter whose roof you're under?'

He could not explain. The essence of his affair with Thelma was its romantic, exciting quality. To fornicate with another woman, with his wife's knowledge and compliance, in their own home – the idea was unthinkable. The suggestion removed any lingering doubt about the need for action, sealed Evelyn's fate.

Evelyn had used up her 'Magical Night'. He bought another bottle, unscrewed it, and with the utmost care added the contents of his phial. When he gave it to her she thanked him, then said with her placid smile that they had had few magical nights lately.

He was going away on the following day, and said with what he felt was false heartiness that if she used it on the day he returned – or even before, if she felt inclined, in preparation as it were – they would see what they would see. He hoped that with this hint the affair, which was the word he preferred to use, would be over before his return. It seemed wise to be absent, and if Heinz should have been mistaken and the procedure was *not* painless, he feared that he might be unduly distressed.

He was therefore not greatly surprised when, on the third evening of his four-day tour, he was told that Inspector Jezzard was in the hotel lobby, and would like to see him. He was prepared to show shock and a touch of grief, the speech ready prepared. 'Good God, Inspector, I can hardly believe it. Evelyn seemed perfectly well when I left home, but of course, now that I think of it, she'd complained of what we both thought were indigestion pains.'

The speech, however, was never made. The Inspector, a sharp-eyed, sharp-nosed man accompanied by a Sergeant, said, 'Mr Courtney Vance? I have a warrant for your arrest on the charge of wilful murder of one Thelma Hartley – hold up, man.'

Courtney Vance had fainted clean away.

His bewilderment was total. How could it conceivably have happened? At first he tried to fence with the Inspector, discover how much he knew. How was Courtney accused of administering this so-called poison?

'No point in playing games, Mr Vance. You know very well it was contained in a bottle of scent called "Magical Night".'

'And you have been able to isolate the poison in the bottle?'

The Inspector smiled, not pleasantly. 'We know where it came from. We know you abstracted a certain amount of a highly toxic plant poison known as NX from your firm's laboratory, and added it to the bottle of scent.'

'I don't accept that for a moment, but I ask again, have you been able to isolate the poison you say is in that bottle?' There was no reply. Heinz had been right, it was undetectable. 'If not, how can you be sure it was present.'

'In the most practical way. Very small quantities from the bottle have been added to food given to rats and mice. They died within half an hour. Painlessly, I understand.'

This was a shock. Perhaps he should have been present at the time after all, to remove the bottle, pour away the contents. The Inspector continued. 'When we contacted your friend at the laboratory, Mr Muller, he confirmed that the effect was exactly that of this particular poison. He then checked the NX bottle and confirmed also that the level was lower than it should have been,

The Birthmark

although the fact had not previously been noticed.'

But why, why did you have any suspicion at all, he longed to ask? Instead he said, 'I admit I gave a bottle of "Magical Night" to Evelyn. I certainly didn't give one to Mrs Hartley.'

'It is not suggested that Mrs Hartley was the intended victim. That was your wife.'

'Then how —'

'Mrs Vance seems to have suspected some joke on your part, a cruel joke she said. According to her, you had an intimate relationship with Mrs Hartley. Do you wish to comment on that? It isn't important, since we have been able to check on some of the hotels where you stayed together. The bottle was meant for your wife. She gave it to Mrs Hartley, saying something to the effect that it had not secured any magical nights for her. Mrs Hartley laughed, opened the bottle, sniffed it, dabbed a little on her hand, then on her face. Within a few minutes she collapsed, in less than an hour she was dead.'

Had Evelyn suspected, had her uncanny understanding of him gone so far that she realised he meant to do her harm, and deliberately passed on the bottle? It was something he never knew.

'And then?'

'Your wife called a doctor. By the time he arrived Mrs Hartley was dead, apparently from heart failure. The death would have been accepted as natural, but for one remarkable thing. It was something your wife noticed. Once it had been pointed out, it was clear that something must be wrong, and that further investigation was needed. We were called in, and took it from there.'

'Yes,' he said. '*Yes?* What was it?'

The Inspector smiled again. 'I think Mr Muller told you not only how powerful NX was, but also of its remarkable properties?'

'He did, but what then? What was it Evelyn saw?'

'It was rather what she did not see. Mrs Hartley had a red birthmark on one side of her face. She had dabbed a few drops of scent near to it. What your wife noticed was that, within a minute or two of the liquid being applied, the birthmark had completely disappeared.'

Miles Tripp

THE CASEBOOK CASANOVA

Gregory Hazelhurst didn't think he was God's gift to women; rather, he preferred to think women were God's gift to him. Sheltering behind a roof parapet he watched the latest gift through powerful field-glasses. She was pacing the square below unaware of being scrutinised by the man who had promised to meet her promptly at one o'clock. It was now seventeen minutes past one. The paved square was busy with office workers hurrying to lunch and few spared a glance for the waiting woman. Dark sun-glasses concealed the expression in her eyes but compressed lips indicated tension, a fact which Hazelhurst noted with satisfaction before putting down his field-glasses to check the time.

She had a long way to go to break the record of one hour six minutes set up two years previously by a housewife from Grantham. But even if she left now she'd been an excellent subject for study. Skill in performance, discretion, marital status, infidelity motivation, sex appeal, intelligence, had all been assessed and partly recorded in code in a journal which he kept in his bedroom. He was a lecturer in sociology at a nearby university and, if challenged, would have said the journal was fieldwork for a serious evaluation of the mores of middle-class married Englishwomen and the code was to protect the identities of his subjects. In due course if his work was published he would provide fictitious names.

But publication was a remote possibility. Without the back-up of a financial grant from some respected institution and without proper control conditions his study wouldn't be regarded as a serious piece of research. There was a slight chance of breaking into the popular market if he could get publicity of some sort but he had no idea how to obtain publicity without paying for it and he didn't possess that sort of money. It irked him that he was little better off financially than he had been ten years before and that he couldn't afford more than a rented apartment. For the time being the journal remained a self-gratifying ego trip, although he would never have admitted this. Nor would he have admitted that he was a womaniser driven by an inner compulsion which not only fed on itself but had the addictive qualities of a hard drug. He was hooked on sequential adulterous episodes and slave to something which, because he kept quasi-academic records, he deceived himself into thinking he mastered and controlled.

His interest in the present subject had almost expired. She wouldn't realise that the episode was terminal and only two columns of reference remained to be completed; the length of time she would wait on a date which never materialised and the method employed for disengagement.

Thirty-five minutes. She moved towards the pedestrian crossing, hesitated, swung on her heel and walked swiftly to the other side of the square where she loitered for a few seconds before returning to the crossing with a purposeful stride. He trained the field-glasses on her. Would she cross the street and disappear from view, fed up with waiting, or would she stay a little longer? For a few moments she lingered indecisively at the end of the crossing and then, with a resigned air, turned round and began pacing the square once more. He put down the glasses and, while still keeping her under observation, mused on the brief history of their relationship.

Stephanie was thirty-three, just two years younger than he, and she had a ten-year-old son at boarding school. She had been owner of a fashion boutique which had gone out of business through over-ordering and general incompetence. She was now taking a course in something she should have studied earlier, business management. It had been after a lecture on the structures of interpersonal relationships in business contexts given by Gregory Hazelhurst that she had been flattered by his attention and agreed to meet him for morning coffee when, he assured her, he would be able to give her useful information omitted from his lecture because of time shortage.

During this first date, seated at a corner table for two in a small restaurant, he learned that her husband was a civil servant.

'Doing what?' he had asked.

'To be honest I don't exactly know,' she said, 'but I think it's quite important.' She gave a little laugh and tapped the side of her nose with a finger. 'Hush-hush, you know.'

'Secret work?'

'Well, it could be. He doesn't talk about it.'

In his journal Hazelhurst had recorded: 'Probably the sort of man who makes a mystery out of a humdrum job to make himself seem more important. Obviously he hasn't succeeded or why is she interested in me?'

The relationship developed rapidly into an episode. He preferred to regard his ventures as episodes rather than affairs. Affairs were of the heart; episodes were basically sexual. It hadn't been difficult to lure her to his apartment one afternoon, but what he really wanted was to gain access to her home. This was always an acid test. Would the subject, God's gift to him, be willing to share her marital bed? With Stephanie, he not only wanted to apply the test but he was conscious of not having performed too well at his apartment. He'd suffered from an unaccountable attack of nausea and been obliged to leave her for a few minutes while he recovered in the bathroom.

The visit to her home had more than compensated for this setback. She had scored nine out of ten for skill in performance although rather strangely, after it was over, she had insisted on him helping with her make-up. He had to stand by the dressing-table and pass cosmetics. He even brushed her hair. Acting as a maidservant, passing her toiletries, hadn't been a displeasing experience. It had taken him time to work out her motivation. It might have been a bizarre form of fetishistic behaviour but it was more likely to be a means of recovering self-esteem. By putting him in a subordinate position she was saying in effect, 'You were in the superior position in bed but now I'm the superior one and so we're quits.'

He liked analysing motivations. Usually they could be reduced to boredom with married life, or desire to reaffirm sexual attractiveness, or from some sort of revenge. But Stephanie didn't seem motivated by any of these and when she did speak of her husband she spoke with affection. 'He's a very understanding man,' she'd said. 'We're lucky. We understand each other. We accept each other's faults while being grateful for the virtues.'

'I'm lucky too,' he had replied, stroking her hair. 'I'm lucky to be here with you.'

'Ah, but you're such a persuasive man,' she had said, taking his hand and giving the palm a light kiss. 'Intelligent, good-looking, sexy. How could any woman resist?'

He had inwardly preened and decided to make a note of her commendation in his journal.

But it was almost time to finish with Stephanie. The farewell shouldn't be too difficult. She wasn't one of those neurotic types who would try to plague him with letters and telephone calls. He might try the 'I feel like a heel and can't go on with this' line, or 'I've lied to you. I'm already married and my wife's coming to join me,' or even tell the brutal truth, 'You're a statistic in a book I'm preparing.' And, if all else failed, he had an unbeatable brush-off. 'Darling, I've been with someone else and I'm afraid' – pause for effect – 'I've contracted something rather nasty. Conscience won't let me . . .'

Fifty-nine minutes. Would she beat the housewife from Grantham? He began to feel quite excited. She was wandering aimlessly round the square like someone who has no home to return to but is waiting for nightfall so that she can shrink into anonymity, dark doorways, and the shadowy seclusion of some forsaken, condemned building.

And then she spoiled everything. Just one minute before equalling the record she went to the pedestrian crossing and walked purposefully out of sight.

That evening, because he'd been obliged to travel to another town to give a talk, he arrived back late at his apartment. He was too tired to write up his journal and went straight to bed.

Sleep was disjointed by bad dreams and when he finally awoke he was feeling depressed. He drew the curtains and looked out at a grey, rain-filled sky. After making a cup of coffee he switched on the radio but the music provided nothing more than a background noise to thoughts which were becoming oppressive. It wasn't often that he indulged in realistic self-examination, but when he did undertake honest introspection he didn't care for what he found. Lecturing on sociology wasn't so much a vocation as a means of earning some, but not enough, money. Its advantage was that more free time was available than in a nine-to-five job and this allowed him to pursue his researches.

Today, however, looking back on his past, the researches seemed a shallow escape from finding a purpose, an objective in life.

He finished his coffee and went for a wash and shave. As he peered into the mirror his hand strayed to the back of his head and he fingered an incipient bald patch. In a few years I shall be past it, he thought, and then what? Settle down with a good woman? If such a being exists! They're all wantons. But what am I? I'm nothing more than a wanton-chaser. I pursue quarries which want to be pursued and the journal isn't anything more than a Casanova's casebook and I'm material for a psychiatrist's casebook, a casebook Casanova.

Depression and self-disgust reached its nadir when he cut himself just below the left nostril. As blood trickled down his upper lip he said aloud to his mirror image, 'It's time you changed your ways.'

During the day his resolve firmed and the depression lifted.

It was while he was preparing notes for an evening-class lecture that the doorbell rang. Two men were outside. An identity card was flashed at him. The photo on the card matched the hard face above it. 'Detective Sergeant Cook. May we have a word, sir?'

'Certainly.' Mystified, Gregory Hazelhurst showed the plain-clothes policemen into a sitting room which, with its chaise-longue and scatter of coloured cushions, had been the setting of many seduction scenes. The junior policeman, young and fresh-faced, allowed his eyes to linger on a bronze reproduction of *The Eternal Idol* which stood on a corner cabinet.

Cook spoke. In a voice smooth with self-assurance he said, 'We're making enquiries. Part of the routine for eliminating possibilities. I wonder if you'd be so good as to answer a few questions.'

They were standing in the middle of the room. Gregory Hazelhurst had no intention of asking them if they wanted to sit down. They were interrupting his work and the sooner they went the better. 'Questions about what,' he asked brusquely.

'You know Mrs Colston, I believe?'

For a moment the name was unfamiliar. 'I don't think so.'

'We have reason to believe you do, sir.'

'Oh, yes . . . Stephanie. Why? She's all right, isn't she?'

The detective assumed a puzzled look. 'All right? I don't quite follow.'

'All right . . . In good health.'

'Ah, yes. I see. Well, you could say she was in good health physically but in a somewhat distressed condition mentally.'

Hazelhurst felt his stomach sink. Surely being stood up on a date hadn't caused Stephanie to have a mental breakdown but, even if it had, that wasn't a police matter. 'I'm not clear what this has to do with me,' he said.

'Maybe it has nothing at all to do with you, sir. Can you tell me where you were between one and two thirty yesterday afternoon?'

'In town. Doing a bit of shopping.'

'I see. And a shopkeeper or some other customer will vouch for this?'

Hazelhurst was badly thrown. He couldn't say, 'I was on a roof spying on a woman I was intending to let down,' but he certainly shouldn't have been foolish enough to pretend he'd been shopping. He attempted to retrieve the situation.

'Sorry. I was thinking of the day before yesterday. No. Yesterday I was here. In this room, as a matter of fact.'

'Alone?'

'Yes. Absolutely alone. Why? What's all this about?'

'Nobody phoned you? No one can substantiate the fact that you were here?'

Hazelhurst felt increasingly nervous and edgy. 'Nobody. Why do you want to know?'

'Mrs Colston was away from her home. She expected to meet you in the market square but you didn't turn up.'

Hazelhurst couldn't help giving a short laugh. 'And that's a police matter?'

'It could have a bearing, sir, because while Mrs Colston was waiting for you her house was entered and some valuable jewellery was stolen.'

'I'm sorry to hear it but that's nothing to do with me. As I say, I was here. I didn't turn up because I wasn't feeling well.'

Detective Sergeant Cook nodded. 'I thought you might say that. So you were never near the house on *that* occasion although Mrs Colston, who has been very frank with us, has made a signed statement that you have visited her there.'

'Well . . . Yes.'

'You didn't happen to notice her spare set of house keys on a table in the hall?'

'No. Why?'

'They've disappeared. Mrs Colston remembers seeing them before you visited her.'

'I didn't take them if that's what you're implying,' said Hazelhurst indignantly.

Cook gave a thin, disbelieving smile. 'If you say so, sir. I'm only quoting from Mrs Colston's statement. She also alleges that a certain amount of intimacy took place in the living room.'

Hazelhurst wished he had never met Stephanie Colston. The silly bitch had given too much away. What the hell would her husband think? He was bound to know, and some husbands could get quite nasty.

'Do you agree with that allegation, sir?'

Absolute denial was useless. He had already admitted visiting the house. All he could do was mitigate the damage done by her stupid statement. Selecting his words carefully he said, 'I'm not sure what's meant by "a certain amount of intimacy". Mrs Colston was still depressed because her boutique business had gone bust. I put my arm round her to comfort her. I think I may have kissed her, but that's all. I felt sorry for her.'

'And this act of compassion on your part took place in the living room?'

'Yes.'

Cook nodded as if approving this positive answer. 'Just one more question, sir. I have to ask it. You didn't adjourn upstairs to continue giving comfort?'

'Certainly not! Why? Mrs Colston didn't say so, did she?'

'No, sir. She didn't.' Cook's demeanour became more relaxed. He seemed glad to have got an unpleasant but necessary question out of the way. 'It only remains for me to ask if you're willing to make a formal statement based on what you've told me.'

'I don't mind. My conscience is clear.'

'Perhaps I might ask you to accompany us to the police station. We'll bring you back, of course.'

'As a matter of fact, I'm rather busy. I've got a lecture to give to an evening class and I'm working on my notes.'

'It won't take long. A few minutes.'

Hazelhurst was uncertain. The blandly cool policeman was not someone to be trifled with. Better to keep on the right side of him and go. 'All right. But it's most inconvenient.'

'Sorry about that, sir.'

Hazelhurst moved towards the door. The young constable who hadn't spoken once said, 'I go to an evening class. Art appreciation.' He indicated the bronze statuette. 'That's a copy of something by Rodin if I'm not mistaken.'

'You're not mistaken,' said Hazelhurst sourly, moving towards the door.

At the police station he made a statement and was then asked if he objected to having his fingerprints taken. Why object, he thought. I didn't steal anything. And anyway, my fingerprints are all over this place.

As his fingerprints were being pressed against a damp pad it occurred to him to ask, 'Where did Mrs Colston keep her jewellery?'

'In her bedroom. In a drawer in her dressing-table.'

It wasn't until he was back at his apartment that the implications hit him. He had been in her bedroom and touched almost everything on her dressing-table. His fingerprints would be all over it. Yet he had signed a statement that the entire period of his visit had been spent in the living room.

No alibi for the time between one and two thirty in the afternoon, and fingerprints on the dressing-table. He hurried to the telephone.

'Stephanie? It's Greg. Is it convenient to talk?'

'Not really. Anyway, I don't want to talk to you.'

Speaking fast, as if afraid she might ring off before he'd finished, he said, 'Sorry about yesterday. I had a terrible stomach. And nausea. Like I had when you were here only much worse.'

'I waited more than an hour.' Her voice was chilly.

'I'm dreadfully sorry. I phoned but you'd gone . . . Incidentally why did you tell the police we'd been in the living room?'

'Why not? It was the truth.'

Hazelhurst felt slightly stunned. 'What are you talking about. We were in the bedroom. You know that.'

'I know nothing of the sort and please don't call me again.'

'But Stephanie . . .'

'Goodbye.'

The line went dead.

* * *

In a restaurant that evening a man and a woman raised their wine glasses to each other.

'To a clever decoder,' she said.

'Working for H.M.G. has some fringe benefits,' he replied. 'I imagine he thought I was in some dreary Ministry drinking innumerable cups of tea.'

'A dull civil servant was the image I presented. It seemed to please him.'

They both laughed.

'And what image of yourself did you present,' he asked.

She cut, forked and ate a slice of smoked salmon before replying. 'I hope it was enigmatic. Thoughtful, but naughty.'

'It was naughty of you to nose around in the poor fellow's belongings while he was suffering in the bathroom.'

'I wouldn't have normally. But there was something I didn't trust. Perhaps I'm computer-conscious because of your job but there were times I felt I was feeding information into a computer. He had a certain particularly alert look when he asked what I felt were key questions. Questions about your status, my attitude to marriage, and so on. It turned out I was right.'

'And he turned out to be perfect for our plan.'

She put down her knife and fork and leaned forward. 'We do have an outlet,' she asked in a lowered voice.

'Leave it to me. The assessor might argue a bit about the value but I don't think we need worry too much about that.'

The woman smiled and spoke normally again. 'So we'll be paid twice over. I wonder how Gregory will wriggle out of this one. Not by suggesting he's got an unmentionable social illness, I'll bet!'

The man laughed and a waiter who had been hovering nearby asked, 'Everything all right, sir?'

'Fine, thanks.' The waiter moved away and the man raised his glass once more. 'Here's to open marriages,' he said.

'And to closed books,' she replied, lifting her glass in response. 'I reckon he'll have closed his book on me.'

In his apartment, miles away from where the couple were celebrating the success of their fraud, Gregory Hazelhurst was staring at his journal, gazing aghast at fragments of paper which showed that three pages had been torn out.

By two in the morning, and after numerous cups of instant

coffee, he had worked out why part of his journal was missing. He was being set up for a fraud on an insurance company. Stephanie's husband was obviously an accomplice in the swindle and was presumably complaisant about his wife's love affairs. No doubt he had access to a computer which could easily unravel a not very complicated code. That would be his hush-hush work in the civil service.

He put the journal down. In the morning he would take it to the police, confess that at the time the robbery was supposedly taking place he was on a roof spying on Stephanie. He would tell them how he had to assist her at her dressing-table. It might make him look small, even despicable, but better to be a casebook Casanova than the fall guy for a swindle.

The postman arrived as he was about to leave for the police station. There was one letter. The handwriting on the envelope was unfamiliar. He opened it and took out four pieces of paper. Three were pages torn from his journal; the fourth was a note from Stephanie.

Dear Gregory,
I deeply regret having told you my husband was expert in code breaking. You seemed to regard it as a challenge and insisted on my taking the pages which are returned herewith. I don't know whether it was his ability you wished to test or whether you wanted to share your private fantasies with me. Perhaps to act them out. In spite of what you have done I feel sorry for you. It was because I felt sorry for you I unwisely allowed you to kiss me. But I wasn't so sorry that I was willing to take you upstairs as you asked. Was it because I refused that you decided to pay me back in the way you did? But that is a matter for the police. I won't comment on it. I hope your punishment won't be too severe and you've learned your lesson.
Sincerely, Stephanie

He read the letter again with increasing disbelief. What was the point of sending him this catalogue of lies? He went to the kitchenette to make a cup of coffee but as he reached for the jar he felt sickened by the thought of yet another cup of coffee. He had consumed more in two days than he normally drank in a fortnight. Anyway, he needed something stronger than coffee. He went to a different cupboard and took out a whisky bottle.

Alcohol, contrary to its usual effect, seemed to clear his mind and he realised she had sent the letter to discourage him from telling the police the true story of his visit. If he had the nerve to show them his journal to support a story that his only interest was in seduction she would give a different version of his visit.

Convinced that he had been set up as a fall guy for a swindle he knew it might be difficult to persuade the police if Stephanie stuck to the line she was taking. Before receiving the letter he had intended to go to the police and say he wished to change his signed statement, but now he wondered if this was sensible. No one had yet come with a warrant for his arrest. Perhaps he should do nothing. In a misery of uncertainty, unable to think of anything but his dilemma, he found himself doing the absurd things which the programmed subconscious mind precipitates when allowed to take over control. He put the whisky bottle in the refrigerator when he had really intended to take an egg out of it.

It was impossible to concentrate on marking up papers. Twice he was on the verge of going to the police and twice he turned back. On the third occasion, late in the afternoon, he made his way there. He asked to speak privately to Detective Sergeant Cook and was shown into a small, barely furnished interview room. They sat down on opposite sides of a plain teak table.

'You have something you wish to tell me, sir?'

'Yes, it sounds odd, and I come out of it very badly, but I want to tell you what actually happened when I visited Mrs Colston. In my statement I said that we were in the living room all the time. That wasn't true. We went to the bedroom. Mrs Colston may deny it and try to make out I'm a fantasist . . .' And then Gregory Hazelhurst plunged into a confession of his 'researches', trying to put across that spying on women to see how long they would wait on an unfulfilled date had a serious sociological purpose.

When he had finished Cook, who had been silent, said, 'What you've told me is interesting, not that it matters greatly. Mr Colston was charged an hour ago.'

The grimly earnest expression on Hazelhurst's face was transformed into a grin of delight. As if he could scarcely believe what he'd just heard, he said, 'Charged?'

A faint reflection of his grin appeared on Cook's face. 'You seem surprised. I was suspicious right from the start. After all, burglaries and housebreakings happen at any time, and often while the wife is out shopping, so why didn't Mrs Colston simply say she'd been out of the house? Why announce something most women would wish to conceal: a date with a man not her husband? And Mrs Colston doesn't seem the sort of person who would hang about in hope for an hour. Why should she be so specific about what she was doing if not to cast suspicion on somebody, if you follow me.' Cook stood up. 'I shouldn't be telling you this.' His pale grin expanded. 'But we are all prone to boast, aren't we, sir. You in your way, I in mine.'

'I can see why you thought it could be a frame-up. Have they confessed?'

Cook opened the door. 'You'll have to wait for the full story. If the court decides there's a case to answer you'll be able to read all the details in the newspapers. Good day, sir. Oh yes, and in case you are wondering, I doubt if your presence will be required. You were a red herring, and red herrings can't give evidence.'

Hazelhurst went home and partly from contrition, and partly as a thank offering, he destroyed his journal. He vowed never again to keep such records.

At the trial some weeks later it transpired that Detective Sergeant Cook had put a twenty-four-hour watch on the Colstons. The celebratory dinner and its cost had been noted. A waiter overheard a remark about being paid twice over.

Colston's job involved shift work and on his day off, which followed the celebration, his car was followed and he was apprehended as he was showing a diamond and ruby necklace to a jeweller. Because the charge of conspiracy to defraud could not be brought against the Colstons (in this context man and wife count as one person, and one person cannot constitute a conspiracy) and since the insurance company had not suffered, the prosecution was based on the fact that police time had been wasted through the false report of a crime having been committed.

The Colstons pleaded guilty. In his speech in mitigation their counsel explained that Mrs Colston had brought a fair amount of capital, including the jewellery, to the marriage, but much had been lost when her boutique business crashed. A number of debts remained to be repaid. In a desperate attempt to recoup losses,

The Casebook Casanova

they hatched a plot whereby they could obtain insurance money and profit from a sale of the jewellery. They were extremely sorry for what they had done. No mention was made of the attempt to frame Gregory Hazelhurst.

The judge, somewhat unfairly, put most of the blame on Colston and sentenced him to three months' imprisonment. Stephanie received the same sentence but it was suspended for two years.

She got off more or less scot-free, thought Hazelhurst as he put down the newspaper. But maybe it's taught her a lesson. And she had the gall to try to teach me a lesson.

He decided to make a note of the case in a new journal he had started quite unaware that he hadn't himself learned the lesson that Casanovas, however much they may repent from time to time, are almost invariably recidivists, and that women are never a gift from God.

Michael Underwood

THE MAN WHO NURSED GRIEVANCES

Philip Manners had gone through life nursing grievances, though it has to be said that he had cause for a great many of them. His first major grievance came at the age of six when he woke up one day and forcibly realised that he was the less favoured of two brothers. Ian, his older brother by three years, was the apple of his parents' eyes. It wasn't that he was simply the favourite of one parent. In the Manners' household both father and mother were unable to hide their stronger liking for their older son. They weren't deliberately cruel or unkind to Philip, but they took no trouble to conceal which child was their favourite.

It was the same thing at boarding school where masters are notorious for having favourites. Philip was nobody's.

He found contentment for the first time, however, when he fell in love and got married at the age of twenty-two. But even this was short-lived and after seven years of diminishing happiness his wife ran off with another man and Philip divorced her. It was his biggest grievance to date. The fact that there were no children – mercifully in the view of most people – had been a further grievance. He had wanted a family, but his wife had always made excuses. It was almost as if she intended their marriage shouldn't last – or so Philip subsequently persuaded himself.

Grievances and self-pity usually go hand in hand and certainly did so in Philip's case. In addition he was capable of appearing extremely self-righteous and friends were apt to find this his most tiresome characteristic. But despite everything he had quite a lot of friends and led as full a life as anyone who had reached the age of forty-eight could wish for.

He had always been determined to be a writer and had applied himself to the task with discipline and industry. He had now published twelve novels and a great many short stories and had contributed articles on a wide variety of subjects to journals all over the English-speaking world. Given his nature it was inevitable, however, that he should feel he had never received his due acclaim, either in a critical or a commercial sense. Other writers always seemed to have the luck, the TV and serial rights, not to mention the bonanza of a film sale, while Philip's books were spurned by those in control of these fickle markets.

'Your last book is just made for television,' friends at the tennis club would say to him.

'I'm afraid my stuff's a bit too literate for the masses,' he would reply in a disdainful tone. 'Anyway, being transferred to the small screen is not the be all and end all of a serious writer's ambition.'

'No, of course not . . .'

'I'd sooner go unrecognised and retain my integrity. Not that I do go without recognition in the quarters that count.'

Needless to say he would dearly have liked to have sold anything to television or in any other market for that matter, but he was used to nursing his grievances privately and to concealing his true feelings about the things that were most important to him. His friends were under few illusions, but generally pandered to his prickly nature, for he could be good company and was regarded as an excellent host.

He lived alone in what the romantic saw as a writer's dream cottage. It was seventeenth century, its outer walls covered with honeysuckle and climbing roses. Its interior had been thoroughly modernised without ruining its charm. Its purchase had been a snip and even Philip came through the transaction without collecting a grievance. Apart from a woman who came in twice a week and cleaned for him, he looked after himself and was quietly self-reliant. For the past eighteen years he had been almost totally celibate.

Next to his writing, his abiding passion was tennis and when not at his typewriter he could usually be found at the club which lay a mile away. He was an all the year round player and the club with its excellent facilities was a catchment area for players from much further afield. The standard of play was consequently high and Philip Manners was one of the club's most stalwart members. He and Tony Priest had won the men's doubles two years running and were set to win it a third when . . .

Tony was sixteen years younger than Philip. He was good-looking, full of easy charm and was devoted to his wife, Jane, and their four children. Jane was as popular a member of the club as her husband though her playing days were considerably limited by having so many small children in permanent tow. The truth was she adored babies more than tennis.

It had been Tony who had suggested to Philip that they should pair up for the club doubles. Philip had been flattered and delighted by the proposal. Their partnership had been an instant success and now neither ever dreamed of playing with anybody else. In addition to club play, they took part in weekend tournaments and various winter competitions.

They presented a slightly incongruous sight on court together. Athletic Tony with a wide range of spectacular shots and an untakeable service when it went in. Philip always working steadily and craftily away to make openings for his partner. And though it was Tony's play that attracted the applause he was the first to pay tribute to Philip's solid ground strokes which were so often the foundation of a winning rally.

Philip had never known such contentment as during the eighteen months of their partnership. And as a result his writing seemed to prosper too. He sold stuff in markets hitherto closed to him and seemed to have far fewer of those frustrating and debilitating blocks that all writers suffer from on occasions. His friends weren't slow to notice that he had mellowed and become more relaxed and would comment on the unlikely bond that had been forged between the two men both on and off the court, for Philip had virtually become a member of the Priests' family circle. Whether he'd adopted them or they him doesn't really matter. He got on very well with Jane, and the two older children always referred to him affectionately as Uncle Tennis. Considering that they didn't have a great deal of money, the Priests were an easy-going family into whose embrace Philip happily fell. Many was the Sunday lunch or supper he enjoyed at their home.

Tony was a salesman with a firm of sports goods manufacturers which enabled him to get his tennis gear at a discount, but with not much money attached to the job. He worked on commission which meant that his livelihood was often precariously balanced to say the least. It was inevitable that Philip should become aware of his friend's financial position and he decided early on in their relationship that he would like to help

Tony when an appropriate moment presented itself. The opportunity came when he overheard Jane telling her husband that their washing-machine had finally packed up and that the repair man had advised against spending further money on it.

Two days later a brand-new machine was delivered to their home and duly installed. While this was being done, Jane was on the phone to Philip.

'I knew it must be you, Philip,' she said. 'You shouldn't have, even though I need it more than anything else in the world at this moment. You're a darling man, but I don't know what Tony's going to say.'

'Tell him you won it in a raffle,' Philip purred, delighted by her reaction.

'Anyway, thank you very, very much. I was beginning to get skinned fingers and a foul temper from all the washing and it was only a matter of days before the children left home and took refuge in the toolshed. You're a real angel, Philip.'

Later he gave them a colour television set for Christmas and he never failed to remember all their birthdays.

On two occasions he gave Tony money.

The first time had been one of those impulsive gestures after a particularly satisfying win in a club match. They were driving home when Tony happened to mention that Jane's old nurse was coming to stay the following week to look after the children and give Jane a bit of a break.

'You ought to take Jane away for a few days,' Philip said.

'Afraid that's not on,' Tony replied. 'I'd like to, of course, and heaven knows Jane could do with a proper break, but it's just not possible at the moment.'

'You mean you can't get away from work?' Philip asked with a frown.

'Oh, it's not that.' Tony paused before going on in a faintly embarrassed tone, 'Money's a bit tight, so holidays are out. Anyway, having Nanny around will give Jane a rest.'

'When did you and Jane last go away together?' Philip asked in a thoughtful tone.

'We had a naughty weekend in Brighton two years ago, from which Jane returned pregnant.' Tony grinned. 'Not that we needed to go to Brighton to achieve that.'

They were nearly at the Priests' house when Philip suddenly

slowed down and said, 'Will you let me give you the money for a holiday? I'd like to and I'm sure it'd do you both a world of good. You could take one of those four-day package trips to Paris. I can just see Jane sitting at a pavement café, relaxed and watching the world go by.'

'I don't know what to say,' Tony murmured. 'It's so unexpected and so incredibly generous.'

'All you have to say is yes. I'll give you a cheque for five hundred pounds which should cover everything and be enough for at least one slap-up meal.'

And so it came about that Tony and Jane went to Paris for three nights. Philip met them at Gatwick on their return and drove them home, where they presented him with a bottle of expensive brandy which they had bought at the duty free with the last of their francs.

'We can never thank you enough,' Jane said as she kissed Philip goodnight.

'I echo that,' Tony said. He patted his stomach and added, 'I'll have to jump around on the court like a dervish to lose the weight I've put on.' They all laughed and Philip drove home in a warm glow.

The next time he gave Tony money was several months later and the sum was then fifteen hundred pounds. He had gone to pick up Tony for a match at a neighbouring club and found him standing in the road with a stranger staring at the roof of his house.

'Won't be a few minutes,' Tony called out. 'Go in and talk to Jane. She's in the kitchen.'

She greeted Philip with a worried air.

'Who's that with Tony?' he enquired.

'He's a builder. He's come to give us an estimate for repairing the roof. We've been putting off having anything done for months, but it's been getting worse all the time and now when there's heavy rain I have to rush about placing buckets in strategic places.'

'That's rather an expensive item, isn't it?'

Jane let out a heavy sigh. 'That's why we've kept on putting it off.'

A moment or two later a sombre-looking Tony came into the house. He gave his wife a thumbs-down look, then smiled ruefully at Philip.

'Has Jane told you who our visitor was?'

'Yes.'

'His is the lowest estimate, but it's still alarming. I reckon they built the emperor's palace in Peking for less.' He gave his wife a quick kiss. 'Philip and I had better be off or our opponents will be claiming a walk-over.'

By the time he drove Tony home that evening Philip had said he would like to give him fifteen hundred pounds toward his roof repairs.

'It's too much, Philip,' Tony said, thoroughly embarrassed. 'Anyway, why should you?'

'Because I can afford it and it pleases me to help you,' Philip retorted a trifle stiffly.

'You really are a heaven-sent benefactor. I know I ought to say no to your generous offer, but in this instance we're all going to be in your debt, by which I mean the children as well as Jane and me, because if the roof falls in, it'll be on all of us.'

'I'll give you a cheque tomorrow.'

It was three months later that the event occurred which was to change all their lives. As so often the initial cloud was no larger than the biblical man's hand and none of those concerned could possibly have foreseen the cataclysm that was to engulf them. Though, for all that, it had its inexorability.

For the second year running Philip and Tony had entered a winter parks tournament. It was the sort of competition in which one was given the names of one's opponents by the organisers and thereafter left to get in touch with them and arrange a date to play. On the day in question – a Sunday at the end of February – they played against a pair who had been runners-up the previous year and who were noted for their guile and gamesmanship. The choice of venue was theirs and Philip and Tony were required to drive about thirty miles to a public park in South-East London where the courts were under the shadow of a railway embankment. There were no proper changing facilities – or facilities of any kind at all – and the court itself was a mass of cracks and crevices. It was not the game of tennis they were used to and their opponents' sharp calls of out to balls that were clearly in did nothing to improve the general atmosphere. It did, however, make Philip and Tony more than ever determined to win, which they managed to do after a closely-fought and rancorous third set.

Afterwards they repaired to a pub to celebrate their victory and resolve never to enter that particular competition again.

'They were outrageous cheats,' Philip observed. 'One really has a duty to report them.'

'Best to forget it as a bad experience. They'd only return any allegations with interest. They're that sort.'

'They still oughtn't to be allowed to get away with it,' Philip remarked with a note of self-righteousness.

'Have another drink,' Tony said soothingly.

Tony became unusually silent on the drive home, so that Philip felt constrained to ask him if anything was the matter.

'One can't escape reality for long, though playing those two experts at cheating gave one something else to think about for a short time.'

'What's that supposed to mean?'

'To put it bluntly, Philip, I'm in trouble. Bad trouble.'

'Is it anything I can help over?' Philip asked after a moment's silence.

'You've already helped me enough.' Tony paused, then blurted out, 'Is there any way you could lend me some money, Philip? I mean *lend*. I'd let you have it back as soon as I could and I'd pay you interest meanwhile.'

'How much do you need?'

'Five thousand pounds.'

'That's a lot of money,' Philip said in a shocked tone.

'I know, but I'm at my wits' end. Very foolishly I borrowed from a moneylender, then I gambled with part of it and of course lost, which made matters even worse. If I don't get hold of five thousand by the end of next month, I'll probably have to sell the house, though that's heavily mortgaged.'

'Does Jane know all this?'

'No,' Tony said miserably. 'I daren't tell her, particularly as she's pregnant again. God, I've been a fool.'

'If I did lend it you,' Philip said slowly, 'I certainly wouldn't want you to pay me interest. I don't regard lending money to a friend as a commercial transaction. If I didn't feel I could trust you, I wouldn't let you have it.'

'Do you mean that you will then?' Tony asked in a quietly anxious tone.

Philip nodded. 'But I want your promise that you won't have further recourse to moneylenders.'

'I've learnt a lesson for life as far as they're concerned,' Tony said earnestly.

A week later Philip called round at Tony's house. Jane was upstairs putting the children to bed and the two men went into the living room. Without saying anything, Philip took a folded cheque from his wallet and handed it to Tony.

'I'll never ever forget this,' Tony murmured. 'But to be more practical, I hope to repay it by the end of July.' Observing Philip's surprised expression, he went on, 'Things are suddenly looking better. I'm pretty sure I can get the money out of a trust fund my grandfather set up for my sister and myself. I've made enquiries and don't think there should be any difficulties. Meanwhile, I can never thank you enough, Philip. You've been my saviour.'

It was with a certain amount of relief that they turned to discussing forthcoming tennis fixtures and, indeed, the matter of the loan wasn't referred to by either of them over the next few months, during which period they continued to prosper together on the courts. Philip's writing, however, didn't show comparable success. An article for an American magazine that normally published everything he sent it was rejected and his agent was clucking unhappily over his new novel.

Six weeks after the July deadline Philip, in as tactful a way as possible, brought up the subject of the loan and enquired if its return would soon be forthcoming. To his surprise and indignation, Tony said in a somewhat offhand tone that the trustees had hit a snag but that he hoped everything would soon be sorted out.

Philip went away and brooded on the reply and decided to let another month go by before raising the matter again. Meanwhile, however, a certain constraint entered into their relationship. They continued to play tennis together, but the partnership had, so to speak, become a marriage of convenience, where previously it had been one of love.

When Philip did mention the loan again, Tony was positively acerbic.

'You don't think I like being in your debt, do you, Philip?' he said sharply. 'You'll get your money back just as soon as I have it. There's no need to keep on reminding me.'

Philip heard this in tight-lipped silence. He felt angry and let down. As soon as he got home he wrote Tony a short, cold note saying that he would not be available to partner him the following Saturday, adding that he proposed so to inform the match secretary. It was the beginning of the end.

A month later he instructed his solicitor to write Tony a letter asking for the immediate return of the outstanding loan of five thousand pounds. The letter was ignored.

'You'll either have to accept the situation or take him to court,' his solicitor said. 'Of course, even judgement in your favour won't automatically get your money back. You can't get blood out of a stone *et cetera*.'

Philip went away and brooded further. By now his whole existence was coloured by what had happened. His writing suffered as his mind became obsessed with how to force Tony into making some honourable amend.

If Tony had only come and apologised and pleaded for more time, Philip might yet have refrained from his next step, but his own sense of self-righteousness precluded any approach on his part. Accordingly, he instructed his solicitor to issue a writ in the local county court.

In the weeks before the case was listed for hearing, Philip became increasingly paranoid. He would go for long walks after dark, but seldom stir outside in daylight. He tried to work, but succeeded only in filling his wastepaper basket with balls of crumpled paper.

On the day of the trial, he put on the suit he always wore on formal occasions and set off for court in the neighbouring market town like someone summoned to perform a distasteful but necessary duty.

He spotted Tony almost as soon as he entered the building. It was the first time he'd seen him for months and he experienced a sudden surge of indignation that his one-time friend should appear so relaxed as he stood talking to his own lawyer. What right did he have to look so much at ease?

After all the weeks of anxious waiting, it seemed totally unrealistic that the case could be over in a single morning. But it was. The facts were, after all, short and simple. It was word against word, with Philip and Tony on opposite sides on this occasion.

Philip gave his evidence stiffly. He looked uncomfortable and his tendency to self-righteousness was manifest. Moreover, he became a target for rebuke when he sought to qualify some of his answers. When Tony's lawyer put it to him that the loan was, in fact, nothing of the sort but a gift, his sense of outrage was obvious.

'Certainly not,' he retorted indignantly. 'It was a loan and the defendant knows it.'

'A loan without any documentary proof whatsoever?' the lawyer enquired with one sardonically raised eyebrow.

'I accepted his word as his bond,' Philip replied pompously.

'Are you sure, Mr Manners, that you didn't make him a gift of the money, just as you had made him gifts of money on previous occasions?'

'Quite sure,' Philip snapped back.

When Tony entered the witness box he was, by contrast, relaxed and at his most charming. He said he was deeply upset by what had happened as Philip had always been a most generous friend to him and his family.

'Did you ask Mr Manners to lend you the five thousand pounds?' his lawyer asked.

Tony shook his head. 'No. He knew I was in financial straits and he offered to help me as he had done on other occasions.'

'Did such generosity surprise you?'

'No, because it was typical of him. In the light of what's happened, however, I wish I'd never accepted it.'

Philip listened to Tony's evidence with suppressed fury. Surely judges had the power to send people straight to prison for such blatant perjury.

Judge Shoreham, however, remained silent as he had done throughout the trial. He was not one of the talkative judges, principally because he had become thoroughly bored with his job and keeping quiet was the least demanding option.

He stifled a yawn as Tony's lawyer completed his final address and sat down. The time had come when indolence was obliged to yield; there was no way he could avoid giving judgement.

'It's always a melancholy circumstance when friends fall out over money,' he said in a weary tone. 'Shakespeare had it right when he said, *Neither a borrower nor a lender be*. In the present case I am confronted by a direct conflict of evidence. Was it a loan or

The Man Who Nursed Grievances

was it a gift? I am required to decide. Having heard both parties, I am bound to say that, on balance, I prefer the evidence of the defendant to that of the plaintiff and I give judgement accordingly. The plaintiff has not discharged the burden of proof that lies on him and I therefore find for the defendant and award him the costs of the action.'

Philip sat frozen in silence. He didn't trust himself to look at anyone, least of all in Tony Priest's direction. Eventually his solicitor tapped him on the shoulder.

'That's it, I'm afraid. I did warn you that judges could be unpredictable in this sort of case.'

'It's outrageous,' Philip hissed angrily. 'There's no justice in it whatsoever. Moreover I've been branded a liar.'

His solicitor knew from experience that the less he said the better. Clients needed time to recover from such blows, though from his knowledge of Philip Manners he reckoned he was going to be a slow healer.

For the next twenty-four hours Philip never left his house. He spoke to nobody and the telephone, when it rang, went unanswered. He had told the truth in court and Tony had lied and yet by some monstrous perversion a judge had reached the opposite conclusion. How Tony must be laughing that he'd got away with it! But he wasn't going to get away with it, Philip would see to that.

He lay awake that night rehearsing in his mind the possibilities of revenge. Tony must pay for his duplicity. But how?

The next day dragged as no other day he'd ever known. He paced about the cottage smoking endless cigarettes and drinking innumerable cups of coffee, but quite unable to settle down to work.

When evening came he got his car out and drove to within a few hundred yards of the Priests' house. He parked up a side turning and completed his journey on foot. It was shortly after eight o'clock when he arrived outside. It was a dark, unfriendly evening with nobody about. Tony's car was parked in its customary place on the grass verge. He was never able to put it in the garage at the side of the house because it was always full of junk. The lights were on in the front room, but the curtains hadn't yet been drawn and he could see Tony and Jane standing there talking without an apparent care in the world. Then Tony left the room and Jane came across and pulled the curtains, blotting out Philip's view. It began to rain quite heavily and he hurried back to his car. He reflected grimly that but for his generosity the same rain would be pouring through their roof.

The next evening he returned much later when he knew they would have gone to bed. It was near enough one o'clock. Their bedroom overlooked the garden at the back of the house so that there was little danger of his being heard. In any event what he was about to do wouldn't involve noise. The idea had come to him as he had stood beside Tony's car the previous evening. Using the key he had purchased that afternoon to unlock the petrol filler cap, he quickly emptied the bag of sugar he'd brought with him into the tank. Then, re-locking the cap, he hurried away as silently as he had come.

'That's just for starters,' he muttered to himself. 'Not that there'll be any starting for Tony Priest in the morning.'

As he made his way home he felt better than at any time since the case had ended. Almost light-headed, in fact.

Halfway through the next morning he decided to get his car out and drive past the Priests' house to assess his handiwork. As he approached he could see Tony's car in its usual place on the verge. The bonnet was up and a breakdown vehicle was parked immediately in front. As he accelerated past he saw a mechanic bent over the engine.

It was time to consider his next move.

Even before he reached home he had decided that a further tampering with Tony's car would be most appropriate. Philip had done his national service in a transport unit and had acquired the mechanical skills that enabled him to carry out the routine maintenance of his own car. He resolved that he would return the next night and loosen a nut on the brake fluid pipe. This should give Tony a thoroughly unpleasant shock when he drove off and found his brakes weren't working.

Though he hadn't yet reached the point of plotting Tony's death, he did darkly perceive it as a logical conclusion.

But to return to his present plan, he reckoned the most likely result would be that Tony would become involved in some sort of minor accident before he had gone very far. The road was dead flat for half a mile in both directions from the Priests' house, so there'd be no question of the car running away with him. He'd most likely run into a ditch after a moment of sheer fright and panic. It was a moment Philip would relish. He had no worries that he might fall under suspicion, and even if Tony did suspect him, he'd never be able to prove anything. Nevertheless, Philip decided he'd better have a change of tactics after two assaults on Tony's car. He must try and think of something really subtle as a follow-up.

That night Philip waited till four a.m. before setting off on his mission. It took him less time than he'd expected to loosen the vital nut and he was home again half an hour later.

Around mid-morning the urge to go and find out what had happened became irresistible. There was no sign of the car outside the Priests' house, nor of any life within. He drove on some distance expecting any moment to come upon Tony's car in a ditch or wrapped round a tree, but he failed to find it. As he returned past the house, a friend of Jane's opened the front door and stepped outside with two of the children. Philip immediately accelerated, hoping he hadn't been spotted.

But what was the friend doing there and where was Jane? Above all, where were Tony and the car?

For the rest of the day he pondered these questions, frustrated that there was nothing he could do to satisfy his curiosity. Moreover, he found it difficult to plan his next move without knowing the effect of his previous one. All he knew was that it must convey a full measure of retribution.

When the telephone rang about half past eight that evening, he was at his desk making notes for an article which was overdue. It was his first attempt at work since the day in court. He reached out for the receiver.

'Yes?' he said in the brisk, deterrent tone he invariably adopted on the phone.

'Philip, it's Jane.' Before he could say anything she went on in a tightly-controlled voice, 'I'm ringing to tell you that Tony had an accident this morning and was killed.'

'Oh, my God!' he exclaimed. 'What happened?' He gripped the receiver and felt beads of sweat break out all over his body.

'Somebody had vandalised the car; it was the second night running it had happened. Anyway Tony had an important meeting and had to get to work somehow. He tried to get hold of a taxi to take him to the station, but there wasn't one and nobody seemed free to give him a lift. So he got my old bike out of the garage and set off in a frantic rush. I told him the brakes hardly worked . . . I should have stopped him.' She paused. 'He failed to take the bend by Armstrong's farm and went head-on into a lorry coming the other way.'

'How terrible! I hardly know what to say or where to begin,' Philip stammered in a voice he hardly recognised as his own.

'Just let me finish saying what I want, Philip,' she broke in fiercely. 'Tony was extremely upset about the rift between you. I've never seen him so depressed. If only I'd knocked both your heads together . . . But by taking him to court, Philip, you drove him into a corner and put him completely at bay. I don't know whether you lent him the money or gave it him and it doesn't matter any more . . . No, don't say anything, Philip . . . Anyway the point is that the money from the trust arrived yesterday and Tony made out a cheque for you. I have it in front of me at this moment. He was going to post it today, but the business with the car put everything else out of his mind and now, of course, he's dead and the cheque's no good. That's all I wanted to tell you, Philip.' She rang off giving him no time to say anything.

For a while he sat stunned by the news he'd just heard. After a short spell of uneasy reflection, however, he was able to satisfy himself that his conscience was clear. No blame could be attached to him, he assured himself. Of course he felt sorry for Jane and the children, but it was the sort of sorrow a bishop might expend on the sins of the world.

In fact it was only a matter of time before the circumstances of Tony Priest's death became a festering grievance.

John Wainwright

A WISE CHILD

It is almost a year, now, since I decided to kill my father. To murder him, as retribution for re-marrying after the death of my mother.

I knew what I was doing. Let that be clearly understood. A modern fifteen-year-old, with a good education, can never claim 'ignorance' on moral issues. I knew I contemplated murder. Patricide, in fact. And, because I was capable of appreciating the moral issues I was, equally, capable of reaching a moral conclusion.

He didn't deserve to live.

Until my mother's death we had been a happy enough family. Just the three of us. Mother had doted on me a little; allowed me the occasional excess while he, in turn, had frowned mild disapproval without openly objecting. Long before I reached my teens, I realised he was a weak man. Mother was the dominating partner and, if sides had to be taken, she was always on my side.

On the other hand, I cannot remember seriously misbehaving myself. Sometimes a schoolboy prank that went a little wrong, or was taken beyond the point of moderation. Now and again, the deliberate playing of one against the other, in order to get my own way. Those were the limits. In the main, I was happy enough to obey my parents, because I loved them and because I respected them.

They, in turn, loved me . . . I make no Freudian excuse of being a 'misunderstood' child.

Perhaps we were too close. Perhaps we were too interdependent. Other than when he was at work, they were always in each other's company. For myself, I was a solitary person and wanted it that way. I read a great deal. Books on every subject under the sun. Travel books and history books; biographies and autobiographies. I read fiction, too – even crime fiction – but always, at the back of my mind, there was the knowledge that fiction was merely the out-pourings of an over-active imagination. The concocted murders were too involved. The alibis were too easily broken. The culprit was far too obvious – or, if not obvious, far too ridiculous.

Most of all, I enjoyed reading about trials. Real trials. Real murderers, who were stupid men, because they'd been caught.

I think the Seddon trial fascinated me more than any of the others. Frederick Seddon. He was called 'the meanest murderer of them all', but I could never understand that. To suggest *that* implies a price on human life. A cash value. I read and re-read various accounts of the Seddon trial and, to this day, I can't accept the proposition that he poisoned Miss Barrow for her money. She had so little. More than that, she was as valuable to him alive as she was dead.

There was just no case to answer. Edward Marshall Hall knew that. So, I'm sure, did Rufus Isaacs, who was prosecuting. Oh, no – the man who put the noose around Seddon's neck was Seddon himself. He was too clever by half. Too fond of the limelight. Had he *not* given evidence – had he declined to take the stand – he'd have walked away from court a free man.

As it was . . .

We were a happy enough family. (*We*, I mean, not the Seddons.) Mother was no raving beauty, but she was pretty enough, in her own way. A somewhat middle-class way, I suppose, but that's what we were – *very* middle class. Father worked in a solicitor's office. He wasn't a solicitor, of course, but he worked in the closed environment of parchment and law books. He was, I think, something to do with the conveyancing side. Something dreary, and not too technical. It must have been a very boring job, but that didn't worry him. He was a very boring man. Not deliberately unkind. Merely monotonous – and *very* boring.

He had jokes and witticisms. An amazingly limited repertoire of jokes and witticisms. He would trot them out with a regularity warranted to make me cringe. Something would be said – some remark a comedian might have described as a 'feed line' – and I'd know *exactly* what that dull-dog of a father would say next. Mother would dutifully laugh. A quick, obliging touch of

A Wise Child

laughter, which never reached her eyes. And, sometimes, she would glance at me, almost appealingly, as if to say, 'Can't we *do* something to stop this irritating man from *always* saying the same ridiculous things?'

We couldn't. We could only tolerate him. I think that, tacitly, we both accepted the burden of toleration until such time as nature took its course.

Odd . . . there was an unspoken assumption that he'd go first.

I rather think the same applies in all families, large or small. In some subtle way, one member is earmarked as being the first to die. Nothing to do with age. Nothing to do with illness. A sort of herd-instinct which prepares the rest for the first shock of close-range bereavement.

I suspect life-style has something to do with it. Father, for instance, was never fully *alive*. Whenever you caught him in an attitude of complete relaxation, the first thing you noticed was that his mouth corners drooped. His natural expression was that of a sad man. An everlastingly serious man. Even a sombre man. Which was quite ridiculous. A fiddling little clerk in the office of some unimportant solicitor, and his attitude suggested that he carried an impossible burden across his shoulders.

Young as I am, I have seen many men of father's ilk. Grey, vaguely unhappy men, without even a splash of colour. And most of them (like father) suffer slight pangs of indigestion. The first signs of quite unnecessary ulcers.

Mother, on the other hand, was quite charming – or would have been, had she not had the millstone of father around her neck. She had a certain spontaneous gaiety which bubbled beneath the surface. On the few occasions when just she and I went out together – to a show, to a cinema, to a concert – she fairly sparkled. She was a changed woman, without him around. She was a delightful companion and (a couple of times, no more) I suspected her of mildly flirting with some man sitting next to her. Nothing serious. Nothing objectionable. Just a happy exchange of pleasantries, accompanied by the sort of smile she so rarely had the chance of using at home.

Then, she died.

I truly couldn't believe it, at first. The head sent for me, from the chemical lab. He made me sit down in his study, then told me. He did his best – but I suspect there's no *easy* way.

'I have some bad news for you, my boy.'
'Yes, sir.'
'Your mother collapsed in the supermarket, earlier today.'
'Oh!'
'It's serious, I'm afraid.'
'How serious, sir? Is she in hospital?'
'I'm afraid she's dead. They think it was a heart attack.'

There was an inquest, and there was a funeral, and not once did I weep. Nor, come to that, did father. With me, it was a hurt too deep for tears. With him, it was – nothing.

I had difficulty in bringing myself to believe she was dead. I think he had equal difficulty in remembering that she'd ever been alive.

In bed, at night, I used to stare into the darkness and wonder what sort of a man he was. What sort of a human being. He wasn't evil . . . God knows, he wasn't *evil*. He wasn't even hard. I could have understood, had he been one of the 'manly' types, to whom tears are a sign of weakness. Had he been like me, with a grief too savage for mere tears. But, he wasn't that. He wasn't that, at all. He had simply erased her from his life. From his memory. Like a misspelled word on a page. She wasn't there any more . . . period.

I once took him to task.

'Don't you miss her?' I asked.

'Of course I miss her.' But, he mouthed the words – he didn't *mean* them.

'You don't show it,' I accused.

'I'm not very demonstrative,' he said, gently. Then, with a quick, half-smile, 'One day you'll know. There's nothing more lonely than a double bed.'

'Not *that*!' The quick spat of disgust made me almost shout the words.

'Not *only* that,' he corrected me. 'You're young, yet. You don't . . .' He stopped, mid-way through the sentence and looked awkward and embarrassed.

'I don't "know".' I ended the sentence for him, then added, 'But one thing I *do* know. One thing I'm certain of. I miss her. I miss her terribly. Far more than you miss her . . . and in a different way.'

He didn't argue, and that was the end of the conversation. Nor did we touch on the subject again. There was this distance between us – this gap – and it couldn't be bridged. He was kind enough. He refused me nothing, within reason, and he gave me freedom which I, in turn, didn't abuse. There was a certain deference between us. But not love. Not even real respect, at least, not on my part.

I had no aunts, no uncles, no grandparents. My parents had been only children and I, too, was an only child. But that didn't matter too much. I was given a key to the house, let myself in when I arrived from school and often prepared our meal for when father got back from the solicitor's office.

I was quite able to live a satisfactory life, without the help of adults. Without the companionship of people of my own age. I counted myself in no way odd. In no way peculiar. I had no real interest in sport, I could see no merit in pop music, I found the bulk of television facile, but having completed my homework each evening, I had my books.

The woman was called Angelica. *Angelica!* Botany lessons had taught me that angelica was a garden plant whose leaf-stalks and mid-ribs were candied for use in Christmas cakes. A sweetmeat. A nothing. I think she had a most appropriate name.

I don't know how or when they met. Neither of them ever saw fit to tell me. They became far too besotted with each other ever to give much thought to simple civilities.

I recall (it was little more than a year after mother's death) that father arrived home from the solicitor's office and announced that he was going to a concert that evening. Some string quartet was performing at the local hall. Part of the local musical society's programme, I think. After the concert, he was having supper with some friends. I remember that quite well. *Friends* – plural – not *a* friend.

I was surprised. It was so out of character. I admit, I was not displeased. My preference was to be alone; to do what I wanted to do, without the slightly strained atmosphere which had gradually built up between us.

Just before he left, he said, 'Don't wait up. I may be a little late.'

Again, there was some slight astonishment on my part, but no complaint. As far as I was able, while still being dependent upon him for a home, I lived my own life.

Nevertheless, and although I was in bed, I heard him return. It was past midnight, and he was humming quietly to himself.

That became the pattern. Twice a week. Sometimes three times a week. A concert. The cinema. Some amateur Gilbert and Sullivan production. That sort of thing. There was always an excuse – always a reason – and always 'supper with friends'.

His character gradually changed, although not towards me. He became less serious. Less hangdog. His choice of ties, while not being flamboyant, became less drab, and he didn't *always* wear a white shirt. In a way difficult to explain, he became 'different'. Not flash – he could never have become in any way flash – but 'different'.

Then, about six months after that first concert, he brought her home, after one more concert. No 'supper with friends' this time. They arrived at about half past nine – shortly after I'd settled down to read one of the *Famous Trials* series – and I heard the key in the lock and the door open and close without taking much notice.

I was a little surprised and a little disgusted, when he brought her into the front room and introduced us. But, in honesty, I kept my distaste to myself because (I told myself) he was a weak man. A basically stupid man. A contemptuous little man living his own contemptuous little life and, for a few more years, I'd have to tolerate him.

But, *after* those few more years . . .

Then, he said, 'I've asked Angelica to be my wife, and she's done me the honour of accepting.'

It caught me completely flat-footed. I was so unready for the remark. So unprepared.

I think the shock showed itself, because she gave a saccharine smile, and said, 'You don't mind, dear, do you?'

'Mind?' I struggled to regain control of myself.

'You see, dear, we don't want to . . .'

'Why should *I* mind?' I closed my book, then repeated the question, but with a different emphasis. 'Why *should* I mind?'

'Of course you don't mind.' The pompous little man thought that, because I was able to hide my outrage, I approved. 'You'll have a mother again . . . won't you?'

A Wise Child

He married her two months later.

It was a quiet enough wedding. The registrar was a paunchy, fussy little man, with loose dentures. The two witnesses were complete strangers to me. I think one came from the office where father worked, and the other was a woman friend of 'the bride'. Everybody dutifully kissed each other, after the ceremony – but nobody kissed me!

'He's at that awkward age.' This, from the Angelica woman, when I backed away from the female witness. 'He thinks it's weak to show any outward signs of emotion. Don't you, dear?'

That was another thing. She would insist upon calling me 'dear'. I didn't want to be her 'dear'. I didn't want to even *know* her.

They went away for a fortnight's honeymoon. Somewhere near Southport. They gave me the address, before they left, but I didn't write. They, in turn, sent me two 'wish you were here' postcards.

Perhaps they did, too – wish I was with them, I mean. They must have been very boring company for each other. The gushing, simpering woman, and the pathetic little man with his limited stock of funny remarks. Two weeks of each other's company must have almost driven them mad. Perhaps they spent most of the time going to 'concerts'. Or having 'supper with friends'.

I never asked, and they never told me.

While they were away, I planned the murder.

I decided upon arsenic. What was good enough for the Borgias seemed good enough for me. I also felt that it had a certain 'romantic' connotation. It is reputed to have aphrodisiac properties. I think some cosmetic preparations include it in their formula. In a typically cynical Continental expression, it is known as The Inheritance Powder, the *poudre de succession*.

Definitely arsenic.

It wasn't difficult to come by. It was there, for the careful filching, at the school lab. I called in at the reference section of the local library, and checked in Glaister's *Medical Jurisprudence and Toxicology*. Three hundred grains was more than enough. Much less than an ounce. I didn't steal it all at once. Four times, and nobody missed it.

Then I stored it in an empty pill box, and hid the box at the back of my books, on a shelf in my bedroom. Then I waited.

The waiting was the worst part. I knew him to be a worrying man, and I knew the worrying brought on the indigestion and the stomach pains. Strangely, his guts seemed not to be causing him as much trouble as they had done previously. He remained the same apology for a man, but seemed not to carry his petty concerns around so heavily. Or, come to that, so obviously.

Perhaps this new wife of his was good for him. If so, she was only going to be good for him for a limited period, and I loathed both of them that little more for that fact. He had no *business* being content. Mother had been his wife – morally, was *still* his wife – not this giggling, empty-headed female with a ridiculous name.

In retrospect, the waiting period worked in my favour. I'd stolen the arsenic from the school lab, and the science master was more than a little lackadaisical in his checking of equipment and materials. Nevertheless, three hundred grains *had* been 'lost'. When a new supply arrived and was added to the little left in the container, I breathed more freely. I had the poison. Nobody knew I had it. And now, nobody would *ever* know I'd taken it. I was quite safe.

Thereafter, Lady Luck walked alongside me.

He came home on the Friday evening holding his middle.

'What is it, dear?' She sounded quite distressed. 'Are you ill?'

'Indigestion. That's all. I've had quite a day.'

'Should I send for the doctor.'

'No, no.' He played the part of the brave little sufferer. 'It comes on, periodically. I have some capsules the doctor gave me. I'll take them for a day or two. They always do the trick.'

I knew those capsules. They were part of the plan. As much a part as the arsenic itself.

The GP was a busy man; too busy to be forever examining a patient with recurring belly-ache. There was a 'repeat prescription' arrangement. Added to which, father was the sort of man who hoards medicines. The bathroom cabinet bulged with bottles and boxes and, amongst them, there was a fine supply of capsules from past bouts of indigestion.

He said, 'Four a day. They'll put me right.'

He went to bed early and, privately, I determined to make sure he would never get up again.

A Wise Child

The next morning, the woman Angelica said, 'I have the weekend shopping to do. I've given your father his capsule. You're not going out, are you?'

'Later. About noon.'

'I should be back by then. He's asleep at the moment. I'll give him his second capsule when I get back.'

That left me two hours, and I didn't need two hours.

I gave her time enough to ensure she wasn't returning for something she might have forgotten, then I moved cautiously into the bedroom. He was still fast asleep. I took the bottle of capsules and returned downstairs. I spread a newspaper on the kitchen worktop, then began the substitution. I did it, one capsule at a time. Emptying the contents down the sink, under a running tap, then carefully substituting arsenic. The capsules were green, and when the two halves were replaced they looked no different from when they'd held whatever it was they'd originally held. As I filled each with arsenic I dropped it back into the bottle. There must have been forty capsules – at least forty – and I doctored every one.

Then, I returned upstairs. Father was still asleep, and I returned the bottle to the bedside table.

On an impulse – a quite imaginative brainwave – I sought, and found, the woman's work-basket. It contained reels of cotton, needles, thimbles (the usual junk) and I pulled the stuff to one side and carefully scattered the barest hint of arsenic in one corner of the silk-lined interior. Then I returned the work-basket, folded what was left of the arsenic into the sheet of newspaper, took it out into the garden, stuffed it into the fire-basket and lighted it.

When the woman, Angelica, returned she said, 'How is he?'

'The last time I looked in he was asleep.'

'Good.' She dumped her basket. 'I'd better go up. It's time he took another capsule.'

It took him all weekend to die. It was very painful and very messy. All the classic symptoms of arsenic poisoning were there. A burning pain in the stomach. Severe vomiting and diarrhoea. The fools thought it was a worse-than-usual attack of indigestion and, because it was the weekend, hesitated about sending for a doctor.

Having been up all Saturday night, on Sunday morning she said, 'He has it bad, this time.'

'Really?'

She described the night's activity, then said, 'Go up and see him, dear.'

'It wouldn't do any good.'

'No. Probably not. He doesn't like to be disturbed.' She frowned, then added, 'I think I'll double the dosage of his capsules.'

'That might help,' I agreed.

I borrowed five pounds from her, took a bus into the country and walked a little. It was a beautiful day. I enjoyed a quiet lunch at an out-of-the-way café, walked a little more, then took the bus back home.

She was in something of a panic when I walked into the house.

'He's getting worse. I'm sure he's getting worse.'

'Indigestion?' I smiled.

'He's in pain. Terrible pain.'

'The capsules have worked before,' I murmured.

'I know,' she wailed. 'He keeps asking for them, and I keep giving them to him.'

'Do you think you should call a doctor?'

The suggestion had to be made, if only for the sake of appearances.

'I keep saying so.' She sighed, heavily. 'He won't have it. He doesn't want to be a nuisance. But if he's no better tomorrow . . .'

It was a 'tomorrow' that never came.

Because he hadn't attended him, the doctor couldn't issue a death certificate. Because there wasn't a death certificate, there had to be an inquest. Because there was an inquest, there was a post-mortem examination.

It was all rather like The House That Jack Built.

The pathologist found traces of arsenic. The police took possession of the remaining capsules. Later that same day the police returned and made a clinical search of the house. Among the things they took away was the work-basket.

Early next morning, they arrested the woman Angelica.

Although I was questioned, and gave the appropriate answers, I discovered that I could watch all this with complete detachment. It was, of course, what I'd planned, and it went as smooth as silk.

A Wise Child

I found myself thinking how like the Seddon case it all was.

The same poison. The same lack of real, or obvious, motive. The same outpourings of indignation when the suspected murderer was arrested, and the same continuation of that indignation at the trial. In so many ways, a perfect parallel to the Seddon case.

Like Seddon, she was convicted.

For myself, I tried to out-do *Mrs* Seddon – and succeeded.

That fine lady (if you recall) was jointly charged, with her husband but, unlike that husband, she made herself as inconspicuous as possible. She allowed her husband to hog the limelight and, from the shadows, defied the prosecution to overturn the Presumption of Innocence. Every scrap of evidence that convicted her husband *could* have convicted her. But it didn't. Figuratively speaking, she crept from the stage, while Frederick Henry made a fool of himself, and was hanged for his trouble. She was acquitted!

I built upon Mrs Seddon's wisdom. My profile was so low, they didn't even charge me. They asked a few questions and, as was becoming in the circumstances, I bravely fought back crocodile tears and answered quietly, but vaguely. They were satisfied.

Even the woman Angelica didn't suspect. She ranted on about 'mistakes'. She raved about the incompetence of the pharmacist. She screamed abuse at the police, and accused them of cooking the evidence.

Like Seddon, she virtually convicted herself.

She was convicted, of course, and, within the first month of her prison sentence, managed to commit suicide.

For myself, I managed quite well. I could (still can) live alone, without any real difficulty. I taught myself to cook simple meals and carefully organised the housework to ensure that keeping the place moderately clean was moderately easy. I had money, of course – not a fortune, but enough – and could take an occasional meal out when I felt like it.

I congratulated myself upon a remarkably efficient removal of certain annoyances. I assure you, I didn't suffer a single bad dream, nor yet the hint of a prick of conscience.

Then, some few weeks ago, the man from the office where father had worked called. He was obviously embarrassed, as he handed me a well-sealed envelope.

'We – er – we all liked your father,' he muttered.

'Thank you.'

'He left this with us. The envelope, I mean. To be given to you, in the event of the death of himself and his wife.'

'What is it?'

'I'm sorry. I don't know. Just that he asked for it to be kept, and when – *if* – you were ever left alone . . .'

His voice trailed off, miserably.

'That's very kind of you,' I smiled.

'Just that – y'know – with all the upset of the trial, and such. We thought it better to wait until you'd had time to settle down a bit.'

'That's very thoughtful of you.'

Then, he left, and I opened the envelope.

I have the letter in front of me. It's from the man I'd called 'father' all my life. He *wasn't* my father . . . and, to be honest, I wasn't too surprised. A little taken aback, that I'd poisoned the wrong man, I think, but not really *shocked*. My mother had been pregnant when he'd married her. He'd 'made her respectable' – his words, not mine. So like him. So much the action of a strait-laced ninny.

Mother had told him who the father was. My *real* father, that is. But the man hadn't known he'd impregnated her. That word – 'impregnated' – was his way of putting it. He was never told.

The name of my real father was there in the letter. And his address.

I made a few enquiries. It wasn't difficult. He'd moved house, and he's now happily married. He doesn't know, of course. He doesn't know how much I hate him, how much I've already learned about him. He certainly doesn't know what's going to happen to him.

I went up to London for the day. Talked to people in the offices of Macmillan Publishers. Convinced them that I had the germ of an idea for a short crime story. They agreed to read it, to 'consider' it. Publish it, if it was good enough.

This is it. You've just read it. My father – my *real* father – likes anthologies of crime stories. That's something else I learned about him.

Hopefully, he'll read this anthology – read this story – then he'll know . . . won't he?

Ted Willis

THE GALLOWS

George Hever had not always been in favour of capital punishment. Indeed, there had been a time when he played an active part in the campaign to abolish hanging, holding that it was both brutal and immoral for society to exact such a summary revenge.

So he had been quietly pleased when Parliament not only voted down the death penalty but liberalised the probation of prisoners. Now even a murderer, with a life sentence on his head, could expect, with luck, to be back on the streets again in fifteen years, sometimes less. George had regarded these reforms as a step forward in the march of civilisation, a victory for humanism and rational thought.

Reason, however, has seldom been able to withstand the onslaught of passion and his views took a sharp turn in the opposite direction following the tragic events of a certain August evening.

It was a little after six when the train bringing him from Canterbury pulled in at Welham station. A dozen other passengers alighted with George, most of them in relatively relaxed and cheerful mood, for it was Friday, the weather outlook was good, and they could look forward to a pleasant pottering weekend.

As they began to file past the ticket barrier a man in faded blue jeans and a loose denim jacket suddenly appeared. Clutching a worn canvas hold-all in one hand and waving a ticket vaguely in the direction of the startled collector with the other, he shoved his way roughly through the group and sprinted across the platform towards the moving train.

The door slammed behind him and he turned for a moment to

look back out of the open window. George had a brief glimpse of a sallow face, the dark line of a moustache, bright staring eyes, and then the train was gone. Had he seen fear in those eyes, on that face?

A bevy of wives waited in the station yard, cars at the ready, and several of his fellow passengers offered George a lift. It was a matter of routine courtesy, for most of them knew that he preferred to walk the two miles to his house on the outskirts of Little Welham, and they were not surprised when he smilingly declined the offers. It was only in exceptionally bad weather that George abandoned his beloved walk and in such circumstances it was usually his wife Jill who arrived with her old but treasured Mini to ferry him home.

For the first quarter-mile he was accompanied by Phil Hazard, a portly and genial solicitor who had a small but comfortable practice in Faversham. George, who liked to strike out briskly, had to accommodate his stride to suit that of his little companion.

'Odd fellow that,' said Hazard.

'Who do you mean?' asked George. He had all but forgotten the incident at the station.

'That fellow who pushed past us at the barrier.'

'Afraid of missing his train, I suppose,' George said.

'No manners. Might at least have said excuse me or sorry.'

'Not much in the way of manners about these days,' said George.

'You're right. Do you know, the other day I was up in London. Offered my seat on a bus to a middle-aged woman. She just glared and told me that she was quite capable of standing, thank you very much.'

'At least she said thank you.'

'Yes. But you should have heard the way she said it. Her voice had all the charm of a dentist's drill.'

They shared a smile at this and walked on in silence for a few moments.

'How is business with you?' asked Hazard. 'Or is that a rude question?'

'Can't complain,' said George.

'People still buying sports equipment, are they?'

'I'm glad to say.'

'I'm thinking of taking up jogging,' said Hazard, patting his stomach. 'Getting a bit on the paunchy side. I'll pop in sometime and get you to fix me up with one of those what-do-you-call-ems? Track suits. And the proper shoes.'

'Any time,' George said. He smiled to himself for he'd had this conversation with Hazard a dozen or more times and he knew that the little solicitor would never get beyond talk of exercise.

By now they had reached the drive that led to Hazard's solid Edwardian house. George declined the offer of a drink.

'How about you and Jill coming in for pre-lunch drinks tomorrow then?' asked Hazard.

'Have a heart. I'm not like you, with a full weekend to myself. I've the shop to run, and we're open on Saturdays.'

'Of course. Sorry. Sunday?'

'Sunday it is.'

George walked on, quickening his pace. He liked Hazard but he was happy to be alone to enjoy his own thoughts. Soon he had left the little cluster of houses and the narrow road behind and was treading the footpath towards Little Welham.

It was, he thought, a perfect evening – a thought which he was to recall with savage bitterness in the weeks to come. The air had a mellow brightness as if reflecting the golden bronze of the cornfields that lay on each side of the path. The benevolent sky, decorated with small pure white clouds, seemed to curve over the dreaming land, creating an enclosed world of gentle peace. And in all that sunlit place there was no sound except the occasional cry of a bird and the faint rustling murmur of the stirring wheat.

George wondered if Jill would come part of the way to meet him, as she did sometimes; but then he remembered that, tempted by the quality of the evening, he had decided to abandon work an hour earlier than usual, leaving Mrs Gale, his assistant, to lock up the shop.

So much the better, he thought, with a smile. He would surprise Jill, not only with his early arrival, but with his good news. Only that day he had signed a potentially lucrative contract to supply sports equipment to one of the larger local public schools.

Climbing the stile which marked the end of the footpath, he reached a narrow lane lined on either side by stands of young Norwegian pine trees. George liked this part of the walk best of all: the subtle resinous scents which flowed from the woods seemed to clear his mind and invigorate his senses, and he strode on with an increased feeling of well-being.

Once it had cleared the trees, the lane climbed sharply for about a quarter of a mile and this, for George, was the homeward stretch. From the summit of the hill he could see his house and the old barn beyond. He felt, as always, a tiny surge of pride as he looked down at the whitewashed walls of what had once been a small farmhouse, and at the garden glowing with colour. It was his piece of earth, his property or – more properly – his and Jill's. They had attained it by their own efforts, their own toil, and together they had lovingly restored the place, fashioning a home which was the envy of many of their friends.

Soon, thought George, soon I must turn my attention to the barn. At the moment it was used as a store and as a workshop, but Jill, with her keen eye, had long ago seen that it could be converted into an attractive home. It was, she always said, an investment for the future: when it was ready they would rent it – to the right people, of course, so that they might have congenial tenants. George was more than happy to fall in with this plan, for their nearest neighbours, the Perryman brothers, were over a half-mile away and he was concerned that Jill spent so much time alone.

When he reached the gate, he saw that the front door of the house was open. Jill must be in the back garden or in the barn, he thought, and with a smile he called, 'I'm home! Hey, it's me! I'm home!'

'Could we just go over it again, sir?'

George looked blankly at the Detective Inspector. His head seemed to be emptied of everything except silence, a vast cold wilderness of silence in which no thought or feeling stirred.

'Sir.' The Detective Inspector leaned forward and touched George gently on the arm, as though to rouse him.

'Yes?' George looked at the other man as if for the first time. The numbness that had gripped his mind for the past hour began to loosen its hold, thought and speech began slowly to return.

Evans? Is that what the policeman had said his name was? He had the tanned clear-eyed look of an athlete and an air of unobtrusive authority. On the young side, too. He could not be much more than thirty and yet he was already a Detective Inspector.

The Gallows

'It would help if you could tell me exactly what you found, what happened.'

'Of course,' George said, but he could not continue. He did not want to think about what he had found or what had happened.

Evans waited patiently for a moment and then said, 'You arrived home at about a quarter to seven?'

'Yes. A quarter to seven.'

'The front door was open?'

'Yes.'

'Was that unusual?'

'What?'

'Was it unusual for the front door to be open?'

'Yes. Well, no. Not really. If my wife –' His voice faltered and he stopped again.

'She might leave it open if she was working in the garden – something like that?' prompted Evans.

George nodded. 'Or if she went over to the barn. We – we keep some stores there.'

'That is where you found her?'

'Yes.' George's voice cracked a little, his mind filling with a vision of Jill's bruised and bleeding face, of her contorted half-naked body, of the look of horror that seemed to be frozen into her lifeless eyes. And he remembered – why should he recall that, of all things? – he remembered the fly that had settled for a moment on her thigh, an obscene black dot on the creamy smoothness of her flesh.

'Why did you carry her into the house?'

'Why?' George looked at the other man in bewilderment. 'I couldn't leave her lying there, could I?'

The Detective Inspector wanted to say that it would have been better if George had left the body untouched, but he did not press the point. The damage, if any, had been done. And something told him that in similar circumstances he might have been driven by shock or impulse to do much the same thing. Murder was murder, tangible and final, but rape was a different kind of violation, it had its own lingering shadowy undertone of shame. This man had carried his wife's body to the bedroom and covered her decently before calling the police and who could blame him for that protective instinct?

'Did you keep much money in the house?' asked Evans, trying another tack.

'Money? Thirty or forty pounds, perhaps.'
'Where was that kept?'
'Jill kept it in –' George's voice trembled and faded again. The familiar name throbbed in his throat and his heart tightened as though a cord had been drawn around it.
'In her handbag?'
George nodded dumbly.
'We found the handbag in the garden. It was empty.'
George nodded again, remembering that as he had laid Jill on the bed he had noticed that she was not wearing her rings or her watch. He – whoever *he* was – had taken everything: her body, her life, her possessions even down to her wedding ring. What kind of animal was he?

In an odd way, the theft of the wedding ring stamped itself on his mind. It seemed to him to be the final desecration, a symbol of all that had happened. And it was in that moment that something snapped in George Hever's mind and the notion of retribution took over.

He had a sudden vision of a sallow face looking out of a railway carriage window with bright fearful eyes.

'There was a man –' he began.
'Yes?' said Evans.

The police investigation rapidly established the fact that there had been three other burglaries in the area that afternoon. In each case, cash and small portable valuables had been stolen but there was no report of injury to any person other than Jill. No one had seen the intruder.

A Ford Cortina, found on the roadside near the village, turned out to have been stolen in Maidstone. The battery was flat and it seemed obvious that it had first been used to bring the thief to the area and then abandoned in desperation when it failed to start. Fingerprints found on the steering-wheel and the driver's door-handle were put to Scotland Yard's computer, which responded with the information that they belonged to a certain Sidney Roberts, aged thirty-two, a man with a criminal record that included robbery with violence.

The idea that there is honour among thieves is a fallacy. The *Kent Mercury* offered a reward of two thousand pounds for information which would lead the police to the man they wanted and within twenty-four hours a former associate of Roberts came forward with an address. An hour later, Roberts was in police custody.

He made no attempt to deny that he had been in the area of Welham on the afternoon in question and that he had stolen money and goods, but he strenuously protested his innocence of murder. He had never seen Mrs Hever. He had gone to her house with robbery in mind, he admitted that much: he had found the front door open, seen the handbag on the table and snatched it up. He had removed the money as he ran and flung the bag away.

Most of the stolen money and valuables were found in an old canvas hold-all at the back of a wardrobe in Roberts' lodgings. The only items of significance that did not show up were the rings and watch taken from Jill Hever.

Again, Roberts stubbornly denied any knowledge of these. Clearly in a panic at the prospect of facing a murder charge, the sweat bubbling on his forehead and neck, he repeated over and over again that he had never seen Mrs Hever, never touched her, never stolen her jewellery. He was a thief, yes, but not a murderer.

He was booked on a holding charge of breaking and entering while the police continued their investigations. At the end of two more days, when the enquiries failed to turn up any fresh evidence or any other possible suspect, Roberts was further charged with rape and wilful murder.

During the weeks leading up to the trial, George Hever amazed his friends by his fortitude. Everyone expected that he would sell the cottage and the barn and move away from the scene of so many bitter memories, but he showed no sign of doing so. After a week he even resumed his old routine, catching the train into Canterbury each day to run his business. The only noticeable difference in his manner was that he was now less outgoing, more reserved, politely refusing the kindly invitations that came his way. It was as though he had retreated into himself and was mourning inwardly.

His friends learned to respect this desire for solitude: they were confident that once the trial was over and the guilty man punished, George would start to recover.

What they did not and could not know was that all George's

emotional energies were centred upon Roberts. As a magnifying glass picks up the rays of the sun and concentrates them into one searing spot, so his thoughts focused on Roberts, on the name, on the man, with a hatred which was white-hot in its intensity. Beneath the superficial calm, his mind was a seething cauldron of feeling: there was scarcely a second, a minute of the day in which he was not possessed by this terrifying passion.

It was a passion laced with guilt, for he blamed himself in part for the vulnerability which had made his wife a victim. Only the death of the murderer would bring relief, only death would balance the books. He had failed Jill once, but he would not fail her again. If he had to wait until the law had taken its course, if he had to wait fifteen or twenty years, he would exact the ultimate revenge on the man who had violated and killed her. But these feelings lay deep within him and he turned a calm face to the outside world.

To the continued surprise of his friends he maintained this repose at the trial even when the case seemed to be going in the defendant's favour.

Roberts was represented by a brilliant if unknown young barrister who made much of the circumstantial nature of the prosecution's case. There was no forensic evidence to link Roberts with the murder, Mrs Hever's rings and watch had not been found in his possession. Just because the man was a thief and happened to have been at or near the scene of the crime did not make him a killer. In his closing speech, the barrister hammered away at the theme of reasonable doubt. It was an impressive performance and it had its effect. After a day and a half of deliberation the jury returned with a verdict of Not Guilty on the charges of murder and rape. The judge, clearly displeased, sentenced Roberts to three years on the lesser charges of breaking and entering and larceny.

There were some protests from the public gallery when the verdict was brought in and Mr Hazard, ever the man for an original phrase, later described the result as a travesty of justice. The Kent police, convinced that they had arrested and charged the right man, put the whole thing down to the cussedness of the courts and closed the file.

George Hever maintained his air of calm and said little. After all, he could scarcely tell his friends that he was quietly rejoicing

The Gallows

at the verdict, rejoicing at the thought that Roberts would be delivered up to him far sooner than he had expected.

On the same night that Roberts began his sentence, George went to the barn and started to build a scaffold.

The barn might have been built for the purpose he had in mind. It was sturdy and high with strong crossbeams to support the roof and along one side there was a storage platform. A man could stand upright on this platform and still have eight or ten feet of headroom above and a drop of twelve feet to the ground below.

The first task was to cut a large square from the floor of the platform. George called this section the flap. He then added a pair of strong hinges and put the flap back in its original position in the platform, holding it in place from below by means of two thick wooden props. When the props were removed the flap immediately gave way and hung down from the platform like a trap-door, held only by the hinges.

So far, so good. The next step, George decided, would be to carry out some tests. Using a block and tackle he hauled several sandbags on to the platform and dragged two of them on to the flap. It held the weight comfortably. He descended to ground level and knocked the props away. The flap flew open and the sandbags crashed down.

Next, he bought some nylon rope of the sort used by climbers and painstakingly fashioned one end into a noose. Then came more experiments with sandbags and these proved to be difficult. One bag slipped the noose and burst on the ground. Another fell through the trap-door but ended up swinging only two or three feet above the barn floor. It became clear to George that distances were critical and he made adjustment after adjustment to the rope until he was sure that he had got it about right.

To make doubly sure, he built a dummy, a sort of scarecrow, stuffing old clothes with sand and tying them up at the legs and sleeves with string. He estimated that Roberts was about five feet seven or eight, but he decided to play safe and made the dummy well over six feet in height. Fastening the head to the body turned out to be a real problem for the neck had to be strong enough to withstand the tension of the rope and the sudden fall when the flap opened. After two frustrating failures, George solved the problem by making a wooden frame and building the dummy around it.

To add a final touch of realism, George put a mask on the head to represent a face and christened his creation Tom.

The first hanging proved to be an outstanding success. George almost applauded as the dummy crashed through the trap-door and the noose tightened on the neck jerking it to a savage halt, with the feet well above the floor. He reached up, patted the dummy in satisfaction, and left it there, the gawdy face swinging in little helpless circles.

After this, George carried out a practise hanging at least three times a week, making small adjustments here and there until the operation was as perfect as he could make it.

He enjoyed these bizarre sessions with his creature, Tom, and looked forward to them with a passionate eagerness. The final drop never failed to excite him, arousing in his body a storm of feeling that was almost sexual in its intensity. He could not help wondering what it would be like to have a human being, a live human being, swinging in the noose. That, he felt, would be the ultimate test of his gallows.

Six months had passed since the conviction of Roberts: he would have to wait at least another eighteen months before the man was released and he could carry his plan to its ultimate conclusion. It was frustrating to have to wait so long. And at the back of his mind there lay a lingering fear that, despite all his tests, something might go wrong when a man instead of a marionette stood on the scaffold.

If only he could test it once, test it with a living person before Roberts was freed . . .

The opportunity occurred, quite by accident, about six weeks later, early on a Saturday evening. George was in the barn, working as always behind locked doors, as he carried out yet another trial with Tom. It worked beautifully. The puppet with the absurd clownish face standing poised on the flap, the noose around its wooden neck: the swift descent by ladder to the floor, the momentary pause as George swung the sledgehammer and knocked aside the props, the sudden crash as the flap opened and Tom came hurtling down, to be checked some three feet from the ground by the tightening rope.

Since his wife's death, George had taken up smoking again

after a ten-year abstinence and, feeling the need for a cigarette, he went across to the house to get the packet of Silk Cut that he had left on the table. He did not bother to lock the barn door behind him, for he intended to go straight back and run one more test.

The telephone rang as he lit up a cigarette and he was delayed for a couple of minutes by Phil Hazard pressing him to go over for a drink and a light supper. He was reluctant to accept but the little solicitor was adamant and eventually George capitulated and agreed to join the Hazards at around eight o'clock. It was now a few minutes past six, he would still be able to drop Tom one more time.

As he crossed back to the barn, his heart quickened suddenly. He was certain that he had closed the door behind him but now it stood wide open. As he drew nearer, he heard an odd whimpering noise from within.

He found Sam Perryman, one of the two brothers who ran the small farm next door, standing in the centre of the barn, staring with big frightened eyes at the scaffold and the still swinging figure of the dummy. Little gurgles of fear came from his throat.

Sam was a large, simple man: some local people went further and regarded him as simple-minded. Certainly he had a childlike quality about him, but he was a hard worker and caused no trouble except on the rare occasions when he escaped from his elder brother's tight control and took too much to drink. At such times he could be unpleasantly violent, using his strength to damaging effect on people and property. Yet when his brother appeared the violence subsided as though at the touch of a switch and he would allow himself to be led away like a naughty child.

As George drew nearer and Sam turned towards him, he caught the scent of raw cider on the big man's breath. The hair was dishevelled, wisps of straw clung to his clothes and his right cheek was marked by a deep scratch over which the dark blood had just clotted.

Without warning, Sam lunged at George with a roar that was half-anger, half-fear, but he stumbled as he came forward and the other man slipped the big grasping hands. As Sam recovered and turned on him again, George, acting instinctively, grasped the heavy chain of the block and tackle that hung just above his head and swung it with the strength of panic in the direction of this new threat. The heavy iron hook hit Sam full on the forehead, a crunching blow that drew fresh blood and sent him crashing to the ground, where he rolled over and lay face downwards, unconscious.

George leaned against the wall for a moment, catching his breath. He could hardly believe what had happened. The big man had clearly been drunk and, equally clearly, he had intended to kill. But why? Had it been the sight of the gallows and the grinning face of Tom?

And it was then that the idea came to him. Here was the opportunity for which he had been waiting, here was the opportunity to make a real test of his apparatus. It would be justice, after all, an eye for an eye: if he had not acted quickly, he would have been the one lying there unconscious or dead.

He approached Sam cautiously. The man was breathing unevenly and as George knelt over him he stirred slightly. This movement urged George to speedier action. He locked the doors, switched on the lights, and cut two lengths of rope with which he bound Sam's feet and tied his hands behind his back. Sweat soaked his shirt and his hands trembled as he released the dummy from the noose and set both the rope and flap in position.

The next stage proved to be less difficult than he had supposed. He linked the iron hook to Sam's leather belt, hauled the still unconscious man up to a point some five or six feet above the level of the platform and tied off the block and tackle, surprised and pleased at the comparative ease of the operation. With a sense of rising excitement he climbed to the platform and carefully dropped the noose over Sam's head, settling it on the neck. He then pulled his victim on to the flap and released the block and tackle.

His calculations had been almost perfect! The noose and the rope jerked Sam upright, his head turned upwards, his feet dragging on the trap-door. This sudden new pressure brought the big man back to an uncertain consciousness: he stared at the noose with rolling frightened eyes and pulled at it with his head. He began to blubber and little bubbles of froth formed on his lips. The blubber turned to a snarl and he thrashed his head wildly in the noose, showing brown stumps of teeth. The smell of the raw cider and of his foul body odour was so strong that George wrinkled his face in disgust and contempt.

Sam's shouting became louder now and George hurriedly

The Gallows

descended the ladder. A moment of fear and apprehension as he grasped the sledgehammer, and then it was all over. The cries died away, there was a final grunt of pain, a sharp crack as if some bone had broken and Sam hung there, twirling on the rope, his eyes bulging.

George sat down suddenly, closing his eyes in relief. He felt exhausted, drained of energy, but deeply satisfied at the same time, like a man who has climbed to the peak of a mountain.

An hour later he went back to the barn. He had bathed and changed ready for his date with the Hazards, for he had decided that he should act as normally as possible.

Sam Perryman was quite dead, the body already growing cold. Tomorrow, thought George, tomorrow I will bury him under the floor of the barn and no one will be the wiser. He locked the barn doors behind him and lit a cigarette, noting that there was no trembling in his hands.

When he arrived at the Hazard's house he was surprised but not disturbed to find a police car in the drive. And when he went inside he was still calm as he came face to face with Detective Inspector Evans.

'Ah, Mr Hever,' he said gravely. 'I was coming over to see you. You've saved me a journey.'

'What's it all about?' asked George.

'You haven't seen Sam Perryman, by any chance.'

George hesitated only slightly. 'No. Not for a week or more. Why? Has he been up to his tricks again?'

'More than tricks,' said Hazard.

'Do you know young Linda Parks?' asked Evans.

'Only by sight.'

'This afternoon, around five, Sam Perryman attacked her in that copse near Welham Common and raped her. Nearly killed her. Thank God, she still had enough strength to identify him. We've got half the county police out looking for him.'

Tonight, thought George, tonight. I must bury the body tonight.

'There is something else,' said Evans.

'You'd better sit down, George,' said Mrs Hazard.

George took a chair by the table, conscious of their half-embarrassed, half-sympathetic looks.

'Sorry to come back to your wife's case,' said Evans, 'but it seems that the jury was right and we were wrong about Roberts. We turned over Sam Perryman's place and found these hidden behind a rabbit-hutch in a shed.'

He produced a plastic bag and shook its contents on to the table. George found himself looking down at his wife's wedding ring, her engagement ring and the gold wristwatch he had given her three years before.

The trembling in his hands began again, his mouth twitched and he began to laugh, violently, hysterically, uncontrollably. Insanely.

Sara Woods

EVERY TALE CONDEMNS ME

I

'Talking of E.S.P.,' said the thin man in the corner diffidently. They hadn't in fact been doing so, but conversation in the first-class compartment had become fairly general, so that he felt it was not an unreasonable way of introducing a change of subject. The stout lady who was sitting diagonally across from him with her back to the engine seemed puzzled and repeated the phrase doubtfully.

'E.S.P.?' she said and looked round for enlightenment. She was a pleasant-looking person with a good fur round her shoulders, a double string of imitation pearls, and an impressive bosom. The Canadian who sat opposite her undertook her instruction.

'Extra-sensory perception,' he said. 'There was an article a week or two back in Maclean's . . . I have it sent over. I don't know if you happened to see it.'

There was a murmur of negation. They were too polite to tell him they thought he was talking about toothpaste . . . all of them except for the youngish man on his left, who had once spent a fortnight in Montreal. He added, kindly but misleadingly, 'Seem to have missed that one.' He was a barrister, Antony Maitland by name, and he was travelling back from Arkenshaw after a conference that seemed likely to lead to a brief in the not too distant future.

Perhaps encouraged by this not very convincing show of interest the elderly man opposite, who looked as though he had spent his whole life climbing the executive ladder to the top of whatever business he was engaged in, added his own comment. 'There has been a good deal of correspondence on the subject in *The Times*.' (An expert in the art of one-upmanship, thought Maitland, amused.)

The clergyman, who had the centre seat with his back to the

engine, crowded uncomfortably between the businessman and the woman passenger, nodded his comprehension. There was an air of authority about the businessman's pronouncement, and though he didn't carry a copy of the newspaper he had mentioned it seemed likely that he was one of the Top People. 'Interesting,' said the clergyman. 'Very.'

'Telepathy,' the Canadian was explaining to the stout woman. He was living in England on a salary that was paid in dollars, and had in consequence a sleek and prosperous look, even by contrast with his companions. 'Telepathy, and clairvoyance, and telekinesis—'

'Spiritualism?' she asked hopefully, but with an apologetic look at the clergyman on her right.

He gave a booming laugh and turned back to the thin man. 'Perhaps,' he suggested, 'our friend will explain what aspect of the subject he had in mind.'

'Well . . . clairvoyance,' said the thin man, still sounding diffident if not apologetic.

'Not ghosts,' said Maitland, answering the question in the stout woman's mind though she had not in fact spoken again.

'I knew a chap,' said the businessman helpfully, 'who dreamed he was running in the Grand National and came a cropper at Beechers. Went out and picked a horse called All Fall Down in the three thirty next day. Thought it was an omen, you see.'

'Did it win?' asked Antony Maitland.

The businessman shook his head sadly. 'No,' he said. 'That was the funny part about it, don't you see?'

The diffident man spoke again into the silence that followed, while the others were wrestling with the logic of this pronouncement.

'A friend of mine had some very odd experiences.' He looked round him, collecting eyes in a determined way. Only the man who sat opposite him, isolated behind a copy of the *Yorkshire Post*, avoided his glance; and as he hadn't spoken during the hour that had passed since the train came out of the station at Arkenshaw it didn't seem likely that he'd interrupt now. 'It started when we were at school together. We'd been out late one night and were all set to get in by the usual route—'

One of the minor public schools, thought the clergyman, eyeing him appraisingly and perhaps a little condescendingly, secure as he was in the knowledge of his own *alma mater*'s undoubted superiority. The stout woman leaned forward and said, 'Boarding school,' helpfully to the Canadian. She was pleased to be able to repay his thoughtfulness, but as she was the only girl in a family of boys and had been well brought up on her brothers' reading matter, disdaining as maudlin stories that were written specifically for the female sex, she was more occupied at the moment in trying to cast the speaker in the role of hero (who broke bounds at night with only the best intentions), or as the depraved boy who went out to drink, or to plead for time to pay his gambling debts. Unaware of these reflections, the thin man was pursuing his story more confidently now. It crossed Maitland's mind that the diffidence, which he himself knew only too well how to assume on occasion, was no more than a cloak for a determination – or perhaps compulsion wouldn't be too strong a word – to tell the story of his clairvoyant friend.

'There was no question in my mind we'd be all right,' he was saying. 'We'd done the same thing a hundred times . . . well, say, a dozen. But all at once Fred stops and grips my arm. Can't go that way he says, old Manning's waiting for us.'

Because he paused some comment seemed to be called for. 'Awkward,' said Maitland drily.

'So what did you do?' asked the stout lady, though to Antony at least it was quite obvious he was in no need of encouragement to proceed.

'Well, we argued a bit back and forth,' said the thin man. 'But Fred was always a determined chap, and as there was another way we could take in the end I humoured him. It was rather a long way round and meant going through the chapel,' he added apologetically. The clergyman looked benevolent and sketched a gesture as though absolving him of blame. 'So that's how we got in. But the funny thing was two other fellows got caught using the regular route. Which proved I'd been right to listen to Fred.'

'Well, I never!' said the stout lady comfortably. There was a murmur of approval from the other travellers, though the man with the *Yorkshire Post* remained silent.

'Coincidence, you say,' said the narrator, encouraged. 'And of course if that had been the only thing that happened . . . but it wasn't. After that it was just as if he knew when circumstances were going to be against him. And when the others began to realise that it made him popular, I can tell you. As long as you kept in with him you were all right, he always saw to it that his friends steered clear of trouble.'

'Did he ever dream the winner of the Grand National?' asked the Canadian.

'No, that didn't seem to be the way of it. But he had the most phenomenal luck,' the thin man went on. 'At school, of course, but I told you about that; I really meant later when he joined a firm of stockbrokers in the city, and later got a seat on the exchange. I went into a bank myself,' he added, faintly regretful.

'Precognition,' said Maitland, and smiled at the narrator. 'If I'd been you I'd have stuck to him like glue,' he added.

'Well, of course, I didn't tell you we were cousins, did I? So we were always friends and saw a good deal of each other. But as for your question, there wasn't so much "pre" about it. What I mean is it was more like the inspiration of the moment, and if he'd stopped to tell me it'd have been too late. At least, that's what he always said. If he went racing he'd go up to put on his stake with no idea in the world what he was going to do, and then, bang, down would go his money on the winner. Uncanny it was, I can tell you, and it wasn't just at the races, of course, on the stock market he always seemed to know exactly when to buy and when to sell.'

'Useful,' said the businessman wistfully.

'Yes, but he stopped going to the races quite early,' said the thin man. 'Said it took all the fun out of gambling. Later, after he was married, he'd only back horses his wife picked out for him with a list of runners and a pin.'

There seemed to be some indignation at this, even the clergyman murmuring, 'How very wasteful.'

The thin man took up his tale again rather quickly. 'It didn't really matter from his point of view, though I did wish sometimes he'd tell me . . . but that's water under the bridge now. But when it came to a question of business he'd no objection at all to making use of his gift. Naturally he didn't tell anyone about it, and when I asked him later he just said he'd outgrown it, but I watched him piling up the money and I must say I wondered. But then his sister was getting married and he sent a telegram at the last minute with some lame excuse for not attending the wedding. Two-thirds of the guests went down with food-poisoning, and if you ask me he knew perfectly well something was going to happen.'

'Were you among them?' asked Maitland. 'You said you were cousins,' he explained when the thin man looked at him inquiringly.

'Yes, I was as a matter of fact, and it was a nasty business but we all got over it. All the same, great offence had been taken in the family, and afterwards when I tackled him about it he admitted he had had a feeling . . . just like when we were at school, he said. And he said perhaps it would have been better to take the risk, because after all it didn't happen so often nowadays. I didn't believe him about that, I was quite sure the feelings had been going on all the time and I didn't feel very sorry for him about the estrangement, even when he was cut out of his aunt's will.'

'Did you benefit from that?' asked the clergyman, to the gratitude of all concerned. His cloth, they felt, entitled him to ask questions that would be unsuitable from anyone else.

'Not a bit of it,' said the thin man. 'She was on the other side of his family, you see, and no relation of mine. But I was saying, I couldn't be really sympathetic about it, he'd plenty of money by then, and many's the time I've wished my relations would stop speaking to me.'

'Yes, indeed,' said Maitland. The businessman and the Canadian both sighed sympathetically. The stout lady, however, bristled, as though she thought there might somehow be something insulting in the remark.

The clergyman put the tips of his fingers together and intoned, 'A sad commentary on human nature, my dear sir. Very sad.'

'Oh, I don't know,' said the thin man vaguely. 'Then when he was thinking of getting married himself, it suddenly came to him that he was courting the wrong sister. So he switched to the other one and found she'd had a fortune left to her by her godmother.'

'Are you sure he didn't know about that beforehand?' asked the businessman rather cynically.

'Unless he was lying to me, and I don't think he was. Because then he admitted to me that the inspirations – whatever you like to call them – had never left him, and of course I asked him to help me out a bit, putting me on to a good thing occasionally, but he said the bank wouldn't look very favourably on one of its employees getting involved in the stock market. Well, naturally I didn't leave it there, and he must have known I'd keep on at him so he wouldn't have admitted it unless it was true.'

'And is that the end of the story?' asked the clergyman after there had been a moment's silence.

'No, it isn't. The queerest thing of all happened only a few days ago. He'd made his pile, and his wife had a packet too as I told you, and for some reason they took it into their heads they'd like to live in the country, in the north. Well, money was no object, as I've explained to you, so there was no reason why he shouldn't take an early retirement. Off they went, and found themselves an estate not too far from Arkenshaw and Fred must have enjoyed himself playing the lord of the manor, or the squire, or whatever, because he didn't come south again until our uncle died.'

'An uncle of both of you?' asked the stout lady, who liked to get anything in connection with family matters quite clear in her mind.

'Yes, this was on Fred's father's side, my father's too, for that matter. The aunt I spoke of earlier was his mother's sister.'

'The question of his non-attendance at his sister's marriage had been overlooked by the family by now, I suppose,' said the clergyman.

'More or less. Anyway, it was his obvious duty to attend.'

'And this time no premonition prevented him from coming?' asked Maitland, with a little scepticism in his tone.

'Nothing like that.'

'Then perhaps his instinct told him he was about to inherit another fortune,' said the businessman, entering into the spirit of the story.

'If he had one of his feelings about that he didn't tell me,' said the thin man. He paused there, but the expectant eyes of his audience proved too much for him. 'Uncle Michael was nicely off,' he said, 'and he left his money half to Fred and half to me. It didn't matter to Fred, of course, but when you've just a bank clerk's salary it meant a good deal to me. Not that I wasn't sorry the old boy had packed it in,' he added. 'He had a stroke, though none of us had expected –'

'Except perhaps Fred?' the Canadian suggested.

'– and he was only about sixty so he should have had a good many years before him. But that wasn't what I was going to tell you.' This time his pause seemed deliberate and he looked round impressively. Obviously the climax of his story had been reached. 'You see he was going to fly back to Yeadon,' he said, 'and I went to Heathrow with him to see him off. And then, just when they called the plane, all of a sudden he got one of his feelings.'

'Now that's something like,' said the Canadian in a pleased tone. 'What I mean, a feeling's of some use if it saves your life.'

'And if it makes you a fortune –'

'Or saves you from getting into trouble at school –'

'Or keeps you from getting food poisoning –'

'Or marrying the wrong girl.'

The man with the *Yorkshire Post* put down his paper suddenly and said in an exasperated way: 'Well, finish your story, man. He went by train instead, and the plane crashed and everyone was killed.'

'Oh no,' said the thin man, 'that wasn't what happened at all. He didn't catch the plane, that's right enough, and we had a bit of an argument about whether he should warn the airline, him saying it was his duty perhaps, and me pointing out they'd just laugh at him. Luckily that time he listened to me, and decided to take the train as you suggested, sir. But he'd be in a bit of a rush to get across town to King's Cross and catch the next one, so he just shoved his airline ticket into my hands to get a refund – he was careful about things like that – and went off to find a taxi.'

'And he caught the train and *that* crashed,' said the man with the *Yorkshire Post*, who seemed to be of an impatient disposition.

'Not that either,' said the thin man, 'but it was his not taking the plane that did for him all the same. He set off to walk from the station to the house of a friend of his who he thought would drive him out to Yeadon where he'd left his car. If any of you know Arkenshaw you'll know the towpath by the canal. Silly, really, to have gone that way, there's never anyone much about, and the long and the short of it is that he got himself mugged . . . hit over the head and his wallet taken. I'm just on my way back from the funeral.'

Everyone, even the man with the *Yorkshire Post*, had some words of condolence for that. It was left to Maitland, who had vivid memories himself of that particular short cut, to add a question to his expressions of sympathy. 'He was found quite quickly then? If he'd been thrown in the canal I'd have thought –'

'He was just left there, dead on the towpath,' said the thin man. 'But it was queer – wasn't it? – that after all that run of luck it should be a premonition that did for him in the end.'

II

The train arrived at King's Cross station just before noon and Maitland, having waited for a taxi with no more impatience than was seemly, directed the driver to take him straight to Astroff's Restaurant where he had a luncheon engagement with his uncle, Sir Nicholas Harding. Sir Nicholas had already taken possession of their usual table by the time he arrived, and to Antony's surprise Geoffrey Horton, a solicitor and a friend of many years' standing, was also with him.

'What the devil are you doing here, Geoffrey?' asked Maitland, seating himself. 'Not that I'm not glad to see you, of course,' he added, 'but I thought you were up to your eyes in that very dull Henshaw business. I warn you, if you want someone to take that on, Derek's your man. The figures involved are far too complicated for my simple mind.'

'It isn't Henshaw,' said Geoffrey, not in the slightest degree put out by this rather unconventional greeting. 'Another matter came up that I want to talk to you about, and as Hill had instructions to put all calls for you through to Sir Nicholas and he was kind enough to ask me to join you –'

'That's good, as long as it isn't so urgent you want to spoil my lunch by talking about it.'

'No, no, nothing like that,' said Geoffrey hastily. Dinner was the only meal at which Sir Nicholas, except in the most exceptional circumstances, placed a complete veto on talk of work in progress, but Geoffrey knew him well enough to realise that to introduce his problem at this stage would not be altogether a popular move, besides which he felt himself to some extent an interloper.

The waiter had by now brought Maitland his usual drink. 'Everything all right at home, Uncle Nick?' he asked, picking up his glass.

'As you've been gone for all of two days, Antony, and spoke to Jenny on the telephone each evening, I imagine you're not really in need of reassurance on that point. However, the house hasn't been hit by lightning since last night, nor have any of us succumbed to some mortal disease. You may take it that in your absence everything has gone on as usual.'

Antony grinned. 'I suppose what you really mean is that because of my absence there have been no alarms or excursions,' he said.

'Precisely,' his uncle told him benignly. 'As for your trip, Antony, how did it go?'

'Another of Chris's forlorn hopes,' Maitland told him. 'No, sir,' he added as Sir Nicholas looked up sharply, 'I mean exactly what I say. I promised Chris I'd go up when the trial comes on if I can possibly fit it in. If not he'll just have to get on as well as he can without me, and between you and me it won't make the slightest difference. However, it was nice to see Chris, as well as Star and my namesake, and I don't think my prospective client will be any the worse for a spell in clink, which I'm pretty sure is what is going to happen to him.'

'If you must use colloquialisms, Antony, need they be quite so dated?' asked Sir Nicholas, pained. He affected an extreme aversion to slang, which – it is sad to report – was one of his nephew's main reasons for never having rid himself of the habit of using it. The two younger men greeted this pronouncement with a respectful silence, and after a moment he went on. 'Your train came in more or less on time, I see. How was the journey?'

'Not without its entertainment. I think they must have reduced the number of first-class carriages though. I had some trouble finding a non-smoker, and then it was pretty crowded.'

'I gather, however, that you found your companions entertaining.'

Maitland shrugged. '*Comme ci, comme ça,*' he said. 'Amiable anyway. There was a man who hid himself behind the *Yorkshire Post*, but we found later he'd been listening to our conversation; a stout amiable lady rather lacking in general knowledge, and a kind-hearted chap whom I judged from his speech to be a Canadian who did his best to enlighten her on the various subjects of conversation as they came up. There was also a prosperous-looking businessman ... at least I'm pretty sure that's what he must have been, though I never found out what his business was; a correctly dressed clergyman who reminded me of nothing so much as the chap who was described as having a "fair round belly with good capon lined", though unless he'd had the capon for breakfast it couldn't have been right; and a thin man who told us he worked in a bank, who'd just come from his cousin's funeral and was absolutely bursting to tell us about the cousin's gift for clairvoyance, precognition, whatever you like to call it, and how it had led to his death in the end.'

'That sounds interesting,' said Geoffrey. Sir Nicholas, meanwhile, by some telepathic method of his own, had summoned the waiter back to their table and ordered another round of drinks.

'As we're none of us in a hurry,' he said languidly when this had been done, 'you may as well tell us the bank clerk's story, Antony.'

'If you really want me to. The stout lady, of course, was hoping for ghosts and goblins but it wasn't anything like that. It wasn't without its interest though, as you'll see when I tell you. In fact, it left me puzzled.'

'By all means tell us then, my dear boy,' his uncle urged him.

Maitland waited only a moment while their drinks were set before them and until the waiter had retired again. 'My fellow traveller and his cousin went to school together,' he said then, 'which is perhaps an unfortunate, though accurate, way of describing him, but I never learned his name. The precognition business started then, but according to my informant it just came over his cousin suddenly, almost without warning. But quite often he and his friends found it useful in keeping out of trouble. Later, however, when they'd both taken up their different professions – the cousin I should have told you was a stockbroker – he doesn't seem to have been so keen on sharing his knowledge. He was fond of racing and always seemed to back the right horse, though he maintained he never knew what he was going to put his money on until the very last moment. Meanwhile, of course, all his investments were doing well, so much so that he found there was no fun in gambling any more, and didn't take it up again until after he was married, when he always made his wife do the selecting. He told his cousin, the man who was telling the story, that his gift had deserted him, but there came a time when he made excuses at the last moment for not attending his sister's wedding and most of the guests got food-poisoning from something they ate at the reception. In the long run though that didn't work out quite so well for him because it alienated his family and some aunt or other cut him out of her will.'

'Not an unmixed blessing then,' said Sir Nicholas thoughtfully.

'All the same I wish I knew a chap like that,' said Geoffrey, almost as wistfully as the businessman on the train had spoken.

'I doubt if he'd have given you any tips,' Antony told him. 'The cousin, of course, the bank clerk, came to the conclusion that his gift hadn't deserted him, and got him to admit the fact. But he still couldn't get any information that might be useful to him financially. The stockbroker had a rather weak, not to say sanctimonious, excuse for not helping him – he said the bank wouldn't like it if the story got about that he was playing the market.'

'Which is perfectly true,' Sir Nicholas pointed out.

'Yes, perhaps, but that wouldn't have mattered if he'd had a good run of luck first. The stockbroker retired early, but I'm getting ahead of my story. He was courting a girl when it suddenly came over him that it ought to be her sister he was trying to fix his interest with. So he changed horses in mid-stream –'

'Your aunt would not like that way of putting it,' said Sir Nicholas, inaccurately as it happened because Vera, Lady Harding, was extremely broadminded where manners of speaking were concerned, and quite often offended in this way herself.

'– and married the other sister,' said Maitland, ignoring the interruption, 'and then it turned out his bride had inherited a fortune from her godmother.'

'That's obvious,' said Geoffrey. 'He'd learned about it from someone.'

'Not knowing the people concerned, I can't argue about that,' said Antony, the humorous look that was so much a part of his nature being very evident just then. 'But taken with all the other things –'

'A series of coincidences,' said Geoffrey flatly.

'You know I find that even harder to swallow than the fact that he really had this gift for knowing what was about to happen,' said Maitland. 'But I haven't quite finished yet. I didn't tell you that having made his pile and his wife having money too, the stockbroker retired early and they took a fancy to live in the country and bought an estate in Yorkshire. That's why this chap was on the train with me today, I told you he was coming back from his cousin's funeral.'

'I suppose you're going to tell us how he died,' said Sir Nicholas in a resigned tone.

'Yes, I spoiled the story rather by giving away the fact that he's dead,' said Maitland. 'He came south for his uncle's funeral, and he and my friend the bank clerk did have a bit of luck over that because the uncle, who was nicely off – I think that was the expression he used – had left his money divided equally between the two of them. But that's nothing to do with the tale. My informant went to Heathrow to see his cousin off on the plane for Yeadon, and all of a sudden the chap had another of these feelings, which was strong enough, apparently, to make him decide to take the train instead. There seems to have been a little argument as to whether they should warn the airline, but common sense prevailed and they didn't do anything about it. There was a train he could just catch if he left right away, so he left his ticket with his cousin to get the refund. Isn't that just like a wealthy man, look after the pence and the pounds will take care of themselves?'

'Perhaps he meant the bank clerk to keep the money,' said Geoffrey charitably.

'Perhaps he did. Anyway by this time, naturally enough, what everyone expected to hear was that the plane had crashed but he'd got home safely by the alternative means of transport; or, alternatively, when the bank clerk denied that that had been the case, that the train had crashed and he'd been killed that way, as a direct result of relying on his intuition.'

'But neither of those things happened,' said Sir Nicholas with a question in his voice.

'No. His car was still at Yeadon, you see, but he had a friend in Arkenshaw, which was the nearest town to where he lived, who would drive him over to collect it, so he took a short cut from the station to the friend's house along the towpath by the canal and got himself mugged.'

'You mean, I suppose, that he was a victim of robbery with violence,' said Sir Nicholas coldly. 'Was he killed?'

'Stone dead,' said Antony dramatically. 'No one saw what happened, it's a deserted spot at the best of times, and the next person who took that route found his body.'

'An edifying story, if rather pointless,' said Sir Nicholas. 'But where does the puzzle you mentioned come in?'

'Yes, I've been wondering about that,' said Geoffrey. 'You seemed ready enough a moment ago to accept this precognition business.'

'It's nothing to do with that, and of course you don't know the terrain as I do,' said Maitland. 'He was presumably found by the first person who came along, and I've no idea whether that was two minutes or two hours after he was robbed, but the mugger couldn't have known how soon it would be, there might have been a hue and cry out almost immediately. So why not roll the body into the canal where it wouldn't be found until . . . well, for some time, anyway?' he added, recollecting that they were about to select their lunch.

'Yes, that is odd,' said Sir Nicholas slowly, but Geoffrey was staring at his friend in complete bewilderment.

'You've told me a thousand times you don't like coincidences, Antony,' he said, 'but it's beginning to sound to me as though you've just dug up the most colossal one of all time. This uncle who died, was his name the same as that of the two nephews?'

'Yes, I think the bank clerk mentioned that it was their fathers' brother. What are you getting at, Geoffrey?'

'And you don't know the dead man's name?'

'No, I told you that. But if the funeral was yesterday, as I daresay it was unless my chance-met acquaintance stayed on for a while after it, there should be a report in the local paper. My raincoat's in the hall and I think I've still got a copy in my pocket, as I never had a chance to read it with all the talk that was going on.' He paused there and eyed the solicitor rather closely. 'Do you want me to fetch it?'

'I think it would be a good idea.'

'What is all this?' asked Sir Nicholas testily, as his nephew disappeared.

'If it's the name I think it is, I'll tell you the moment we find out, Sir Nicholas,' Geoffrey promised. 'I don't like coincidences any more than you and Antony do, but the trouble is, whichever way it turns out coincidence is involved.'

Maitland didn't take more than a moment before he was back in his place and spreading out the paper in front of him.

'Obituaries,' he said, consulting the list of contents at the bottom right-hand corner of the front page. 'No, that would have been in days ago, I'll just have to go through each sheet, but he must have been a fairly important person in the district so . . . ah, here it is!'

'Are you sure you've got the right man?' asked Geoffrey sceptically.

'Give me credit for a little sense,' Maitland adjured him. 'I remember now that his name was Fred, and there can't have been many Freds murdered tragically on the towpath by the canal a week ago.' He hesitated. 'A week? Of course, there'd have to be time for the inquest. This is it then, not a shadow of a doubt, Geoffrey. Frederick Waring. Does that help you?'

'Bernard's the uncle's executor,' said Horton, speaking of his partner. 'He told me about it because as things have turned out it's rather an unusual story. And that you should have met the legatee coming back from the funeral . . . well, I've never heard anything queerer.'

Maitland was staring at him. 'Shouldn't you have said the other legatee?' he asked. 'After all, uncle whatever-his-name-was –'

'He was Frederick Waring too.'

'– predeceased the nephew who was buried yesterday, so there's no question that the inheritance wouldn't pass to his estate.'

'Oh yes, there is, that's the oddity that made Bernard tell me about it.' (Geoffrey took care of the criminal side of the practice, while Bernard Stanley looked after what might be called the domestic cases.) 'The residue of the estate was equally divided between the two of them, but whichever of them died first the other one scooped the pot. Sorry, Sir Nicholas,' he added quickly, seeing that gentleman's outraged expression.

'So that's why the body was left on the towpath,' said Antony, taking no notice whatever of this exchange. 'If it had been chucked into the canal it might never have been found.'

'It would have come to the surface sooner or later,' said Sir Nicholas disdainfully.

'It might not have done, it might have been caught in the weeds, or anything. I don't know how much my friend the bank clerk stands to gain, but he looked as if he could do with it. And there's another thing too, he told that story because he *had* to. I thought at the time it was just because his cousin was dead and the circumstances were very much on his mind, but I also got the impression – and I'm not being wise after the event – that he'd been jealous of the other man's success.'

'Now look here, Antony,' Geoffrey protested, 'if you're trying to tell me that this chap murdered his cousin for the sake of the extra money it would bring him, how could he possibly have done so? He was in London, and Frederick Waring was killed in Yorkshire.'

'I can answer that I think, and only part of the answer will be guesswork, Uncle Nick, so you needn't jump on me until after I've finished. Let's suppose that while they were arguing about Fred's taking the train his cousin said, What about your car, that'll be at Yeadon, won't it? And Fred said, That'll be all right, my friend so-and-so will take me out to fetch it, and if I go along the towpath his house is only ten minutes' walk – or whatever it may be – from the station. All right so far, Uncle Nick?'

'Pure speculation, but I presume you don't intend to rest your case there.'

'No, of course I don't. I was just about to point out to this doubting Thomas here that my friend the bank clerk had in his pocket an airline ticket from Heathrow to Yeadon, which he could very well have used.'

'It's a fair distance from the airport at Yeadon to Arkenshaw,' said Geoffrey doubtfully.

'Well, it's nothing to do with me,' said Maitland, picking up the menu which had been lying neglected beside him, 'but it seems to me there'd have been time. The plane had already been called, if you recollect, so he wouldn't have had long to wait for take-off. And when you travel to Arkenshaw by train, which I daresay you've never done, Geoffrey, there are only a couple of stops until it gets to Leeds, but after that it stops at every station.'

'I am bound to agree with you as to the time element,' said Sir Nicholas, 'but surely your friend would not have used the airline ticket if he believed his cousin's assurance that the plane would never reach its destination.'

'He wouldn't, but I think I can explain that too.'

'Given your over-active imagination I'm sure you can.'

'No, really Uncle Nick, it's quite reasonable, and Geoffrey already agrees with me.'

'Do I?' asked Horton, mystified.

'You queried the precognition business and now I think you were right. At school Fred may well have had the gift, there are any number of well-attested cases where children have shown supra-normal powers that have later worn off. Suppose that's what happened, as Fred said. His cousin believed him at first and may not have been telling the truth when he told us he'd changed his mind.'

'And the other things?' queried Sir Nicholas.

'He was good at his job and made a fortune on the stock market. It isn't unknown.'

'And the gambling?'

'One of Geoffrey's coincidences. He had a run of luck, which later deserted him. Geoffrey was probably right too when he said that Fred must have found out somehow that the girl he married had come into money. As for not going to his sister's wedding, perhaps he just didn't want to. I don't think I mentioned to you that he only admitted to having had one of his feelings about it when his cousin suggested it to him afterwards. From that point on Fred seems to have believed in his gift himself, but I doubt if the chap you call "my friend" shared his conviction.'

'From what he told you he seems to have done,' Geoffrey objected.

'That may have been just to make a good story. He wanted to talk about Fred's death and had to have some excuse to do so. So when Fred got one of his feelings about the plane his cousin didn't believe a word of it, but saw his chance and grabbed it. He may even have put the idea into Fred's head. What do you think of that?'

'On the whole,' said Sir Nicholas slowly, 'I prefer it to all this talk about precognition. But it is, after all –'

'I know . . . guesswork. But it can easily be checked. Not the details of my theory, of course, but whether the plane ticket was used or turned in for a refund.'

'But what do you expect me to do about it?' asked Geoffrey plaintively.

'It's nothing to do with me, thank goodness . . . or with you either. Put it up to Bernard and let him decide,' said Antony with a sudden brilliant smile at his companion. 'The only thing that concerned me was the question of why the body was left on the towpath, which would seem on the face of it to have been particularly stupid. But now you've put my mind at rest about that and I'm very grateful to you.'

'In that case, perhaps we may be permitted to eat our lunch in peace,' said Sir Nicholas. 'There is still, of course, the question,' he added, turning to catch the waiter's eye, 'of – ah – Fred's clairvoyance as a boy. And if it indeed existed then, as your informant would have you believe, how did it come to abandon him? When you say such things happen as childhood is left behind, Antony, I feel you may be thinking of poltergeists. Which really, when you come to think about it, have nothing to do with the case.'

BOSTON PUBLIC LIBRARY

3 9999 00704 951 1

WITHDRAWN
No longer the property of the
Boston Public Library.
Sale of this material benefits the Library.

WINTER S CRIMES   Ruleo J W

PZ1   A1W54

87822597-32

DU